The Inn in Rhode Island

ALSO BY
JUDY PRESCOTT MARSHALL

BE STRONG ENOUGH
STILL CRAZY

THE INN IN RHODE ISLAND

Book Two
Be Strong Enough Series

JUDY PRESCOTT MARSHALL

For information, please address
Writing Studio 12 May Knoll Dover Plains, New York 12522
ISBN 978-0-99-10273-6-1 (hardcover)
ISBN 978-0-99-10273-8-5 (e-book)
ISBN 978-0-99-10273-7-8 (paperback)
ISBN 987-0-99-10273-9-2 (audible)

Audio read by Susan McGurl

For David W. Marshall,
my every breath, dream and desire!

BE STRONG ENOUGH SERIES
Book One – *STILL CRAZY*

Julie Holliday discovered a handwritten note that had the power to destroy her.

For quite some time, she suspected her husband Dan of having extra-marital affairs. During an intense argument, Dan confessed to an affair from ten years ago. The next day, Julie packed an overnight bag and disappeared without a trace.

Three days later, she was touring an old farmhouse located in Point Judith, Rhode Island. It seemed as if the house had waiting just for her. Room by room, one garden at a time, Julie turned the five-bedroom home into a twenty-five room inn.

The inn gave her purpose. It allowed her to fulfill her dream of becoming an innkeeper, and running her own business gave her back her self-worth.

As much as she loved her inn, welcoming her guests, working alongside her employees and enjoying a cup of tea with her tea partner, Teresa, her heart was still missing the only man she had ever loved.

Everyone working for Julie knew she was hiding something about her past. Frank, the general contractor and Julie's confidant, knew exactly what he needed to do to make her heart happy again.

After searching for almost three years to find Julie, Dan received a phone call, but he was so excited he disconnected the call. Thankfully, Frank called him back.

BE STRONG ENOUGH SERIES
Book Two – *THE INN IN RHODE ISLAND*

On a gorgeous day in October, the Hollidays will celebrate their love by renewing their wedding vows.

Across town, like an owl lurking in the dark, Erin and her son Kyle in danger, run into the middle of the night.

CAST of CHARACTERS
BE STRONG ENOUGH SERIES

Julie Holliday ~ Baker/Innkeeper
Dan Holliday ~ Contractor
Jesse ~ Arborist
Lynnae ~ Baker/Bella Napoli Bakery
Sam ~ Lynnae's son
Max ~ Lynnae's son
Barry ~ Builder
Brooke ~ Cake decorator/Bella Napoli Bakery
Stephanie ~ Artist/Bella Napoli Bakery
Aimee Jo ~ Lynnae's babysitter
Barbara ~ Therapist/New York
Kelly ~ Restaurateur/Rhode Island
Geri ~ Real Estate Broker/Rhode Island
Frank ~ General Contractor/Rhode Island
Gina Marie ~ Budget Master/Rhode Island
Jessica ~ Contracting Supervisor/Rhode Island
Sabrina ~ Architect/Rhode Island
Teresa ~ Receptionist/Rhode Island
Cathy ~ Spa Owner/Rhode Island
Amanda ~ Daycare Owner/Rhode Island
Kourtnee ~ Bookkeeper/Rhode Island
Kevin ~ Landscaper/Rhode Island
Michael ~ Chef/Rhode Island
Christine ~ Pâtissie/Rhode Island
Mary ~ Bakery Owner/Rhode Island
Christina Stellate ~ Model/NYC
Michelle Eggink ~ Model/NYC
Molly ~ Interior Designer/Rhode Island
Tina ~ Writer/New York
Debbie ~ Spiritual Shop Owner/ Rhode Island
Chad ~ Pilot
Erin ~ Student
Kyle ~ Erin's son
Lady ~ Chocolate Labrador/Star of the show!

When two hearts are meant for each other,
no distance is too far,
no time is too long,
and no other love can break them apart.

~ Unknown

THE INN IN

RHODE ISLAND

Chapter 1

With the morning sun beaming on my face, I rolled over onto my back, and opened my eyes.

I tried to focus on the day ahead of me. Our six p.m. ceremony down by the pond, then a celebration dinner outside on the back terrace.

Dan and I had written our own vows. No minister needed, just those near and dear to our hearts. We both wanted something simple yet elegant.

I glanced over at Dan. He was sound asleep. I wasn't the only person, he, too, snored like a baby. He was the man of my dreams and I was still crazily in love with him.

To think three years ago I ran away from it all. Our home, my bakery, the only man I ever loved, but he found me. *Thank you, Lord.*

I prayed for this day – Dan no longer the same narcissistic person seeking comfort from other women. A new man with a desire to be with his wife and only her.

I closed my eyes for a second but then quickly opened them. A chill ran up my spine. Last night, I dreamt I was sitting in my rocking chair, outside on the front porch. All of a sudden, I heard Dan hollering my name. I ran down to the pond to meet him. Dan reached for my hand. He told me he loved me. He promised me he would never break my heart again. Dan kissed the back of my hand, before adding, "I only have eyes for you, you're my one and only love. I love you, Julie Holliday." Then his hand slipped out of mine and he was gone.

I blew out a sigh of relief when I heard Dan yawn, followed by,

"Good morning, beautiful."

"Ahh, you're awake. Good morning, my love." I kissed him on the cheek and started to get out of bed. I needed to shake that dream. "I'll pour our coffee?" I said.

Dan reached for my arm. "Are you marrying me today?" He raised an eyebrow and gave me that seductive smile of his. The one that stops my heart every time.

"Oh, yeah!" I replied, glad for the reality check and feeling ready to start my day.

"I love you, Julie. I want to move forward with our lives. Today is the first day of our *new* life together. I'm going to make you feel my love every day. You'll see."

"Dan." I inhaled. "I believe you and I'm so happy you found me."

"I started searching for you the day you—" Dan glanced over at the clock. "Holy crap, I have to meet Rose in twenty minutes."

Dan was in the shower before I could throw back the covers.

I went to the kitchen, sipped my coffee, scrambled some eggs, buttered the toast, thinking, *It's a good thing this woman, Rose, is his therapist!* I took another sip, cradling my cup with both hands, hoping, *our time together was as special as the love we shared.*

When I heard Dan clear his throat, I set our plates on the table.

Dan sat down, took a sip of his coffee, shook his head and said, "Rose is nothing like Barbara. Barbara was more like what brought you here? How can I help you? How do you think therapy can help you? And how do you wish your life were different. Not, Rose! She goes straight to the matter of things."

"How?" I asked as I studied his facial expressions.

Dan smirked. "She's tough!" Then he devoured his breakfast and kissed me goodbye. "I love you."

"And I love you, Dan." I smiled warmly at him, thinking about the day when I would be able to sleep an entire night without those damn nightmares. To help take my mind off last night, I put a Norah Jones CD in the player. While Norah and I sang, "Come Away With Me", I cleared the table and washed the dishes.

After I took my shower, Lady and I headed up to the inn. Lady was such an obedient dog. We never had to put a leash on her. I wanted to make sure all of my welcome baskets were in each of the guest rooms. Lynnae's room had a few extra goodie baskets for the boys. She promised me they would be here by eleven. I hated the fact that my dearest friend lived in New York. I wanted her here with me in Rhode Island.

As soon as I saw Jesse's truck pull in, I stopped walking, waiting for him to park. The big lug had made it. We knew he would. He was Dan's best friend and best man. He may have had the physique of a lumberjack and the tattoos of a biker, but to me, he was a big old teddy bear. In New York, he never missed a Friday night out. Jesse loved sending Dan and me photos of whatever meal he was dining on. He dressed as if he was posing for the cover of *GQ*. Women never knew how to take him, or how to hold onto him. I told him he needed to wear a sign on his back that read: "I'm not here for a long time. I'm just here for a good time."

When he turned the engine off, I waved and told Lady it was okay to go see him. My beautiful chocolate Lab bolted for his truck. She loved Jesse and he usually loved her. But he ignored her and went to the passenger side, helping a woman and a young boy get out of the truck. That was odd. He hadn't said anything about bringing— "Oh, no!"

Jesse hitched his chin my way. The woman turned her head in my direction. From where I was, I could see the weariness in her eyes and the rips in her clothes.

"Is that *blood?*" I ran to assist Jesse. Up close, it was worse than I imagined. She appeared weak and bruised. Both eyes and her chin were black, blue, and covered in blood.

"Julie, this is Erin and her son Kyle." Jesse sounded choked up, and I thought I saw tears in his eyes.

The woman quivered as I reached for the little boy, who was clutching a brown stuffed animal by one of its feet.

When Jesse took Erin in his arms, the sweatshirt, his sweatshirt, slipped down between them. Erin, looking even more frightened, pulled it back up, clutching it to her chest as if it were a lifeline. With her head resting on his shoulder, he carried her toward the front porch of the inn.

"Come with me, Kyle," I panted. When I picked him up, his teddy bear must have fallen to the ground. A moment later, Lady scampered ahead of me. I stopped and bent over. Kyle reached down and patted Lady on her head before taking back his teddy bear. Lady barked joyfully, certain she had done a good job. Kyle held his teddy close to me as we followed Jesse inside.

"*Oh my God!*" Teresa screamed in a spine-chilling tone and ran from behind the reception desk. "*What* happened?"

"Teresa, grab the first aid kit," Jesse yelled to her. Then he went into the library and sat Erin down on the sofa.

I stopped in the doorway and told Lady to stay in the lobby. With my foot, I closed the door and sat Kyle down next to his mother. On the other side of the door, I could hear Lady whining.

Kyle looked past me, his eyes searching for Lady. When I let her in, Kyle immediately moved to the floor and hugged her.

"I'm sorry. I… I had no idea where I was going." Her voice was broken. We could barely hear her. "I just knew I had to get away from him before he—"

"Who?" Jesse asked, making a growling sound.

"My husband," she replied, glancing down at her son.

"C'mere," Jesse said to her as he knelt down and embraced her in a gentle bear hug. "No one is going to hurt you. Not while I'm around." He held her face in his hands. "I promise."

Erin's voice was barely above a whisper as she looked into his eyes and bawled, "You're sweet."

Her pain was so keen we both felt it. When she started crying, I bit down on my bottom lip. The urge to cry was so strong. I had to look away for a moment.

"It's okay," I said, wondering if I needed to call the police or a doctor. "You and your son are safe. We'll take care of you." I heard the door close behind me, then I felt a hand on my shoulder.

"Here." Teresa handed me the first aid kit and a warm washcloth. She took off her sweater and wrapped it around Erin. Erin was trembling so hard Jesse's sweatshirt was in her lap. Her right breast was exposed. Teresa gnawed at the inside of her left cheek as she tried to help Erin put her arms in the sleeves.

I pulled myself together, opened the kit, and said, "Erin, this is Teresa. She's the receptionist here at the inn." I turned to introduce Teresa to Kyle, but he and Jesse were gone.

My heart was bleeding for this woman. From the color of her pale skin, I could only assume she hadn't been out in the sun in a long time. I bent down, squeezed the cloth and gently wiped the dried blood from her cheeks, neck, and right hand. I could not believe my eyes. Everywhere I looked, Erin had another bruise. I looked closer at her nose. "Erin, can I touch your nose?"

She pulled back, shivered, but nodded for me to go ahead.

"Not broken," I said. Noticing how skittish and nervous she was, I added, "Erin, you're safe. You're okay, sweetheart."

"Julie." I felt Teresa's hand on my shoulder again. "Jesse took the little boy to the kitchen for something to eat. I heard him tell Jesse he was hungry. Would you like me to get something for Erin and bring it in here?"

I asked Erin, "Are you hungry?"

She shook her head and wiped her tears with the back of her hand.

"You should probably eat something." I swallowed hard, fighting back tears. My blood was boiling. Who could do such a thing? I didn't mean to cry. But the moment I made eye contact with Teresa, I, too, started bawling my eyes out.

Chapter 2

After we cleaned Erin's wounds, she agreed to drink a cup of tea.

Teresa told Erin, "I'll give you something to wear and then we'll go into the kitchen."

Where would I put her? The inn was booked solid, all the extra rooms were for the wedding guests and getting involved with Erin meant involving the inn, which did not include scandal on its list of amenities. I could let her stay in the cottage, just not tonight. When Teresa offered her own room to Erin and her son, I had to admit, I felt relieved.

Erin said all she needed was a quick shower.

"Perhaps you should soak in a hot bath," I suggested. "It might do you some good."

"I don't want to impose."

The better part of me kicked in. "You are not an imposition. You're welcome to whatever we have. Erin, you and Kyle can stay with us for as long as you need."

"That's right," Teresa echoed me.

"But I don't want to put you out of your room," Erin said and sniffled.

"It's okay." Teresa explained, "I can stay with my boyfriend, Sal. Besides, a month from now, the inn will have plenty of rooms available."

"A *month?* I can't stay here, I…"

"Erin, we'll figure that all out later." I touched her on her knee. "Let's start with a nice bath and a cup of soothing tea."

"A hot bath sounds good right about now." Erin's face looking more somber than before, she added, "But I don't want to bring you any more trouble."

"You're no trouble. Trust me," I said as I handed her a tissue.

I looked over at the books neatly categorized and thought about all the badass female characters that I had read about over the years. Thanks to them, I knew I could handle whatever was coming our way. Lord knows, I would love to get my hands on the beast who did this to her.

Teresa curled her upper lip, telling Erin, "Don't worry; she's got a gun the size of my leg."

I rolled my eyes. "No one is getting shot. Dan and Jesse will step in if needed."

"Hey, where is everyone?"

I quickly turned around knowing Lynnae, Barry, Max and Sam had arrived.

"I've got this," Teresa said to me. "Go."

I knelt down in front of Erin. "You're safe. I don't want you to worry about anything." When she inhaled, I gently moved her hair from her face. "Promise me you'll try to eat something."

Erin nodded.

I opened the library door, and my heart skipped a beat. "Aunt Julie!" Sam and Max both ran into my arms.

I was still hugging Barry when Dan walked in from outside. "I figured that was your SUV out there," he said.

Lynnae hugged him. "It's Friday!" She winked. "Time to kick this weekend off."

"How are you?" Barry asked, shaking Dan's hand.

A second later, Teresa and Erin slowly made their way up the stairs. Teresa tried to shield Erin with her body. Dan looked at me, and I shook my head. Just then, Jesse, Kyle and Lady entered the lobby. Kyle's hand was on Lady's head.

Jesse extended his hand out to Dan and then Barry. "Come here, you," he said as he picked Max up. Holding Max in his arms, he bent down. "Sam this is my friend, Kyle. Kyle, this is Sam and this little monster is Max." Then he tickled Max until he squirmed his way to the floor.

Lady never went to Sam and Max. Nor did she run to Dan. She sat next to Kyle the entire time. I looked up at Dan and swiped my fingers across my forehead. Indicating my head was about to explode. Followed by a wide-eyed look. One he's seen many times.

"Umm, who wants to go fishing?" Dan winked at me as he called out to the boys. "I stocked the pond two weeks ago and yesterday I caught a brown trout."

Sam's hand shot up in the air. "Me!"

"Me, too!" shouted Max.

"Come on, Kyle, let's show these men how to catch a fish," Jesse said as he tapped Kyle's shoulder. "What do you say?"

"I'll get the bags later." Barry grinned at Lynnae. "It's fishing derby time!"

The boys ran out of the inn, across the yard and down toward the pond as though they had wings on their arms.

Lynnae and I stood in the doorway and watched as they headed down the path. I put my arm around her. "Come in the library, I have a favor to ask."

"Hey!" Bea shouted to Lynnae as she came into the lobby looking like the fashionista that she was.

I turned to Lynnae. "Lynnae, you remember my assistant, Bea."

Lynnae hugged her and said hello. "Of course, I do. Frank's niece, right?"

Bea smiled and nodded. "Oh, my goodness! Wait until you see Julie's outfit. She looks amazing in vintage."

"I'll bet," Lynnae, chirped.

"Bea, can you cover the front desk for a few minutes?"

"Absolutely!" Bea walked around the desk and sat in the leather chair. Bea not only assisted me in the dining rooms, often she would cover the phones for Teresa.

Lynnae and I went into the library. "What's going on?" she asked.

"I don't know exactly." I shook my head. "Jesse arrived with a woman and her son, Kyle. That's all I know."

"What do you mean? Julie, the kid is going fishing in his pajamas. What'd he do, pick them up along the way?"

"I think so."

"Is he bringing her to the wedding?"

"Lynnae, she's not his friend or his girlfriend. She ran away from her husband."

"You can't make this shit up. Only Jesse. So now what?" she asked me.

"Can you please take care of her son? Ask the boys to play with him. Make him feel—"

"Stop! Of course," she replied, as I knew she would.

"Thanks." I blew out a breath. "I'll try to make some time later to sit with Erin and find out what happened."

"Yeah right. Like you got time for that." Lynnae shook her head. "I'll take care of Erin."

I looked at her.

"What?" she rolled her eyes. "I got this!"

"Uncle Frank," we heard Bea holler. "You're not wearing *that*!"

I opened the door so Lynnae and I could see him. I smiled seeing his cheeks glowing red upon his chocolate skin. "Hello, handsome," I called out as I extended my arms out to hug him.

"Hey, Frank, how are you?" Lynnae kissed him on the cheek. "Bea's right. You're not wearing that to walk her down the aisle."

"Still as fresh as ever." Frank touched Lynnae's chin. "I'm glad Barry's here; he can help me and Dan with my gift."

"Frank!" I protested. "I told you, no presents."

"Okay. Contribution to the inn."

Frank took my arm and we followed him outside.

My hands flew to my heart. "It's beautiful!" Behind Frank's truck was a flatbed trailer, carrying an amazing wedding chuppah.

Frank helped Lynnae and me up onto the trailer. It was even more beautiful on the inside. I touched every detail. I could not take my eyes off it.

"This is incredible. Good job, Frank!" Lynnae said as she jumped down.

Frank held his hand out for me as I got down. "Frank, thank you. I love it!"

"I'm glad. I thought it would look nice down by the pond."

"Frank, it's perfect." Lynnae placed her hand on his back. "I can see why she loves you so much."

"Where's Dan and Barry?" Frank asked, brimming with pride.

"They're all down at the pond, fishing," Lynnae said. "You're in luck, Jesse's with them."

"Good, I'll drive down. They can all help me unload it." Frank kissed me on my forehead. "I'll be back to get you later."

"You're still the best." I returned his kiss, feeling even more wedding frenzy.

It didn't take Frank long to go from being the inn's contractor to my confidant and friend. I leaned on him more times than I could count.

When Lynnae and I went back inside, I asked Bea if Teresa had come downstairs yet.

"She just headed to the kitchen with a guest, I think."

"Lynnae, how are you?" Kourtnee said as she stepped out of the office and came into the lobby, holding baby Delilah in her arms.

"Let me see that precious little girl." Lynnae held her arms out, and Kourtnee handed Delilah to her.

I looked at Lynnae. "I'm going to the kitchen, I'll be right back."

Just then, I heard someone say, "Oh, this is lovely, absolutely gorgeous! Is Dan Holliday here?"

"He's not, but I can help you," Bea said to the woman.

I turned around, and I knew exactly whom she was. Dan's therapist from New York. "Barbara?" I asked as I extended my hand out to her, pleased to see that she had arrived safely.

"Yes. You must be Julie." She tilted her head and shook my hand. "It's a pleasure to meet you."

"I'm so glad you could make it. Dan was so excited when he received your RSVP."

"Oh, good," Barbara said.

The front door flew open as more guests arrived carrying an armload of garment bags. "Heyyy," Bea called out to them.

"What a wonderful day it's going to be." Barbara looked around the room. "Dan wrote me a lovely letter," she said, smiling. "I'm delighted for both of you. Well, you must be extremely busy running the inn, on your wedding day."

"Busy, I can handle," I replied.

Except there was Erin and Kyle to worry about. My mind steeped in visions of her face, those damn bruises, her poor legs badly banged up, so weak she could not go any further.

Delilah cried for her father the second she saw Kevin walk in the door and I was back in the moment. Wedding guests were arriving. My heart started racing when I saw my old bakery staff had arrived from New York. Brooke and Stephanie approached the lobby holding an enormous amount of boxes.

Guests of the inn were checking in right alongside my family and friends. And before I knew it, my cell phone was ringing. Cathy from the salon was calling. "Excuse me, I have to take this call," I said, as I answered my phone. "Yes. Sounds good. Thanks, Cathy." I took it all in: my hair appointment, Dan's therapist, the inn bustling, renewing our vows. "Love wins," I said to myself, and that was just fine with me. I looked around the room. Everyone and everything was moving so fast.

Kourtnee asking Barbara if she would like something to eat. Barbara agreeing to a quick cup of herbal tea, explaining she had a hair appointment soon.

Then… Michael came out from the kitchen and by the look on his face, I knew exactly what he was going to say. "Julie, what the hell is going on? Christine and Teresa are eating breakfast out on the side porch with a woman who looks like she got hit by a cement truck."

I grabbed his elbow. "Chef, I don't know any more than you do right now." Michael knew I was serious when I referred to him as chef.

"Was she in a car wreck?"

"No. She came with Jesse."

Michael looked at me with wide eyes.

"For heaven's sake *no*. Jesse wouldn't hurt a possum. He picked her up along the road. I think. Oh, dear God, I don't know! Michael, all I know is her husband did that to her. Her son is fishing with Dan and Jesse right now."

"Michael, can you help us?" Brooke asked from behind an enormous floral bouquet.

Michael touched my arm. "Sure. What can I help you with?"

"We need help carrying the wedding cake, flowers and candles to the terrace."

I watched Michael go out the front door with Brooke, followed by Stephanie. I slipped out of the lobby and headed to the kitchen but then remembered Michael had said they were out on the side porch. Before I could open the door, I saw Molly. Molly was not only a talented interior designer, she was also the best party planner I had ever seen. She was simply magical!

"What can I do?" she asked.

"Go to my hair appointment, greet seventy-five guests, I'm kidding. I've got this!"

"Seriously? Tell me how I can help. Wow!" Molly's eyes widened.

I turned around and saw an enormous floral arrangement go by the kitchen window.

We were standing in the middle of the kitchen watching one floral bouquet after another go by when I realized every person I loved and treasured so deeply in my heart was at the inn. I just started crying.

Molly patted me on my back. "I'm so happy for you." Seeing my face, she said, "I hope those are happy tears."

I wiped my eyes and hugged her. "They are indeed." Then I waved back to Brooke. Stephanie stopped outside the window, blowing me kisses.

A minute later, Christine came into the kitchen, holding a tray of dirty dishes. "Teresa's taking Erin up to her room. She's going to try to take a nap. I'm going to see if Kourtnee has anything that will fit Erin. Teresa's yoga pants are like capris on Erin."

"Is she okay?" I asked, hoping she said something, anything to them.

"She was silent for the most part. We told her about tonight, the inn and about everyone who works here. She's the sweetest twenty-three-year-old I've ever met," Christine said after a long exhale.

"Did she say anything more about her bruises?" I asked, hoping they were able to get a little more out of her.

"Bruises? Someone got hurt?" Molly stammered. "Who?"

"Jesse gave a woman and her son a ride," Christine explained as she set everything in the sink. "She's banged up, but she assured us she doesn't need to go to the hospital. A little tired but she'll be okay." Christine looked at me. "She was able to eat some scrambled eggs."

I gave a sigh of relief.

"Aunt Julie, look what I caught!" Sam yelled, running into the kitchen.

Dan was holding up a stringer of fish. "Everyone caught a fish."

"Not everyone," Max shouted. "Only me and Sam… oh yeah, Kyle."

"I'll take care of those," Michael said as he watched Dan place the fish in the porcelain sink.

I gave Dan a kiss and thanked him for taking the boys down to the pond. "Oh, I almost forgot. Barbara is here."

Dan flashed a broad smile before asking me, "Where is she? Is she in her room?"

"She's not staying with us. She's staying with her sister in Narragansett. I think she's in the dining room. No, wait." I thought for a minute. Barbara called yesterday and asked where she could get her hair and nails done. "She has the first appointment with Cathy. Check the salon."

Dan spun around and headed toward the lobby.

"Where's he going? He almost knocked me over." Christine, the inn's baker, said, holding a large tray of cookies.

"What is everyone doing in my kitchen?" Michael roared.

I looked at the boys and made a scary face. "We better get washed up for lunch."

At noon, we were to gather out on the lawn for a luncheon. Michael was serving lacy cheddar crisps, buttermilk-honey fried chicken fingers, chopped Caesar salad, Hungarian-style stew and for dessert, s'more bars and pumpkin cheesecake.

I had to admit, I was relieved when everyone said *they* wanted to take care of all the details. Dan made me promise not to interfere, and so far, I hadn't. Well, except for peeking at the menu cards.

We were in the lobby when Lynnae bent down and asked Kyle if he wanted to go with her and the boys, but he told her no. She kissed him, whispered in his ear and handed him a small duffle bag. The minute he put his hand on Lady's head, I knew he wasn't leaving her side. Lynnae grabbed the boys and went up to their room.

"Come on, Lady," I said reaching for Kyle's hand, to go down to the cottage. "Kyle, when your mommy wakes up, how about the three of us find something for you to wear?"

"I have clothes. That lady gave me some," he said with a wrinkle in his nose.

"She did? That's great." When we reached the cottage, I held the door open and Lady ran inside. She went straight to her bowl. "Kyle, would you like to feed her?"

"Uh-huh."

I lifted the cover on the bin and scooped up a small amount.

Kyle put his hand out and dumped the food in Lady's bowl. "I like Lady."

"Well, I think Lady likes you. Do you have a dog?"

"No. Daddy says I can't have one. But Mommy said when I'm ten. Where's Mommy?"

"Mommy's sleeping. As soon as I change into my dress, we'll go see her. Oh, boy, Dan's here," I said holding up my dress.

"Kyle," Dan said, "do you want to help me pick out a shirt?"

"No."

I pointed to the duffle bag on the kitchen floor.

Dan picked up the bag Lynnae had given to Kyle, smiled at Kyle and told him, "Lady's coming."

Sure enough, Kyle jumped up and followed Dan into the bedroom.

I went into the living room, and took off my jeans and sweater and pulled the dress over my head, wondering if Kyle had witnessed anything himself. Unlike Erin, he appeared fine. Stable in fact. I put my boots on and grabbed my poncho. Dan said the pumpkin color looked good on me.

I freshened my lipstick and from behind me, I heard Dan whistle. I turned around, noticed both men had changed their clothes. When I saw Kyle reach for Dan's hand, my heart smiled.

Chapter 3

Dan, Kyle, Lady and I walked around the inn to the backyard. It was a vision of gorgeousness. Tables adorned in fall shades of tulle. Yellow, sage and ochre colored candles glowing. There were small floral cachepots overflowing with garnet hydrangea, black magic roses, poppy pods, garnet dahlias, chocolate cosmos and velvety coxcomb. On the buffet table sat large dark-colored baskets filled with golden yellow chrysanthemums, amber sedum, rose hips and viburnum berries.

Dan hugged me. "This is incredible." Even he sounded choked up.

"Mommy!" Kyle spotted his mother standing in the doorway and ran to her. Erin bent down to hug him. She looked better. Rested. I felt relieved knowing she was safe. She was wearing Kourtnee's tan pants and a brown turtleneck sweater. Even though Max was seven and Kyle was only four, Max's clothes fit Kyle perfectly.

"Come sit," Michael said as he held out his hand.

Dan shook his hand. "This is great. Everything looks—"

Michael put his hand on Dan's back. "You're both very special to us." He looked at me. "This is *your* day. This is the day *we* have all prayed for."

Dan hugged me once more before we sat down in the middle of the enormous farm table. It must have been forty feet long. Our eyes met as Dan wiped mine with his napkin.

In the middle of the table, a vine of bittersweet ran from one end to the other. Russet, rust, deep orange, warm red and peach roses coordinated beautifully with autumn fruits, apples, berries, gourds and mini pumpkins. The entire table reflected the warmth of an October afternoon.

Dan squeezed my hand and said, "He looks good," as Jesse came out of the inn.

Jesse walked past me, put his hands on Dan's shoulders, kissed the back of Dan's head, came back, and sat down next to me. I gave him a kiss and told him he looked very handsome.

Lynnae came outside. I felt her fingers go across my back as she went by and sat down next to Dan. As soon as she sat down, everyone else came outside and stood across from us. Everyone was standing in one large group. Even Erin and Kyle. Jesse and Lynnae both stood up.

"I want to." Lynnae started to say.

I looked at her; she had tears in her eyes. When her tears fell, I lost it.

A hush fell over the crowd.

Lynnae made a sound. Then it sounded like, "Ugh!" She took a sip of water, shook her head and said, "Thank you. I want to say thank you to everyone who took care of my fairy godmother." She was blushing. "Julie and Dan have taught me so much. Most of all, they have shown me what forever looks like."

When she sat down, Jesse looked over at Dan. "Never give up. That's what you taught me. I can't thank you enough for showing me... dammit." Jesse started to cry. "I love these two. I've known them longer than anyone. They belong together and I'm glad they found each other again."

Jesse sat down, cleared his throat, and I hugged him.

Michael motioned for everyone to sit down. "Please," he said. "Sit and enjoy." He turned and waved to his staff to serve lunch.

Erin and Kyle sat down next to Barry, Sam and Max. I was glad to see them. I was thankful for every person sitting at the table.

Chapter 4

The boys were enjoying their s'mores, and the adults were feasting on pumpkin cheesecake. Lynnae handed me a mock Bellini and said, "The boys think their grown-ups. Someone told them there's alcohol in the punch."

I looked over at the boys; they were laughing and having a good time. "Thanks for giving Kyle some of Max's clothes."

Lynnae looked over at Barry and smiled. "Barry assured Erin she was welcome to join us at the table and that she would be safe with him. He told her he wouldn't leave her side. When Erin cried she felt out of place, Barry insisted she come downstairs and eat."

I mouthed, "I love you," to Barry and told Lynnae, "Erin looks better, thanks again for looking after her."

Lynnae tilted her head. "I didn't do anything. Bea did her makeup. Teresa's been tending to her the whole time."

I looked over just as Teresa and Jesse sat down next to Erin. Teresa offered Erin a sampling of her s'mores.

"Okay, sunshine, you need to get ready for tonight," Michael said.

I looked up at him and smiled. "Michael, my goodness. Everything was delicious."

Michael pulled my chair back, and I stood up. "I need to clear this table and get it ready for dinner," he reported.

"It looks fine," I said. "What time is it? I'm so full—"

"It's one-thirty and you better not be full," Christine chimed in, rubbing her baby bump. "Remember, four-thirty is cocktail hour."

"Then you're marrying me." Dan kissed me on my cheek. "Right?"

"Oh, yeah!" I turned to face him and noticed everyone heading inside. Erin and Teresa were escaping to the rose garden. I only had a half-hour before my hair appointment. I wished I had more time to talk to Erin.

Dan put his arm around me and whispered in my ear. "She's fine. She told Jesse she feels safe here, and she's glad *he* found her."

I turned to face him. "My heart is bleeding—"

"I know it is. I know what you're thinking. You'll have plenty of time tomorrow to sit and get to know her." His lips curved into a sexy grin. He kissed me on the forehead, hard, leaned back and looked into my eyes. "I promise."

Chapter 5

Dan and I strolled hand in hand down to the cottage.

"I need to change," I said.

"Again?" Dan teased.

"Cathy told me to wear a button-down shirt so I don't mess up my hair."

Dan stopped and looked back. "Where's Lady?"

"I said she could stay with Kyle. Jesse's keeping tabs on them."

Dan held the door open. "The next time you see me, I'll be…"

I raised an eyebrow. "My husband."

"A better husband." He kissed me and this time he held me in his arms so tight, I could not move. "I'm jealous," he added.

"Of…?" I asked, captured in his embrace.

"Frank gets to see you before I do."

"You better behave or I'll run away with Frank."

Dan let go of me. "That was the worst time of my life. I don't ever want to imagine a day without you in it."

"I didn't—"

Dan held his finger to my lips. "Julie, I'm going to make you so happy."

I took his hands in mine. Kissed them several times. "You can start right now." I reached down and touched him.

"Oh, no you don't. I have plans and you're not stopping me. Woman, get a move on."

"Fine. But you don't know what you're missing."

I took off my dress and put on a flannel shirt. From the bedroom, I hollered, "I do believe I'm excited."

"I am, too," Dan said as he took off his sweater and draped it over the couch. "Wait until you hear what I wrote. Nope, you'll have to wait for that, too."

I stepped into the living area and watched him grab his sweater and hang it up on the rack near the front door. I was so glad he was neat. Our home in New York was five thousand square feet. The cottage was under a thousand, and yet everything was in its place. I could not take my eyes off him. Dan tossed some paper, kindling and logs in the fireplace. He looked up at me. "I'm lighting a fire tonight."

I stood there, taking it all in.

"I can be very romantic and you know it!" He stood up, laughing. "What?"

I kissed him. "I love you so much."

Dan held me close. "Every day, Julie. For the rest of my life, I'm going to show you my love." He tapped me on my nose. "You'll see." He opened the door, but then approached me from behind. "You better put this on. Temperature is dropping."

I smiled. "Still taking care of me?"

He patted me on my derriere. "Get going!"

On my way up to the inn, I passed Bea, Molly, Brooke, and Stephanie. They had our guests, models, Christina and Michelle, helping them carry flowers down to the pond.

"Don't look," Brooke shouted.

"I'm not looking. Thank you for doing this. The table was absolutely gorgeous at lunchtime."

Stephanie yelled, "Wait until you see what we're doing for the ceremony."

I kept walking, thinking *that's some entourage.* The temperature outside was still warm. Too warm for the sweater wrapped around my shoulders. I took it off and carried it the rest of the way.

The foliage on the katsura tree was bright yellow. In the fall, the tree released the smell of caramel corn and cotton candy. I stood near the garden, taking in the fragrance and the beauty of the angel coneflower, eternal fragrance daphne, and the sweet autumn clematis clinging to the arbor hovering over the resting bench.

The white clematis and the black beauty snakeroot were striking together. I looked up at the sky. Back at the cottage was *the* only man I had ever loved. I had prayed hard for Dan to open his eyes. I stood there a moment longer. *I pray he continues going to therapy.* I wanted only the best for him, for him to recognize his illness. My heart was happy, knowing Dan was truly worthy of my love. Our best is yet to come.

I continued walking until I saw the inn. Staring at all that I'd accomplished. I had everything I desired, all I had dreamt of having in my life, and yet there was the overwhelming feeling that something bad was going to happen. I took a few more steps. To my left, the salon. I put my hand in my right pocket, hoping for a tissue, and felt an envelope instead. I opened it and read the words, "*Forever After!*" I stared at it for a few seconds.

"What are you doing? Cathy's waiting for you." Kourtnee was coming out of the salon.

"You look great," I called out to her. "Am I late?"

"No. You're next."

I kissed her on the cheek. "Thank you for taking care of Barbara earlier. Oh, and thanks for lending Erin your clothes."

"No prob! I have to go, Kevin still has to shower and I want to see Delilah before Amanda comes and gets her."

Amanda offered to watch all of the children in the daycare, but I insisted she attend the ceremony and dinner afterwards. She agreed to do so only if Delilah was her date.

I stepped inside. Lynnae was sitting at the small table getting her nails done. "You curled your hair. It looks nice," I said to her.

"It's a special day." She raised her eyebrows. "How do you feel?"

"I'll let you know later."

Cathy smiled at me and held up an apron. I gave her a hug. "Thank you. Everyone looks great." I sat down as she put the apron around my neck.

"You're my last appointment. I'm starving."

"Didn't you eat lunch?" I asked as she began to pour warm water on my hair.

"No time. I scheduled Gina Marie, Sabrina and Jessica during that time." Cathy held her hand on my forehead as to keep water out of my eyes.

"I'm sorry." I closed my eyes, and for thirty seconds allowed myself to relax. Lady A, "Need You Now" was playing on the radio. And I thought *I seriously need to take a deep breath and enjoy every second of the day.* Except, I could not stop thinking about Erin or her four-year-old son.

"Okay, you're all set. Sit in the first chair, I'm going to clean up your ends before I dry and curl your hair."

"Cathy, I'm so sorry you didn't get to eat."

"Believe me, I'll be fine. I'll eat during the cocktail hour."

"Good, because there'll be plenty of food. Coconut shrimp, quesadillas, pastry triangles with spinach and feta, potato crisps with smoked salmon and herb cream cheese, and Dan's favorite –garlicky mussels. No wait, I saw Michael crossed them out and is serving that at dinner."

"How the hell do you know that?" Lynnae hollered over to me.

"I read the menu board. Thank you! Wait, mini pizzas, too."

"Pizza! Yum," Cathy said as she curled my last strand.

"Love you, Cathy. Thank you, thank you, thank… you."

Cathy blew me kisses in the mirror and said, "Okay, I'm going to take a shower. Everyone is tan, nails are polished, and their hair is curled. Ciao, my *bella mias*!"

Chapter 6

Michael told me not to go near the terrace. Like the wonderful woman I was, I opened the front door and went straight to the library. My blouse and skirt were hanging on the bookcase that Frank had built for me a few months ago. Bea and Molly picked out my outfit. They chose a vintage gray pleated skirt and a three-quarter sleeve button-down blouse. The tag read: "Bouffancy and Retro Style." Whatever that meant. All I knew was, it felt elegant the moment I had tried it on.

"Knock, knock, I'm coming in."

"Lynnae, is that you?"

"Yes, it's me." She opened the door and came in holding a bag. "I want to do your make-up."

"I can do my own lipstick—"

"Your hair looks great. Sit your ass down. I want to do your eyebrows and just a little mascara."

I laughed, sat down, and watched her create magic. Cathy had pulled my hair back on the left side. And on the right, she gave me this big lush curl. Lynnae did more than just my eyebrows; she used eyeliner and deep crimson red lipstick. When I looked in the mirror, it felt as if I had stepped back in time.

"Details. It's the little things that make a difference." Lynnae slapped me on the shoulder. "You look frigging amazing."

I could not believe my eyes. "It *feels* amazing. I hope Dan recognizes me."

"Okay, Cinderella, I'll see you at six."

"Where are you going?"

"It's four-thirty. I'm a guest. I'm going to a cocktail party." And out the door, she went.

I loved that idea. I thought more people should adopt it. Let the guests have an hour of cocktails and appetizers before the ceremony. I asked Michael to plan it that way, purposely, because both Dan and I would want to sit down and eat dinner immediately after the ceremony. "Ceremony! Oh, my goodness!" I jumped up. "I left my vows down at the cottage."

"Would you like for me to get them?"

I turned around and saw Frank standing in the doorway. "Wow you look fantastic!" He was wearing a royal blue peak lapel dinner jacket with a black bowtie that made his dark skin blend beautifully. I gave him a kiss, reaching for his hand. "Come sit with me."

"I know I'm a bit early, but I want to say something before we go down to the pond."

I sat in one chair and watched as Frank pulled his chair closer.

"Young lady, I have never met a woman like you. You mean a lot to me. So listen up. 'Cause I got something to say. I've never seen you happier than the day that man showed up. I want you to open your heart and find forgiveness. He loves you. I can see it."

I smiled.

"Don't let jealousy come between the two of you. Men do stupid things from time to time. It doesn't mean he don't love you. Now, he swore to me those days are over. And I believe him."

I reached over and patted his knee. "I'm so blessed to have you in my life."

"If you ever wonder again, *talk* to him, Julie. Tell him how you're feeling. Don't run away."

I could have cried. His words touched my heart. "I won't," I replied as I leaned forward and hugged him. "Frank…" I bowed my head, looked up at him and added, "Dan is an answered prayer."

"Amen!" Frank looked at his watch. "It's time."

My heart started racing. "I'm so excited right now."

"You should be," he said with a smile.

"Frank, thank you for calling Dan and telling him where I was. I don't know that he would have found me, if not for you."

"Dan told me about the cad working for him. That devil wanted you all to himself."

I hadn't thought about Chad since Dan arrived. *I pray he finds love again.*

"I'll wait for you in the lobby, while you get dressed," he said and we both stood up.

Frank closed the door behind him, and I slipped out of my jeans and shirt. Put on my skirt and my heels. When I was ready, I opened the door.

"Hot damn!" Frank slapped the side of his leg.

"You're funny." I took a deep breath. "I'm ready if you are."

At a quarter to six, Frank held out his arm and I laced mine inside.

We were almost to the cottage when I stopped walking. Frank looked over at me. "You all right?"

I was feeling overwhelmed.

Frank held me in his arms for a few seconds.

"I'm okay," I said and giggled. "I'm nervous and I don't know why. I think I'm more nervous now than the first time I married him."

"He's probably more nervous than you." Frank patted the top of my hand. "Remember what you told me, it's just a celebration of two people in love."

He was correct.

We strolled past the shade garden and the cottage. To our right was the pond. I could see the first row of chairs. I didn't need my vows; I knew exactly what I wanted to say.

We stopped just short of the path.

I could smell the eucalyptus. On the back of every chair, an ivory sash held a bouquet of hanging green Amaranthus and large creamy white roses. The chuppah adorned with seeded eucalyptus. A large centerpiece of cream and white flowers in the center. As we stepped closer, I could see Casablanca lilies, carnations, roses, freesia and ranunculus.

I looked over at Frank. "It's gorgeous."

Every seat taken. Everyone had arrived. Michael whistled as we went by. Kevin winked at me. Kourtnee said, "You both look stunning," to us as we walked past her.

A warm grin appeared on Teresa's face. I didn't cry again until I saw Dan and Jesse. Tears were streaming down Dan's face. He reached over and placed his hand on Jesse's back, and said, "She's even more beautiful this time."

When we reached the chuppah, Frank and I turned to face everyone. Dan moved closer to us. Every molecule inside me surged when Frank put my hand in Dan's.

Frank nodded to everyone. "I built this," he held his hands above his head, moving from side to side, "as a symbol of the new home and life Julie and Dan will build together. Marriage is a gift – an amazing blessing from God. Cherish every moment together."

Frank kissed me. He turned to Dan, holding his hand in his own. "She's a treasure." When he sat down next to Jesse, Frank's bottom lip quivered.

Dan turned to face me. "Julie, you are my world. You're my best friend. I want to share everything with... you." He brought our hands to his mouth and kissed the back of mine, and all I wanted to do was hold him. "We have the best *foundation* all around us. Good *friends!* Friends who care about us. They'll go to the end of the earth." He looked away, then back at me. "My friend Barbara said something to me one day that I'll never forget. 'If you say I'm sorry, know exactly what *it* is you are sorry for.' Julie, for the rest of my life, I take responsibility for my actions. Every day, I plan on showing you my love."

I took a deep breath. "Lord, today and every day, let laughter echo in our hearts and in our home, our inn and in our lives. May there be joy in every room. Let the radiance of Your face shine all around us. Help us bear each other's burdens, even as we cast our cares upon Your shoulders. Dan, may we choose to see the best in each other, even in the worst of times."

I heard Frank shout, "Amen." Echoed by others.

I reached up and wiped away Dan's tears.

We kissed, and everyone stood up, whistling and clapping.

Barbara gestured gracefully to Dan. I mouthed the words, "Thank you." to her, as I placed my hand over my heart. Then I blew her a kiss.

Lynnae hugged me. "This is a happy day…"

When she hugged Dan, he picked her up and spun her around in a circle. "Mwah!" Lynnae shouted as she kissed her palm and then waved it in the air.

Jesse gave Dan a bear hug.

I was grateful for the opportunity to introduce Dan to everyone who had been with me since day one. "Kelly is the person who introduced me to Frank. Geri's the maestro who made all of this happen."

Geri held out her hand. "I was the listing agent for the property. It's a pleasure to meet you."

"Hey, beautiful." Michael kissed me. "Dinner will be served in twenty…"

"Sounds great!" Dan shook Michael's hand. "Geri, this is Michael, best chef in Rhode Island!"

Geri looked at Michael. "So I've been told."

Cathy hugged and congratulated both of us, then added, "Did I hear the word food?" Geri, Barbara, and Frank followed Cathy back up to the terrace.

Michael, Christine, Kevin and Kourtnee said they would meet us on the terrace in a few minutes. "I can't wait," I told them.

"Dan, I'm Gina Marie, I work for Frank. It was a beautiful ceremony."

I motioned to Jessica and Sabrina. Gina Marie turned to them. "This is Jessica and Sabrina. They also work with Frank."

Jessica held her hand out to Dan and he shook it. She gave me a warm hug. "You look gorgeous."

"Yes," Gina Marie echoed Jessica's sentiments.

I looked over and saw Jesse and Barry talking and my heart sank. *Tomorrow, they'll be gone.*

"Aunt Julie, I'm hungry," Max said beckoning me to follow him.

"Me, too!" Sam yelled.

I picked Max up and kissed his cheek. "Okay, let's eat." I looked over at Dan. "Ready?"

"There's one more person I want you to meet." Dan waved to a woman sitting in the second row. She was talking to the owner of the bakery, Mary. Both women stood and came over to us.

I put Max down and kissed Mary on the cheek. "Thank you for coming."

"It was a pleasure making your desserts. I hope you like them."

I tilted my head. "I *love* everything you bake. Mary, this is my husband, Dan."

Dan nodded. "It's nice to meet you. Do you and Rose know each other?"

I looked at her. Rose was not what I expected. She was voluptuous by nature, younger than I assumed. I extended my hand to her. "Rose? Dan's…"

She smiled. "Therapist. Yes, it's nice to meet you. Thank you for inviting me. Barbara has told me great things about you." She chuckled, adding, "Dan never stops singing your praises."

Dan put his arm around me and kissed my cheek. "I wanted Rose to see for herself the reason I breathe."

When he said that, my heart came back to life.

"My husband was planning to come," Rose said before adding, "We heard the *food* is out of this world. But our sitter called at the last minute and said she couldn't make it."

"Call him and tell him to come. Seriously, we love children." I looked over at Dan.

"Yeah, they can run around with the boys."

"Thanks, but my youngest is eleven months. She goes to bed early. Next invite, I promise."

"Ready?" Mary asked Rose with a nod as she turned to leave. I watched as they walked away.

The awkwardness became excruciating. *Please God let us talk about this so we can get on with our lives.* Apparently, God was listening, because.

"Julie, she's…" Dan reached over and cupped my face in the palms of his hands. "She's my therapist." Dan's eyes leveled on me. "You are the only woman for me."

For a moment, we just stood there, in a silence that felt heavy, like a blanket. I had to admit I got some satisfaction that the subject at least made him feel uncomfortable. I was doing it again. Letting my own insecurities get the best of me. I saw Rose as a beautiful woman instead of recognizing her for the person helping my husband.

"Hey, lovebirds." Behind me, I heard Teresa say, "Umm, did I miss something?"

Sal chuckled. "It's their day. Give them a moment."

"I loved your vows. Perfect! But, I'm starving." Teresa's eyes opened wide. "Let's go, for heaven's sake."

Dan and Sal shook hands. I hugged Sal, and the four of us headed up to the inn.

Teresa put her arm around me. "How are you holding up? Because it looked like you just saw a ghost."

"Nah, I'm just worried about Erin," I replied.

"She's fine," Teresa said, adding, "don't worry about Erin. The entire staff is taking care of her. You're okay, right?"

I looked up. Dan and Sal were in front of us. I grinned from ear to ear. "Oh, yeah."

A moment later, Dan reached back for my hand, whispered in my ear, "I love you more and more every day!"

Chapter 7

Michael had transformed the farm table into an enormous buffet.

On the terrace, under twinkling lights, were eight round tables. At each place setting sat a small gift, wrapped in silver paper and tied with a satin ribbon. Inside, were personal tokens of affection keyed to the recipient's passionate interests.

Silver beakers filled with white, ivory and cream roses sat in the center of every table, surrounded by five sterling silver candlesticks. To my surprise, *new* cloth napkins bore the inn's logo. A silver anchor.

The moment Dan and I stepped onto the terrace, everyone held their glasses up.

"Salute!" Gina Marie shouted.

"Wahoo!" someone else cheered.

Dan pointed to the crowd. "Thank you for coming. Please, eat."

We followed our guests to the buffet table. When it was our turn, Dan filled his plate with a sampling of butternut squash ravioli, and Butterfield Cornish game hens with rosemary dressing. While Dan helped himself to the roasted rack of lamb with mint pan seared dressing and garlicky mussels, I opted for the mixed baby greens with fresh herb vinaigrette and grilled chicken.

Everyone took his or her seat, and Teresa offered the blessing. "Father, we thank You for this bounty. For those who are here to share in Your blessings and generosity. Amen"

"Amen," I echoed, and watched each one pick up a fork and begin to eat. I heard sounds of joy and laughter, and then I noticed Erin and my heart stopped. Her chin was blue beneath her makeup.

"Are you happy?" Dan whispered in my ear.

"About? Oh, sorry. Yes." I kissed him. "Very much," I replied as I watched Erin and Kyle, move to fill their plates with a dessert or two.

The Venetian table was an enormous success. I think the mini cakes were the guests' favorite, although Dan said, "The custard *crema frittata* was unbelievable."

First, Dan and I danced to "How Sweet It Is To Be Loved By You", then everyone joined in when "All Summer Long" played. As much as I loved Kid Rock, I enjoyed sitting back watching my entire staff get down on the dance floor.

By quarter after nine, everyone left. I didn't see Rose, Geri, Barbara or Mary before they left. The flower entourage said they were heading over to Newport for an early Halloween party hosted by the Fashion Institute.

Lynnae and Kourtnee both said they had children to put to bed.

I looked for Erin. She was nowhere in sight.

"Good night, sunshine." Michael kissed me on the cheek. "Dan's waiting for you."

I turned around and saw he was standing alone at the end of the terrace.

"We'll see you tomorrow morning." Christine gestured gracefully as she put her arm through Michael's. "This momma's got to get off her feet."

I blew her a kiss. Her due date was in less than a month.

Dan was leaning against a pillar. He was staring at me intently. "Ready?"

"Yeah…"

"What?"

"I can't believe they came." I took his hand. "I don't want it to end."

"It's not over yet," he said as he put his arm around me.

We strolled down to the cottage. Dan was humming. I listened closely as he said the words, "I Cross My Heart" aloud.

My heart leveled on him as I rubbed the small of his back. Dan pivoted to face me as I told him. "I love you so much—"

In the glow of the evening, he promised to love me forever. Then I heard him say, "Make a wish!" he pointed to a shooting star.

I looked up, "Please don't let them leave."

Dan lowered his voice. "Don't think about tomorrow. Lynnae and Barry will be back before you know it."

I started walking again. "You're right. Tonight is very special." I smiled. "I'm so happy you found me."

Dan opened the door, and my eyes took in the room. The fire was glowing. He had champagne on ice. And in front of the fireplace, three packages stacked on top of one another. All wrapped in silver paper. The small package on the top had a tiny bow on it.

Dan poured two glasses. I sat down on the floor in front of the fireplace. I took off my shoes and leaned up against the sofa. My legs stretched out in front of me, I breathed in the scent of burning wood, cinnamon and vanilla scented candles.

Dan sat down beside me and kissed me. "I love you more than you can imagine."

"I will always love you," I replied, meaning it more than ever.

He handed me the large box from the bottom. I opened it and saw a beautiful short black lace nightgown. "It's gorgeous. Thank you." Then he handed me the middle box. Inside was a pair of matching boxer shorts. "Seriously? You're not wearing these." I snickered at the thought.

Dan kissed me on my cheek. "Open this one."

I opened the box and found a small black velvet box inside. "Oh, my…" I looked at him. "It's… it's beautiful." Of course, I started to cry the moment Dan slipped the necklace around my neck.

"I know you're not big on jewelry, but I want you to always remember this day. Think of it as chocolates from the jewelry store."

I kissed him, and while he was kissing me, he somehow managed to pull out a card. I looked at him. "I didn't get you anything."

Dan inhaled and then blew out a slow breath. "You are all I want. You're my... everything."

He handed me the envelope. When I opened the card inside, two plane tickets fell onto my lap. "Oh, Dan." My heart started racing. "Italy!"

"The travel agent said May is the best time to go." Dan inhaled before adding, "I'm sorry I didn't take you sooner." He tilted his head. "From now on we are going to live life to the fullest. I'll take you wherever you want to go."

"Well," I said, "maybe I'll take you! Right after I make myself comfortable."

Dan stood up, and I jumped into his arms. In the bedroom, I slowly took off my skirt, then my top. He picked me up. Sat me down on the edge of the bed and knelt down in front of me. Our eyes locked as Dan moved his hands from my knees to my thighs, and before I knew it, my panties were on the floor.

One kiss on my lips before he whispered in my ear, "I'm going to make love to you all night long."

Chapter 8

The next morning, I woke in a pool of sweat, and it was *not* menopause!

I had that nightmare again. On top of that, I dreamt about Erin being abused by her husband. I sat up and looked at myself in the mirror. My hair plastered against my face. My heart was *full* of worry. I needed a shower.

The water was streaming down my face and body. I had yet to pick up the soap, when Dan opened the shower door. "We need a bigger shower." He kissed my right shoulder, and I heard the door close.

I turned to kiss him, but Dan spun me back around. I felt his hand on the top of my head. One hand held my forehead, and the other massaged shampoo in my hair. After he rinsed my hair, we washed both our bodies. I rinsed myself off and then stepped out of the shower.

I was toweling off when Dan started singing, George Jones's "Walk Through This World with Me". When I heard him singing "share all your dreams with me..." I wished I could tell him about last night's nightmare but I couldn't. It was our time. I prayed my worries would go away.

When Dan looked at me, I could see all the heaviness that he had been carrying around the past few years. *Now he's uprooting his entire life so we can be together.*

"Is my beautiful wife ready or not?" Dan teased me.

At eight-thirty, we headed up to the inn. I missed my baby girl. Couldn't wait to wrap my arms around her. "I can't wait to see Lady," I said.

Dan patted my hand. "Me, either."

The moment I stepped on the front porch, I could smell freshly baked croissants.

Dan held the door open for me. "I smell coffee," he said, smiling at Teresa.

"Good morning," Teresa said and set her teacup down.

Dan gave her a kiss on the cheek. "Thanks for everything. Sal's coming, right?"

"He's inside with Lynnae, Barry, and the boys," she replied.

"Lynnae's downstairs already?" I asked, surprised.

"Yeah, she said they were leaving by ten."

My heart sank knowing I wouldn't see her until Christmas.

Dan put his arm around me. "Let's get some breakfast."

In the billiards room, Michael had put a drop cloth, then a sheet of plywood, on the pool table. Covered it with a piece of plastic and a tablecloth. He also set a few café tables for our wedding guests. The sign on the door read: Private Party.

In less than an hour, Lynnae, Barry, Sam and Max would head home to their normal lives, leaving a hole in mine. My *saving grace*: believing Barry. He assured me Lynnae would never have to look at a price tag or tell the boys to put something back.

"Morning," Barry said, and then stood up to shake Dan's hand.

"Good morning," Dan said, extending his hand.

I kissed him. "Good morning." Then I looked at Lynnae. "You're leaving—"

"Barry's got a lot of things to do this weekend." She curled her lip before adding, "I have a bakery to run."

Dan asked if anyone had seen Jesse yet, and when Barry told him he went into town early this morning, I was afraid he was out looking for Erin's husband.

Dan and I filled our plates, sat down, and watched as everyone came in and did the same. I heard laughter, baby

Delilah cry, and I thought, *please make them stay*. But when Barry stood up and shook Dan's hand, my heart stopped beating.

"Bye, Aunt Julie," Sam said, sounding as sad as I felt.

I hugged him and Max at the same time. "I love you both so much."

"I…" Max looked at me and then ran over to Barry. When he picked him up, Max buried his face. Lynnae hugged me goodbye. Brushed her hand on Dan's cheek and took hold of Sam. We followed them outside.

A stream of tears rushed down my cheeks as I watched Barry's SUV go down the driveway. My cheeks were burning, and even though the ache in my chest was as heavy as an anchor, I smiled and waved goodbye.

Dan held me close in his arms. "They'll be back for Christmas."

Lady ran between us. "Lady, how's my girl?" Dan bent down and hugged her.

I looked over and saw Erin holding Kyle in her arms. The sun was glowing on her raven waves as they brushed against her shoulders. Our eyes met. Erin put Kyle down. I heard her say, "Go!"

Kyle came over to where Dan and I were standing. "Thank you."

Dan picked Kyle up. Glanced over at Erin. "You're welcome." He set Kyle down and asked if he wanted to go for a ride in the canoe.

Kyle nodded and looked back at his mother.

"Um… sure," Erin said.

I was thankful, and I knew what Dan was doing. Because every time things went awry, Dan stepped up.

I bent down and hugged my baby girl before she ran after Dan and Kyle. I put my hand on Erin's shoulder and told her, "Don't worry. Dan will make him wear a life vest and wrap him in a

Woolrich blanket. I was just about to make myself a cup of tea. Would you like one?"

Erin nodded, and together we went back into the inn.

A few minutes later, I handed Erin her cup.

"Would you like to take a stroll with me? The rose garden has a way of keeping secrets fiercely private."

We walked in our own silence. I held the gate open. Without saying a word, Erin walked over to the resting bench, sat down, and began sipping her tea.

I sat down next to her. "This is my go-to place. I enjoy the peace and tranquility the garden offers." I drank my tea, wondering why I felt I had to be so careful-around her. When my cup was empty, I set it down and patted Erin on the leg, "You're welcome here for as long as you—"

"Julie... I feel so ashamed of myself."

"Erin, there's nothing to be ashamed of."

"My life's a mess," she said.

"It's not. I assure you, you're going to get through this. Erin, my life wasn't always like this. Three years ago, I walked away from everything that I loved. In order to be where I am today, I had to believe in myself. It wasn't easy for me." I looked at her. "I promise you better days are coming."

I saw her dissolving into her own memories. She rolled her eyes and ran her fingers through her hair, her wary green gaze directed at the walking path. With the scent of roses still prominent in the air, she inhaled.

Erin set her teacup down. "I didn't know where..." She paused, fidgeting with her hands. "Julie, I have nowhere to go." She sat back and inhaled again. "My parents..." Then she looked at me. "When I was born, my birth mother left me in the hospital. My parents traveled all the way to Ireland to adopt me. I was eight months old when I came to the United States."

She kicked her legs out. "We didn't have a lot of money. My mother always paid our rent six months in advance because she never knew how long my father could keep working the way he did. Life was hard on my mother and even harder on my dad. If no one picked him up, he walked two to three miles to and from work every day. He was a stubborn old Irishman. Worked on the Seven B's in Narragansett all his life. I was twelve when my dad died. He was only fifty-nine. Mom said as long as I was in school, she could collect Dad's social security. Her heart broke when he died. She held on until I graduated from high school. Four months after she died, I met Josh."

"I'm sorry about your parents. Erin, is Josh the person who did this to you?"

She started shaking her legs. "I was so stupid. I… believed him."

"Erin, you're not stupid, and you're definitely not alone. A lot of women—"

"No, Julie! I don't want to be like them. We might have been poor, but I promised my mother, I would never let a man treat me that way. I wanted to go to college." Erin held out her hands and then rested them on her head. "What happened to me? Why didn't I know?"

Loneliness, I thought, but didn't say it.

Her hands were now at her side. She sighed, long and hard. "Josh was so kind, and smart, too. I was working at the new Chocolate-Coffee Shop in Charlestown, trying to save enough money to buy myself a car so I could go to community college, when I met him."

She looked at me. "When Josh paid for his coffee, he told me I was the most beautiful girl he'd ever met. I thanked him but when he left, I rolled my eyes and said, 'He'll never be back.'"

She shook her head. "The next day he sent me flowers at the shop. And every day for a week one bouquet after another arrived. On Saturday, Josh walked in with a picnic basket. He sat at the corner table until I got off work. We went to the park across the street, ate the take out he had from Aunt Carrie's, and talked."

Erin gathered her hair behind her head and began twirling it. "The next day, a package arrived for me. Inside was a beautiful Pandora bracelet with a picnic basket charm. I opened the card. He wrote me the most beautiful poem. We spent every weekend together. Took so many mini romantic vacations."

She looked down at her hands, then up at me. "A month after we got married, I told him I was pregnant. He yelled at me. Julie, I was terrified. But Josh quickly apologized and said he would never raise his voice to me again." She shook her head and sounded choked up when she added, "I hate myself."

I reached over and held her in my arms.

Erin leaned back. "I'm sorry. I'm ruining your beautiful moment."

"Right now is your moment in time. I've had my share. Erin, I care about you. I want to help you, but I have to know more about you, Kyle, and especially about Josh." I looked at her. Our eyes locked. "When you're ready to share your backstory, I'll be waiting."

"Thank you," she said as she took a deep, shuddering breath.

I knew exactly how she felt. Lost, confused and broken. I hated domestic violence. Hearing only a part of her story, I knew I had to help her. First, I needed to see what the local government had to say about Josh accusing her of kidnapping their son. If he cared at all. As if we were reading each other's minds, we both stood at the same time.

"I don't think Josh even misses us," she said.

I didn't know what to say. Side by side, we made our way past the English roses. I closed the gate to the garden, not knowing what was to come next.

We were on our way over to the inn when she said, "Julie, thank you for all you've done, you and your friends, but... um... maybe Kyle and I should go to a shelter—"

"No! This is your safe house. You and Kyle can stay in the Newport room. The girls are leaving this morning. I'll have Teresa block *that* room off for the rest of the season. As soon as Brooke and Stephanie leave, you and Kyle will move in to that room until we figure this all out."

"Are you sure?" She looked at me.

"Absolutely," I declared.

"I don't know what to say." She put her hand to her mouth, mumbling something, but I didn't quite understand what. Then I heard her say, "Thank you."

"You're welcome. The Newport is a suitable room for you. You'll have a view of the rose garden and the daycare. Amanda is phenomenal with the children. She can take care of Kyle while you look at colleges."

"I... no... no, Julie."

"Yes, you can and will," I said in my best firm voice. "I'll have Dan put a bed in your room for Kyle." I sighed, then tipped my head back to look up at the sky before adding, "God has placed you in my path for a reason. What that reason is... I don't know. But what I do know is you are not going back to that monster." I put my hands on her shoulders. "I do not tolerate domestic violence."

A pause, then she slowly nodded.

Out in the distance, we could hear Jesse hollering for Dan. We caught up to him and told him that Dan had taken Kyle for a canoe ride.

"My little buddy went without me?" Jesse said jokingly and then teased us. "What are the two of you up to?"

Erin reached up and hugged him. For a minute, I didn't think Jesse knew what to do. He looked at me, tilted his head, and patted Erin on her back. He exhaled in a low, whistle-like sound. "Mmm, better now?"

Erin stepped back from him. "Thank you for stopping."

"You're welcome." Jesse placed one of his enormous hands on Erin's shoulder. "Whatever you need, it's yours." He turned to me. "I'd better head down to the pond and check up on those two."

I shook my head. "That's Jesse for you. Erin, I have to ask. Where is your husband right now?"

"He's probably in his office." Her voice was suddenly frantic. "He works from home."

"Okay and where is that?" I asked, still unaware of where they lived.

"Scarborough Hills."

I thought for a minute. "It doesn't matter. He'll never find you here."

"I'm so sorry. I had to carry Kyle. I... I couldn't go any farther." She rubbed her face.

"Erin, it's okay. I'm grateful to Jesse for picking you up and bringing you here—"

"But..." she drew in a shuddering breath.

I waited for her to comment further. When she didn't say anything, we both started walking again.

"Julie! Erin, wait," Dan hollered.

Dan and Jesse were holding Kyle's hands, swinging him high in the air.

"I have a great idea," Dan said to us, as they got closer. "Kyle has never tried oysters. I was telling Jesse the oysters at Ballard's are the best reason to go to Block Island. That's when Kyle said, 'Let's go now.' But Jesse and I were just saying to Kyle that it's too cold to go for a ferry ride, so let's cook our own. What do you say?"

I giggled. "I don't eat oysters. Do you?"

Erin shook her head. "Ewe."

"Mommy, I saw a deer."

Erin's face lit up. "You did? Where?"

"Near the pond."

I leaned over toward Jesse. "Jesse, what time are you leaving tomorrow?" I asked, hoping he would still be around to help Dan with Kyle's bed.

Jesse ran his hand over his chin. "Huh, I'm not. I've decided to stick around for a while."

I was pleased to hear that. "Great, can you go into town with Dan and buy a twin bed?"

Jesse looked at me. "What? Oh, right. Sure I can." He rubbed the top of Kyle's head.

"We'll go now," Dan said as he looked in his wallet. "Plenty."

"Mommy?"

Erin picked Kyle up.

"Can I go?"

I tugged on Kyle's foot. "Kyle, why don't you, Mommy and I check out the daycare? Amanda's there and she has a lot of games, books and toys."

"Kyle." Dan moved closer to him. "There's a train set in there. And if you're good this afternoon, Jesse and I will come over and show you how to make it go *fast*."

I left Erin and Kyle with Amanda for a few minutes. Stopped on the front porch greeted a couple checking in for the weekend. Said goodbye to some guests.

"We'll be back for the garden tour," the woman said.

"Sounds good. We look forward to your return. Drive safe. Bye now."

I stepped inside, stopped at the front desk and informed Teresa to block the Newport room off for the rest of the season.

I went into the library, closed the door, and dialed Frank's number. "How's my favorite person in the world?"

"You're funny," he said. "Dan's not in the room, is he?"

I laughed. "No."

"How's my girl? You looked beautiful last night."

"Thank you. Well, you looked very handsome yourself." I sat down in my favorite chair. "Frank, do you know a local judge?"

"Sure, I do. Abrams. He's a good friend of mine, fishing buddy. Tries to get me to play golf with him every Friday."

"Frank, Erin's husband is the person who beat her up."

"Dan told me something about her. Said Jesse picked them up in their pajamas at the end of your driveway. What do you need me to do?"

"Can you call him and ask what the law has to say about a woman leaving with a child?"

"You planning on keeping her there?" Frank's voice was firm. I had never heard him use that tone with me.

"I—"

"I'll take care of it," Frank said flatly. "You call me day or night." He hung up the phone.

I thanked God for Frank.

I was grateful for Jesse. Glad he decided to stay awhile longer.

The curtain moved, and it startled me. I closed the window and latched it all the way. As I lay sprawled out on the carpet, trying to relieve the tension in my back, I was trying to figure out the best way to help Erin.

Ten minutes later, I stood up, stretched, and noticed a man outside the window. My heart started to race. He walked alongside the building, looking in every direction. I watched him walk toward the backyard. He frightened me. I didn't know what to do. I called Dan on his cell phone. "Where are you? There's a man walking around the inn. I think it's Josh. Dan, please turn the truck around."

"Julie, where's Erin and Kyle? Julie, where are they?" he shouted in my ear.

I looked out the window again. This time I didn't see the man. "They're in the daycare. I left them alone..." My heart raced faster and faster. I needed to sit down, but I ran out of the inn. Directly to the daycare and locked the door behind me. I didn't say a word to anyone, I just sat in the rocking chair watching the door, listening to Amanda read, *The Frog Prince*. Twenty, maybe thirty minutes later, Dan and Jesse knocked on the door. Kyle ran to them before I could get close enough to find out what happened.

Dan hugged me and whispered in my ear. "Apparently, the Land for Trust had an appointment to walk the property today." Dan leaned back. "You're shaking." He hugged me again. "You're okay. Next time, one of us will stay with you. Jesse and I won't leave you here by yourself."

"I panicked, I shouldn't have," I said.

Chapter 9

I was sitting on the window seat in the bedroom when I sprang to my feet. I decided to call a staff meeting. I hadn't had one since Dan arrived in August. I headed up to the inn, feeling good about asking Dan to attend the meeting. I knew he was proud of me, but this would allow him to see me in action. I didn't care if anyone heard me. I started singing, "It's Your Love" by Shania Twain.

Teresa was on the phone when I walked through the lobby, so I just gave her a quick wave hello. I went into Kourtnee's office, and she was on the phone. She was speaking to a bride about her cake.

"You can have whatever top you want." Kourtnee rolled her eyes at me and pointed to the chair. "Sounds good. Send me the picture and I'll give it to Christine. You got it." She hung up. "She's changed the cake topper... ten times."

I laughed. "At least she doesn't want teepees."

"Remember?"

"I thought the teepees were fine. Can you schedule a meeting for this Friday?"

Kourtnee looked at her computer screen. "Nine? No, wait." She moved the cursor. "Nine works. I'll let Michael know right away. How's Erin today?"

"I've convinced her to stay here for a little while. Kourtnee, she's petrified of her husband." I shook my head. "She has no one else."

Bea tapped on the door, and of course, I jumped. "Can I see you for a minute?"

I turned to face her. "Kourtnee or me?"

"Actually, both of you." She sounded ecstatic.

"Come on in," Kourtnee said to her.

Bea sat down next to me. "I got accepted at FIT."

"Wow!" I reached over and hugged her. "You're talking about the Fashion Institute of Technology. Yes?"

Bea nodded. "My friends introduced me to an instructor and she loved my work. I wanted to let you know right away." Bea put her hands to her cheeks. "I haven't told Uncle Frank yet. I'm planning on surprising him tonight. I'm taking him to dinner at Kelly's new restaurant."

"Kelly from the diner?" Kourtnee asked.

"Yeah, it's on Great Island Road. It's really cool. You should check it out. Mulligans' Tap Room, right next to the coffee shop."

"We will," I said. "Bea, I'm sure your Uncle Frank is going to be delighted. I'm so proud of you. Wow, FIT. Good for you."

"I don't start until next fall," Bea said. "Even so, I wanted to let you know so you could hire another person. I'm planning on moving to New York City the first of the year."

Kourtnee looked at me. "I'll take care of it."

"Bea, this calls for a celebration." I hugged her again and told her, "I'm going to miss you."

Both Bea and I left Kourtnee's office at the same time.

After I told everyone about the meeting, I strolled down to the pond. I was happy to see Dan sitting in one of the Adirondack chairs. "It's beautiful, isn't it?" I said.

Dan reached up for my hand, kissed the back of it, and shook his head. "You did a good job. Inlet, outlet."

I sat down next to him. "You taught me so much. I have to tell you, every time I had to make a decision, I wished you were here." I looked out at the pond. "I almost dredged out the pond on the upper piece, but then I heard this voice in my head saying, 'it will grow stagnate.' I didn't want to put a pump in, or plant anything so I put it close enough to the stream."

"How big is the pipe?" he asked.

"Twenty-four-inches. Would you like to take a walk and see how I did it?" Dan and I strolled around the entire pond. It felt like old times, Dan stopping to kiss me, telling me how proud he was and discussing our future as innkeepers. It was a beautiful moment.

Two days later, the air was cold, but I didn't care. I was sitting in the same Adirondack chair, wishing I had a tissue. Praying for a positive resolution for Erin. Right in front of me, deer were feasting on my hydrangeas. The pond had more ducks than ever before. I could have cared less.

"Young lady, those better be happy tears."

I turned around. "Frank!"

Frank sat down next to me. "My wife, she used to cry every day when she got her cycle. During those three or four days, she would bake like crazy. I miss her. Miss her sweet smile. I'm guessing those tears you're shedding are about something," he said, looking at me with that twinkle in his eye.

"I'm not sure how to help Erin. My heart hurts, Frank. I don't know what to do. There's more to her story than she is telling me."

Frank reached over and patted my hand, and said, "I spoke to Abrams. He suggested we take pictures of those marks on her."

"Okay, I can do that." I swallowed and sniffled again, wiping my nose on the back of my other hand.

"Maybe Erin can fill in for Bea," he said, sounding unsure.

"That's a great idea," I said and then added, "I'm so proud of Bea. It's not easy getting into FIT."

"I always knew she would succeed," Frank said, smiling. "I told her I'm just a call away."

"You're the best uncle, and friend, in the world."

"Everything's happening so fast. Bea moving to New York, and—"

I looked at him. "And?" I leaned in closer.

"Julie?" Dan was hollering for me.

"Wait, and what Frank…?"

"Another time," he said. "It can wait."

"Julie!" Dan shouted.

Frank and I stood up to face the cottage. "I'm right here," I hollered back to him.

"Michael needs you. Christine's in labor."

"Oh, my Lord. It never ends." I looked at Frank. "Quick tell me. You said *and*. And what?"

"Go, you have a baby on the way." He touched my cheek. "We'll talk later."

By the time we reached the inn, Michael and Christine were gone. I kissed Frank goodbye. Dan and I followed him down the driveway. On our way to the hospital, I told Dan what Frank and I had discussed. Dan thought it was a good idea to take the pictures. A few days had passed since Erin and Kyle had arrived, making her bruises more noticeable than ever.

"Are you okay?" he asked me.

"I'm fine. It's a good thing I built the daycare when I did."

Dan reached over and took my hand in his. "Were you crying?"

There was no hiding anything from Dan. "I'm worried sick about Erin." I looked over at him. "One minute she's willing to talk to me and the next she's fidgeting and uncomfortable."

"I'm sorry. I wish there was something I could do to help you. Julie, I know how bad you wanted to have children but you can't take every person under your wing and expect them to take to you like Lynnae did. Give Erin some time. I have a great idea. Let's go to New York for Thanksgiving?" He squeezed my hand. "We'll have dinner with Barry and Lynnae."

I looked at him. "That would be great, except they're going away that week."

"Well, where are they going, maybe we'll join them?"

"No. They're going to the Snapdragon Inn in Vermont. Sam wrote a paper on famed editor, Maxwell Perkins. Barry wants to surprise Sam. The inn was once the home of Perkins. Then Barry's taking them skiing at a family resort, Bromley."

A moment later, Dan pulled up to the front door of the hospital. "Go on in, I'll park the truck."

Thanks to Kourtnee, I knew exactly where the maternity unit was located. I was sitting in the waiting room when Dan came in. He stood in front of me and held out his hand. "I just saw Michael. Care to see the newest addition to our family?" Dan was grinning from ear to ear. "Michael said Christine was only in labor for a few hours. They're in room 202."

Christine gave birth to a baby girl. They named her Brin, after her maternal grandmother.

With Michael at the hospital that night, Dan and I cooked dinner for our guests. Dan made his famous meat loaf, barbecued potato skins with cheddar cheese, and golden beets from the garden. I made the endive salad. And for dessert, I made apple cake with apple cider glaze. It felt incredible being in the kitchen with Dan. Watching him sway to the sound of Willie Nelson made me feel good.

The next morning, I waited for Kyle to go to the daycare. I knocked on Erin's door. Then I sat down with her and told her what Judge Abrams asked us to do.

"I, uh, I didn't want to be one of those stereotypes. I.—" she cried.

"Erin, it's important that we protect you."

"Ugh." Erin rubbed her face. "Sorry, I, uh, I'm pretty banged up!"

"That's why it's important. We have to do it, in case…"

Erin blew out a breath. "I know." She wrapped her hair up in a high ponytail.

I got up and locked the door. Erin went into the bathroom. When she came back, she had a towel wrapped around her. Wearing only a pair of panties, Erin dropped the towel.

I tried not to show any emotions. Her thighs were purple. The upper part of her arms, black and blue.

"One more and we're done." I reached up and lifted Erin's chin. I took a snapshot of her jaw. Then I picked the towel up and handed it to her. "I'm proud of you for running as fast as you could."

Erin held the towel together with her left hand. With her right hand, she reached down and grabbed a tissue. Tears were running down her face.

Mine, too. I sat down at the foot of the bed.

Erin went back into the bathroom to redress. When she came out and sat down next to me, I asked her if she would like a cup of tea.

She nodded. "Yes, ma'am."

We went to the kitchen. I put the water on and set four shortbread cookies on a small plate. A minute later, I sat down next to Erin.

"Thank you." She sipped her tea. "Oooh, hot!"

I stood up, opened the kitchen drawer, and handed her a folder. "I found a few colleges that offer home study. Southern New Hampshire will hand deliver your diploma right to your door."

"I don't know what to say. I, I have no way of re-paying you."

"Erin, please," I said. "I'll make you a deal." I pointed my finger at her. "I'll give you work but you have to go to college."

Her face lit up. She nodded. "Okay…"

"Great!" I ate a cookie, drank my tea, and listened to Erin tell me another chapter in her story.

"Julie, I didn't realize what Josh was doing until now." Her mouth twisted. "When I first met him, he gave me a cell phone. I thought it was for…" she shook her head. "The phone was so he could keep track of me. It took me awhile to figure it out, but one day when he asked me where I went, I told him I was at the library. Just to see what he would say. Later on, when he asked me what I picked up at the drugstore, I knew."

Erin sat back, laced her fingers, and continued. "I looked at the applications on my cell and saw an app called, Family Locator. He frigging monitored my phone."

She was getting stronger. I could hear it in her voice.

"Last night, while Kyle was sleeping. I sat in the chair in my room, trying to come up with a reason why. Why I allowed him to treat me like that. I can't believe how dumb I was."

"Erin—"

"No, Julie, it's true. For five years, I thought Josh was doing everything for me because he loved me." Her voice got a little louder. "I thought he was taking care of me. Julie, when he put gas in my car, I thought he was being nice. But now I know why he did it."

She drank her tea. Started tapping her fingers on the table. "He'd say to me, 'You went through a lot of gas this week. Where did you go?' And I'd be like, nowhere. Not realizing he was keeping track of everything. He bought the groceries, cooked all of our meals, he even bought my clothes. He would say things like, 'Just make yourself pretty.'" She shifted in her seat. "One day a man came to the house to pick up his income tax returns. He told Josh that if I wasn't his wife, he would ask me out on a date. When he left, Josh opened his desk drawer and pulled out a gun. He said he wanted to kill that man just for saying that to him. 'Burn his files! Every damn last income tax file,' he screamed."

Oh, dear Lord. I looked at her. "Erin, have you ever been to New York?"

"I've never been nowhere but Rhode Island." She picked up a cookie and broke it in half. "Why?"

"Dan and Jesse are planning to go to New York for a few days. Perhaps you and I could go with them. You could help me pack up some of my belongings in the house, while Dan and Jesse pack up Dan's tools and load up his heavy equipment."

"I would love to help you, but what about Kyle?"

I looked at her. "Lady and Kyle will go with us."

Chapter 10

Friday, October 18th, when Dan opened the front door at the cottage, the sky cracked with thunder, and the downpour was instantaneous. By the time, we reached the inn and stepped up onto the porch, thankfully, the rain had softened.

I asked Dan and Jesse to attend the meeting because I wanted them both to know how the inn operated. And I wanted to formally introduce Erin to the entire staff.

Inside, Erin was sitting in one of the two accent chairs in the lobby. "Good morning," I said to her.

A moment later, Kevin came down the stairs carrying Delilah. "Dan, I need to see you for a sec."

"Sure." Dan reached up and took the diaper bag from him.

Kevin looked back at me. "We'll be right back. I have to take Delilah to daycare."

I kissed her on the cheek.

Teresa set foot in the lobby, holding a cup of tea. "Crap, you guys want one?" She asked, holding up her cup, smiling at Erin and me.

"I'm good." I looked at Erin. "Erin?"

"No thanks," she replied.

Kourtnee came downstairs, followed by Jesse and two of our guests.

"Good morning, Mr. and Mrs. Canton," Teresa said. "Are you having breakfast before you leave?"

"We ate in the dining room earlier, thank you," Mr. Canton replied. "We were hoping to beat the rain, but it doesn't look like we succeeded."

"It's let up, if that helps," I said as I held the door open for them.

"Great, because I hate driving in downpours," Mr. Canton admitted.

I smiled warmly at them both and said, "Thank you for staying with us."

"Hang on," Teresa said, and held an umbrella over Mrs. Canton's head as she went to step off the front porch. Teresa ran back inside, put the wet umbrella in the stand and announced, "Winter is coming. I can feel it in my bones."

When Dan and Kevin came back, Dan gave Jesse two thumbs up.

I saw Jesse give Kevin a nod. "Good job."

Not knowing what that was all about, I said, "Okay, let's go."

We all gathered in the kitchen. Everyone except Christine, who was tending to her newborn. "Good morning, please help yourself to breakfast and take your seats. I have a lot to go over."

Dan sat down between Kevin and Jesse. The three men each had a sampling of pancakes, scrambled eggs, bacon, and sausage on their plates.

I waited for everyone to take a seat before saying, "I would like to start by introducing our new house guest, Erin, to everyone. Erin will be working with us. She has a four-year-old son. And for those of you who have not met him, his name is Kyle. They will be in the Newport room."

"Welcome," Michael said.

Erin nodded. "Thank you. Umm, congratulations on your new baby."

I held my coffee cup up, smiling. "Cheers to Michael and Christine. Christine, by the way is upstairs with the baby. And for the next week, I'll be baking all of our desserts."

"Oh, boy," Teresa said under her breath.

I pointed my finger at Teresa. I haven't lost my touch yet. "Erin, let me start with the couples. Kevin is married to

Kourtnee. Kevin is in charge of lawn maintenance. Kourtnee takes care of the books. Michael is our chef and Christine is our baker. You know what, why doesn't everyone tell Erin who you are and what job you perform?"

"Jesse. Bodyguard."

I laughed and then added, "He has a successful tree business. Jesse's an arborist."

Teresa smiled and winked at Erin. "Receptionist."

Kourtnee raised her cup. "My closet is always open."

Erin grinned.

"I'm Cathy. I run the day spa. It's nice to meet you, Erin."

"My name is Bea." She looked at me and I nodded. "I assist Julie in the dining rooms. But in January I'll be leaving to settle in an apartment in New York. I've been accepted to FIT!"

When the room erupted with loud cheers, Jesse put his hands over his ears. "Jeeez."

Teresa, Molly and Kourtnee all jumped up and hugged Bea.

"Well, that leaves me. I'm Molly. Designer. I'm in charge of the floral arrangements and decor."

"Molly is our inn-house decorator, so to speak," I echoed. "And, she's the best interior designer in the world." I looked at Dan; he was staring at me, smiling. I winked at him. "Erin, besides Amanda, there are a few others that you may see from time to time. Frank is the contractor who put the addition on the inn. His architect's name is Sabrina. Gina Maria and Jessica also work directly with Frank. We try to schedule repairs and renovations during the days when the inn is closed."

"Never," Michael said. "When the mood strikes, she gets it done."

Everyone laughed.

"Stop. I've been very good." I looked over at Dan, who was *looking* at Jesse. They both had two thumbs up again. "Okay, since Dan's been here," I added.

"What?" Dan said.

I waved him off. Wondering what in the world he was up to now. "I want to let you all know that next week, Dan, Jesse, Erin and I are going to go to New York to pack up the house."

Michael jumped to his feet. "Yes!" At that. Everyone started cheering. Michael and Kevin shook Dan's hand. "You're going love it here," Michael told Dan.

"Tell me you're bringing some iron with you?" Kevin asked, with his hand on Dan's shoulder. "You know, some heavy equipment!"

"I'll be bringing back whatever Julie needs," Dan replied.

"Dan is retiring," I said with a smiling heart. "We've sold our home in New York."

Chapter 11

The following Monday, Dan, Jesse, Kyle, and Lady drove down the driveway in Jesse's truck. Erin and I drove Dan's truck. Thankfully, both trucks had crew cabs. Dan had put Kyle's car seat behind the driver's seat so he could see him at all times.

Lady sat in the back with Kyle. Jesse's truck already had tinted windows, but for added protection, Dan hung black screens on the two side windows. Kyle was small enough that no one would see him from the windshield. Dan also hung the screens in his truck and asked Erin to sit behind the passenger's seat. He reassured her that once we were out of Rhode Island, she could join me in the front seat.

Erin agreed to ride in the back until we were in Connecticut.

"What type of music do you like to listen to?" I asked her."

"Mostly country," she replied. "But I'm fine with whatever you like."

"Country it is," I said happily.

Before I could turn the radio on, Erin asked me what I thought about Kyle not asking for his father. "He hasn't asked once. It's like… umm, he doesn't even miss him. Do you think… he's okay?"

I glanced in the mirror. Our eyes met. "Was he close to his father?"

Erin's mouth twitched several times before saying, "No, not really."

I stopped at a red light and turned to face her. "Erin, Kyle is four. Amanda says he's very smart. Who taught him to read?"

"Umm, that would be me."

"Very impressive."

"You think so?" she asked. "I had to do something with him. I read to him to keep him quiet." I heard her feet stomp on the floor. "Josh was such an ass! When Kyle was teething. It was hard for me to keep him quiet. No matter what I gave him, all he wanted was for me to hold him..." Her voice drifted away.

Silence.

Following Jesse's every move, I put my blinker on and turned right at the corner. I glanced in the mirror and said, "All babies— "

"Julie, that's when Josh moved my desk to the basement," she said with sadness in her voice. "In one corner was Kyle's playpen and in the other, my new file cabinet. The only time Kyle and I went upstairs was dinner and at bedtime."

I could hear her breathing. I wondered if Josh put her in the basement to prevent other men from seeing her, or if he really was that cruel to his own son.

She continued, "So in between filling out income tax forms, I read to him. I think it was right before his third birthday when he started reading along with me. From that moment on I started pointing to the words."

I looked back at her. Tears were running down her face. Once again, silence.

"Erin, are you hungry?" I asked her, hoping she was. "There's a cooler with water and seltzer on the floor next to you." I grabbed a small bag and handed it back to her. "I'm not sure what he packed, but Dan always packs a great snack bag."

Up ahead, Jesse turned his signal on for us to pull over. He came back to the truck and asked us if we were both okay. "We're fine," I said.

Jesse tapped on my doorframe. "Good. Dan says to turn your damn cell phone ringer on. He's been trying to call you."

"Yikes," I said, reaching for my phone.

"Is Kyle okay?" Erin asked.

"He's fine. He's singing country…" Jesse winked at me. "Dan just wants to make sure *you're* okay." He looked back at Erin. "Ya okay?"

Erin nodded.

Jesse went back to his truck and I put my cell phone in the car cradle. "Thank God for hands-free." I laughed, adding, "but it only works if it's on." I glanced back at Erin. "Obviously, Kyle likes country as much Dan and Jesse."

She smiled. "I used to let him listen while wearing my headphones."

"I'm glad you're coming with us," I said and meant it. "You'll get to see my house. I used to have some amazing gardens. I'm sure they've turned to weeds by now."

I thought for a minute about Dan being there without me. As I thought about the house, my whole body was racked with guilt imagining Dan sitting home alone, wondering if I was dead or alive. I smiled knowing Dan would always be the only fox in my hole.

"Julie…?" From the backseat, I felt her reach out and touch my arm. "Why did you leave your home?"

"Erin, what if I told you that Dan is the person I trust and lean on because no matter how serious or bad the situation, like a good soldier, Dan knows exactly what to do under fire? And yet, three years ago, I left Dan. Moved to Rhode Island, bought an old farmhouse, put an addition on it and opened the inn…"

"By yourself?" she asked.

"Yes, in spite of my love for Dan, I left." I looked back at her. "I don't know where I would be without Frank. He is not only a building contractor, he's my angel. Frank is the person responsible for bringing Dan and me back together."

"Julie, because of jealousy?"

"Suspicion," I corrected her and then looked out at Jesse's truck and thought about my own thoughts had killed everything inside me. I almost lost the most important person in my life.

Me. "Erin, Dan cheated on me and I could not live with myself, the mounting suspicions in my heart or in my head. So I left. Let me tell you, leaving Dan was the hardest thing I have ever done in my life. I hit the floor. Hard."

"How did you survive leaving him?" she asked.

"I brushed myself off. Stood up and made a new life for myself. When Dan found me, he was a changed man. I took him back... knowing that I was stronger. Strong enough to survive whatever storm comes my way."

"You and Dan, remind me of my parents. Teresa said you're much happier now."

"I am. I love him so much."

"Umm..." Erin's voice was slow with hesitation. "All of your friends are really nice. Especially Jesse."

I tried to keep my eyes on the road. I glanced back at her. "Jesse is definitely a big teddy bear. He's a good friend to both Dan and me."

Erin leaned forward. "Is he going to move to Rhode Island?"

"No, he lives and works in New York. Right down the road from where I used to live."

"Oh..."

She sounded disappointed. I shot her a look.

I turned the radio up just as Zac Brown was singing, "As She's Walking Away" and thought *great timing*.

Chapter 12

An hour and a half later, we stopped at a gas station. Jesse pulled up to the side of the building and pointed to the restrooms. I asked Erin if she needed to go to the bathroom.

She sat up and looked around. "Where are we?"

"Somewhere in Connecticut," I replied.

Jesse got out of the truck. I saw Dan get out, holding Kyle in his arms. I had no idea where the small hooded sweatshirt had come from. I couldn't even see Kyle's face. Dan went into the men's room. Jesse took Lady over by the bushes and motioned for us to get out.

"There's no one around," I said. "I have got to pee."

Erin unbuckled her belt and gingerly opened her door, looking around. After we all used the restrooms, Erin got back in the truck and sat in the front seat. Dan put Lady in Jesse's truck and then he, Jesse and Kyle got in the backseat of our truck.

"Mommy!" Kyle stood on the hump and Erin hugged him.

"Are you being a good boy for Dan and Jesse?"

"Uh huh. We're singing and telling stories."

"Who's telling stories, Dan or Jesse?" Erin asked him.

"No, Mommy. Me." Kyle laughed. "Pete the Cat, and The Mitten one, too."

"He's quite the storyteller," Dan said. "Okay, about another two hours and we'll be home..." Our eyes met. "We'll be in New York." Dan stopped outside my window and I kissed him.

When Dan opened the back door, Kyle waved to his mother. I saw Dan's lips move, and Kyle blew us a kiss.

"Dan and Jesse are fantastic with Kyle. He likes them," she said as she watched them drive away.

I fastened my seatbelt and started the truck. I laughed, agreeing with her. "That's because they're both big kids themselves. Wait until you see them at Christmas time. You'll see."

"Teresa said you guys don't have any children."

I reached over and touched her arm. "We have been blessed with many. Including, yourself. Now, buckle up."

"Yes, Mama." I heard her chuckle.

We drove past the sign for Hartford. I never enjoyed driving through big cities, especially Hartford.

"Erin, the next thing we have to take care of is ensuring that you and Kyle are both protected from Josh. Do you suppose you could write a letter to the judge telling him what you just told me?"

We were sitting at a stop sign when a group of children and one adult crossed the street, caught my eye and distracted me for a second before I quickly remembered to add, "Especially about Josh moving Kyle to the basement." I glanced over at her and thought, *that's why she's so pale.*

"If it means protecting Kyle, I'll do it. Do you think he…? He can't take Kyle from me. Can he? I'm a wonderful mother. I—"

"No, no. I just want to make sure you never have to see him again." I didn't want to say it, but it had to be said. "Erin, I don't want Josh to accuse you of kidnapping."

"But why?" Her hands were over her mouth. I felt horrible when she cried, "Kyle is my son."

"Please don't cry. Erin, you need to be strong. I hate to say it but from now on, stay two steps ahead of Josh and his corrupt mind." I stopped at yet another stop sign. "Erin, ask yourself, what is he capable of?"

"He's turned out to be such a mean person. I don't want to think about him. I…"

"I know you're an excellent mother. Erin, look at me. Kyle is a good boy. He's smart, caring and loving. You said it yourself.

You raised him. Be proud of that. Don't let Josh upset you. He's in the past and that's where he'll remain."

"Okay," she said, sounding calmer.

I was glad for the entertainment of music. Erin closed eyes. I began praying harder than ever. I asked the Lord to place a hedge of protection around Erin and Kyle. A moment later, I heard her snoring and thought we're going to get along just fine. I turned the music down just enough not to wake her. Erin didn't wake until we were in Danbury.

Up ahead, I read the "Welcome to New York," sign. "Erin, you just crossed two state lines. Welcome to New York, sweetheart."

Chapter 13

Forty-five minutes later, we arrived at our destination. "Oh, my." I looked at Erin.

"Wow, Julie, your home is absolutely beautiful."

I put the truck in park, opened the door, and got out. My gardens were amazing. I looked around. I could not believe my eyes. Leaves were flowing down the river. Bright colors of red, orange, yellow and green. To my right was my favorite maple tree, and the statue was still there. Surrounded by dahlias, Mon Cheri roses, miniature Antonia Ridge roses, viburnum berries, and my favorite, Arabian Night dahlias.

Dan approached me from behind. I spun around. "My gardens look unbelievable."

"I had help." Dan motioned to Lady. "Right, girl?" He kissed me on the lips. "Although she let me put my hand on the sharp prickles on the thistle plant."

I looked down at Lady. "Good girl."

Then I slid my hands up from Dan's arms to his chest. I could feel *goosebumps* forming as I did. Dan's eyes were wide but steady on my every movement. I took another small step forward and kissed him. I kissed Dan in the presence of Kyle. Dan kissed me back, one hand sinking into my hair and the other hand wrapped around my waist. For a moment, my body melted against his, and it was easy to ignore the deafening silence around us.

"Enough of that," Jesse teased, as he picked Kyle up. "Erin, what do you say I show you around the old homestead?"

When Dan opened the front door, I stepped inside. My heart started beating a little faster. I remembered the day I was dancing in the living room. Dan had come into the room, and I discovered he had been watching me the whole time. I glanced to my right and saw our kitchen. "We've had a lot of good times in this house," I told him.

"Are you okay?" Dan kissed the back of my head.

"I'm." I turned to face him. "I love you so much. I'm so thankful you found me."

He kissed my forehead. "I'm going to make you so happy in Rhode Island. In fact, I'm going to start right now. Jesse's moving to Point Judith."

"What?"

"I offered to give him my snow plowing customers. He said, 'Rhode Island has trees.' And wherever we go, he's going. Then he said something about loving the salt life."

I looked out the window. I could see Jesse, Erin and Kyle. They were sitting on the bench near the river. Lady sat down in her own little world. She loves water as much as her momma does.

"Make me a list of what you want, and Jesse and I will pack it up for you. The movers can grab everything else."

"I want my father's bench. We'll put it down by the pond."

"He would love that. You got it." Dan turned around and opened the front door. "They're here," he hollered to me.

"Who?" I asked, but then saw Barry and Lynnae's SUV.

I rushed to the passenger side and hugged her so tight.

"I love you with all my heart," Lynnae said, as we both watched Sam and Max run down to the river and hug Kyle, Lady and Jesse.

That night, we all cooked dinner. While Lynnae and Barry were dancing to the Black Eyed Peas, Kyle, Sam and Max were playing hide-n-seek with Lady. "Where's Erin and Jesse?" I asked.

"Downstairs. Jesse's letting Erin win."

"Ahh, playing pool," I replied.

"I knew this would make you happy," Dan said, drying the last plate.

"Incredibly," I said, smiling on the inside.

Chapter 14

On the drive back to Rhode Island, Erin and I spoke about Amanda tutoring Kyle and her decision to pick a program for herself. It impressed me when she said she had been a straight-A student in high school. But then she started chewing on her fingernail and stated she wasn't sure if now was the right time for her to start her studies.

"Erin, I'll stand behind whatever decision you make."

Our conversations quickly turned lighter. Erin and I talked about our favorite flowers, perennial gardens, books, and games for Kyle. We even sang a few words from each song playing on the radio.

"Julie, can I ask you a question?"

"Anything," I said.

"Last night, after we all cleared the table, Jesse asked me if I wanted to grab Kyle and go to his house to help him pack up his clothes. Do you think it was wrong of me to say no…?"

"Can I ask why you didn't want to go?"

"Honestly, I'm not ready to be alone with a man."

That broke my heart. Especially knowing Jesse and the way he treats everyone he cares for. "Erin, I give you my word." I looked at her and winked. "You can trust Jesse to protect you and your dignity. Knowing Jesse, he wanted to show Kyle his equipment."

She smiled warmly. "I hope I didn't hurt his feelings." Then she closed her eyes.

Up ahead was the sign for Narragansett Bay. As much as I loved seeing my old house, I was glad to be home.

The moment our caravan pulled up to the inn, Kevin ran up to Dan.

"I have got to use the bathroom," I blurted out, but then realized she was once again sound asleep. I reached over and tapped her on the arm. "Erin, we're home."

She opened her eyes. "Home? Home…"

"I'll see you inside. This chick has got to go to the bathroom."

She stretched her arms out. "Me, too."

I ran inside, sang hello to Teresa, Bea and Molly and then bolted for the bathroom.

When I stepped back into the lobby I said, "Man that was a long ride. Where is everyone?"

"Dan wants to see you." Teresa pointed toward the front door. "He's waiting for you on the porch."

I turned to face the door. Dan, Jesse and Kevin were standing outside, rubbing their hands and blowing warm breath on them. I opened the door and heard Kyle say, "She's here."

Dan picked Kyle up and commanded, "Come with us."

I followed them down toward the small stream. I could not believe my eyes. There was a new garden. Full of small trees, bushes and a new arbor. "Are they grape vines?" I screamed.

As soon as Dan put Kyle down, he ran over to a basket filled with my favorite – concord grapes.

"Oh, my goodness. I… love it!"

"We're glad you like it. I wanted to give you something that would last a lifetime. I know how much you love —"

I kissed him. Turned back around and studied every detail, tree and bush.

"Julie, I didn't do this on my own. The orchard was my idea, but Jesse did all the digging before we left for New York, and Kevin did the planting while we were gone."

I had tears in my eyes. I kissed and hugged them. "Thank you."

Kyle handed me an apple, and I took a bite. "Mmmm, this is good."

"We bought them. From a store." Kyle looked up at Dan. "Right?"

Dan put his hand on Kyle's head. "That's right. Julie, there's raspberry, blueberry, blackberry bushes and apple, pear, peach and plum trees. Kevin planted three grape vines."

"Three?" I smiled. "Unbelievable!"

Kyle and Lady ran back up to the inn. As we followed them, I told Kevin and Jesse they did a fantastic job.

"Next year, you'll be picking your own berries," Kevin said, beaming from ear to ear and then added, "the fruit trees are small, but in about three years they should start to produce."

"I can't thank you enough," I said.

For several days, everyone seemed to fit in perfectly.

For Halloween, Dan and Jesse took Kyle trick or treating in every room at the inn. We opted for clothes, games, and books instead of candy.

By November 5th, Erin was busy deciding on her future. Christine and Michael couldn't stop looking at baby Brin or her cute dimples. I loved her jet-black hair. Kourtnee and Kevin were both in the daycare when Delilah took her first step. Jesse declared, "From now on the salt life is the only life for me. Beaches, babes and a good beer is all I need."

"A Corona and a pickle. Right?" Dan said, laughing as he slapped Jesse on the back.

As for Teresa, she couldn't hold it in any longer. As soon as we all sat down for lunch she said, "Umm, does anyone care that the inn is booked solid! Next year, we are rocking, baby!"

Later on, I was able to take a few minutes to write in my new journal.

Dear Lord, thank you for loving me, guiding me and for bringing Dan back to me!

Chapter 15

After I ended the phone call with Frank, I leaned back against the headboard, happy to hear his voice, laughter, and let him know that Erin had written her letter. I thought about Teresa's comment. With the inn booked, solid, that meant I would have my best year to date. Maybe… I could have my swimming pool after all.

It was still cold outside, raw, in fact. I didn't want to go up to the inn. All I wanted to do was curl up in front of the fireplace with Dan, a new book, and a cup of tea.

"I got it!" Dan shouted from the kitchen. "I'll make garlic mashed potatoes."

I got up and stood in the bedroom's doorway. "I made them last year. Teresa can't eat garlic."

"Huh. What are you making?" He held up my empty cup, and I nodded.

I sat down at the kitchen table, picked up a newspaper and answered him, "I'm making homemade cranberry relish. Did you put this here?"

Dan frowned and cleared his throat before he handed me a cup of coffee. "Yes, I was looking to see if there was any news of a woman and child missing." He pursed his lips and added, "Nothing."

I sipped my coffee. Looked up and countered, "I don't think he cares enough about them."

"Let's hope. Julie… I just don't know. I mean, I hope we're doing the right thing. I can't believe a control freak like Josh would let his wife and child walk away and do nothing about it." He shook his head in bewilderment.

"What do you mean?" I asked, but knew exactly what he was thinking.

"It makes me wonder what he's capable of and I'm worried about you getting close to them..."

"And one day, they're out on their own. As long as they're not living with that monster, I'm good with them living anywhere else."

He grinned. "What am I going to make?"

"You picked potato, stick with it. Oh, make your potato gratin. Yum," I said.

We were still drinking our coffee when Dan asked me, "Was it your idea to have the entire staff cook together and eat family style?"

"Nope, that was Michael's idea. We used to sit down every night before we served our guests, but that didn't last very long." I thought about Bea. "I'm going to miss Bea, she was such a big help in the dining rooms."

"You'll find someone else. Ask Erin to help you."

"Great idea! I'm hungry. Let's have soft-boiled eggs."

Dan boiled the eggs, browned the sausage and poured two glasses of orange juice while I made the bed.

After breakfast, we headed up to the inn. Jesse was on the front porch, holding two cups. He held up one cup and shouted, "Morning!"

Dan gave me a kiss. "Jesse and I are going to see Frank. Kevin is staying with Erin and Kyle in the daycare until we get back."

I felt nervous, but replied, "Okay. Give Frank my love."

"I will. We'll be back for lunch. Do you want anything from town?" Dan asked, getting into his truck.

"No, I'm good. Thanks." I stepped inside, thankful for the warmth coming from the fireplace in the library.

"Good morning, Julie. Erin's waiting for you in the library."

"Good morning, Teresa. Thanks." I looked back at her. "What are you cooking this year for Thanksgiving?"

"An appetizer, but I haven't decided on which one yet. I heard you're making cranberry relish. I love homemade cranberry relish."

"With garlic, right?" I teased.

Teresa stuck her tongue out.

I went into the library and found Erin looking out the window. "Good morning," I called out to her in a low voice. "You look so peaceful standing there. I didn't want to scare you."

"Good morning. Do you have a second?"

We each sat down in a wingback chair.

"Um," she began slowly, "I wrote everything down, but I was wondering…"

"Erin, look at me. Whatever's bothering you, you can tell me."

"I'm not sure I want to go to college for accounting. I… I would like to become a teacher."

"I think you would make a brilliant teacher." I started to stand up.

"But…" she hesitated. "It will cost more and I'll…"

I sat back in the chair. "Erin, the inn will pay for your education. You can work every cent off…"

"Julie, it's a four-year program."

"Erin, you need to take care of Kyle and yourself. Going back to school is step one toward your future. Getting a degree and being able to provide for yourself means you won't ever have to depend on anyone. You need to do this," I said, sounding more and more like a mother.

"Yes, ma'am." She sucked in a breath. "Oh, yeah. Michael told me to write on the shopping list what I needed for Thanksgiving dinner. I would like to make my mom's popovers."

"Popovers? Dan and I love popovers."

Her eyes lit up. "Really?"

"Yes, now tell Kourtnee what classes you need to sign up for."

Erin hugged me and I thought, *you can't hide how you feel. A person's eyes will always speak the truth.* Her eyes were smiling.

Monday morning, I was saying goodbye to my last guest for the 2010 season. Mrs. O'Brien.

"I'm so glad I chose the Americana room. I was able to get so much writing done. Julie, would you allow me to have a book signing here at the inn? I could read from my novel. Your library would be perfect..."

Teresa spoke before I could respond. "That sounds like a great idea!"

"I totally agree. In fact, I'm honored. Call us and let us know when. Teresa will put you on our schedule. Care to share what the book is about?"

"I just love writing women's fiction with a hint of romance," Mrs. O'Brien said.

"This is so exciting. What's the title going to be?" Teresa picked up a pen.

"The Day After. I'm excited as well. Thanks for saying yes. As soon as I have a release date, I'll call you."

"Great. We'll serve tea and cookies," Teresa added.

When she left, Teresa looked at me. "We are growing more and more. Garden tours, weddings, book signings, my goodness what's next?"

"Dinner. I have to let Michael know what I need for Thanksgiving dinner."

"Go," she said, and waved me off.

When I reached the kitchen, Christine was nursing the baby. "Good morning, Christine. Good morning, Brin." As I stepped closer to them, I whispered, "Is Michael around?"

Christine shook her head. "He went shopping." She pointed to the whiteboard. "Write down what you need and I'll text him."

Next to the whiteboard was the menu board. I smiled when I read Julie's apple pie, in Dan's handwriting.

Three days later, we celebrated the last light of the golden autumn sun in family style. First, we all gathered in the kitchen to prepare our dishes. Kourtnee insisted on playing Christmas music. After she baked the brie, Kevin added the peach preserves, chopped pecans, red pepper flakes, honey and whiskey.

Brin's bassinet was in one corner and Delilah's playpen in the other. I had no idea how those babies slept with all the noise. But they did!

At five o'clock, the turkey was ready. So was the dressing, gravy, and relish. Jesse and Kyle made mini chocolate cream pies to go with my apple and Teresa's pumpkin. Christine, not permitted to lift a finger, found the time to bake some pear and ginger tarts.

Everyone sat down, and I gave thanks. "Dear Heavenly Father, we thank you for the food that we are about to eat. Lord, we thank you for bringing us together. Amen."

"Amen," everyone said.

We started with Teresa's squash soup and Erin's popovers. By the time we finished eating dessert, no one could move.

Michael wheeled the bassinet to the library and Kevin carried Delilah. Everyone was talking about his or her plans for the winter vacation. Dan wanted to know why we closed from December 1st to January 2nd.

That's when I decided. "We don't have to close anymore." I looked around the room. "What? You all come back in a few days. Fine, we'll close."

"No!" they all shouted, and Delilah started crying.

"Can you imagine? We'll all be together on Christmas," Teresa gushed.

I looked at Teresa, smiling. "That will be the best present ever."

Chapter 16

By eight o'clock, the adults were falling asleep. Kyle and Lady were sitting on the floor playing with a ball. Every time Lady hit the ball with her paw, sending it back to Kyle, he laughed so hard everyone else chuckled.

"Goodnight, everyone." I stood up. "I'm exhausted."

"Don't go to the cottage. Stay here. It's too cold to be walking down there." Teresa looked at Dan. "Tell her."

"Sounds good to me," Dan agreed.

"Goodnight." Erin stood up and tapped Kyle on the head. "Kyle, what do you say?"

Kyle stood up and hugged Jesse, Dan, and then me. "Thank you."

I kissed him on the cheek. "You're welcome. Goodnight, my prince." I looked at Lady. "Goodnight, baby girl."

Dan and I went up to the Jamestown Room. Closing the door, he said, "I'll go down and get our clothes in the morning. When the sun is shining," he added shaking his head.

"Can you light a fire?" I asked, knowing he would.

"For you… anything."

I grinned, knowing all he had to do was flip the switch and the gas logs would burst into flame. I took my clothes off and grabbed the robes hanging in the closet. I put the bigger one on the bed and wrapped myself up in the other one.

Dan looked at me. "Where's mine?"

I pointed to the bed and sat down on the floor with the extra pillows from the closet.

Dan grabbed the throw blanket draped over the chair near the window and sat down next to me. "Julie, I've been meaning to talk to you about something."

I rested my head on his shoulder as he covered my legs with the blanket. "Mmmm...?" I said, as I pulled the blanket up higher.

"I'm glad you got to meet Barbara. And Rose." He kissed the side of my face. "They've helped me so much. Seriously. I never believed in therapy until I met them. Honestly, I didn't think anyone *could* help me. Julie?"

"Yes?"

"Are you okay with me talking about this?"

"I promise you. I'm okay talking about it. As long as you're truthful with me."

Dan nodded. "I promise. Can I tell you how different Barbara and Rose are?" He continued as I glanced at the fire. "Barbara would ask me things like. Tell me what you like about yourself and what you don't like. Rose, handed me a mirror and said, tell me who you see? Julie?" He held his breath as the tension on his face eased. "I looked at my reflection so long Rose asked me if I was okay. I thought about you, and that made me feel good inside. I handed her back the mirror and said I see Julie's husband, and he's the happiest man alive. That's who I see!"

I had goosebumps hearing him say those words. I sat motionless, staring at the flames. I wanted him to know how I felt. "Dan, you can talk to me about anything..." I looked up at him. "I love you with all my heart. I promise you no more pretending. From now on open dialogue."

He kissed the top of my head again. "I want to talk about it for a reason. A reason that I *hate*."

I hugged him.

"Barbara told me that an affair was less about the sex and more about the betrayal. She told me to imagine you with a thousand cuts… for every time I had betrayed you. That killed me."

I heard him sniffle and swallow.

"Julie, Barbara gave me detailed advice on helping you to overcome the trauma I've caused you. She said the only way to restore your trust in me is by me telling you the truth. I can't ignore the fact that I cheated on you. We can agree the affairs should never have happened. I don't have to tell *you*, infidelity has a tenacity that marriage can only envy. We both know there are two commandments in the Bible, one against doing it and one just for thinking about it."

I rubbed his hand. "I prayed for you. Dan, I asked God to forgive you."

"Julie, I ask Him every day to forgive me. I thanked God for Frank. Did Frank tell you he had to call me back? I was so relieved to hear you were okay, I immediately had to call Lynnae and Jesse. I lived in hell. Every day I asked myself why. Barbara said, 'If your life was a living hell without your wife, then *why* did you cheat on her?'"

Dan held me tighter.

"Julie, I was bored. Not with you. With myself. Every affair was *my* mistake."

"Dan, you have no idea how much those words mean to me." I pulled the blanket up to my chin. "I used to blame the women. I suppose that was my way of protecting our relationship."

"I'm sorry you had to do that."

"Dan, it's hard for me to think about you with another woman. Let alone talk about it. But… I cannot turn my head, nor will I close my eyes. I love you so much. You… were my world. And even though deep down I knew you *were* having an affair, I knew if I confronted you, and you would not have told me the truth." I felt Dan sit up straighter, inhale, and turn toward me, moving in even closer. I patted his hand. "I feared losing you."

"You will never have to live in that fear again. I promise you." Dan scratched his head. He was breathing heavily. "At one of my last sessions, Barbara looked right at me and said, 'Dan, your first marriage is over. Would you like to create a second one with Julie?' My heart started beating. She gave me hope for the future. I prayed so hard that night. The next day, Frank called the house."

I sat up. Our eyes met.

Dan had tears in his eyes. "And a day later, I found you. I'm so thankful you opened your heart and –"

I kissed him. "Forgave you?"

"Yes."

Chapter 17

As soon as we woke up, Dan and I went down to the cottage. I needed to get ready for my lunch date with Frank. I was bringing him the letter Erin wrote. I also wanted to invite Frank to the inn for Christmas.

"Are you ready?" Dan hollered from the kitchen.

I peeked out from the bedroom. "Two seconds. I can't find my long black coat."

"It's probably up at the inn."

"I found it." I stepped into the living area. "It was hanging in the closet under one of my other coats. Thanks for taking me to see Frank."

Dan reached for my coat. "I know what I'm getting you for Christmas." Then he helped me put it on.

"Surprise me." I buttoned my coat. Put my scarf and gloves on. "I'm ready."

Dan handed me the envelope containing Erin's documents. "Now you're ready."

I grinned. "What would I do without you?"

"Believe me… you'd survive."

I winked. "Frank's meeting with the judge tomorrow morning. I'm praying he can do something for Erin. I don't want any trouble from her husband. I just want her to make a new life for herself and Kyle."

"Me, too." Dan closed the door behind us. "Yesterday, she was sitting on the floor in the corner of the billiards room, crying her eyes out. I asked her if she was okay. She told me she wished her mother were here."

"Why didn't you tell me?" I blurted out.

"Julie, she was crying about her mother. There's nothing you could've done. I'm sorry, I didn't get you."

I thought for a moment. "Which one? Erin was adopted. Born in Ireland. Her birth mother left her in the hospital—"

"What? She left her?"

"Yeah, she was around eight months old when her adopted parents brought her to America."

"Damn, I didn't know that. If I see her crying again, I'll find you. Poor kid."

It was so cold outside we both picked up our pace. I couldn't help wonder *how* an elderly couple with no money were able to adopt a child all the way from Ireland.

Dan opened my door. "I'm building a road to the cottage. This is ridiculous walking on frozen turf."

"Stop it!" When he got in, I told him about Erin's decision to become a teacher.

"Sounds good. She's great with Kyle. You should spend some time with Kyle. He's smart as a whip."

"He is adorable. I think he's adopted Lady."

"You mean Lady's adopted him." Dan pulled out onto the main road. "She was the same way with me after you left."

I looked out my window. His comment made me feel sad. A chill came over me.

A few minutes passed. I looked over at Dan. "I like the idea of Erin becoming a teacher. She'll be able to take care of Kyle on her own. When he's out of school, she'll be off from work."

Dan's cell phone rang. "Grab that for me."

I lifted it from the stand. "Hello. Hey, Joe, how are you? Seriously? Great! He's right here. Hang on a second." I tapped Dan on the leg. "Joe Sagsveen would like to make an offer on the house *and* the property outback." I put the phone back to my ear. "Yes, we're driving. Umm, *okay!* Let me speak to Dan, and we'll call you back in a little while. Say hello to your mom and dad from us." The call ended.

"What'd he say? Julie…?"

"He offered us two point five. He wants to grow hops…"

"He always wanted to start his own brewery. Good for him! What do you think?"

"Wow… I don't know. We'll have to…"

Dan reached over and put his arm around me. "Julie, with two and a half million dollars, you can design another home. I'll build you whatever you want. You already have enough property for us to enjoy. I thought *this* is what you wanted."

"I do. Wow!"

Dan turned into the driveway. "Frank's standing in the window, waiting for you. I'll be back in two hours." Dan put the truck in park. Leaned over and kissed me. "If you don't want to sell…"

I tapped Dan on his leg. "I'm glad Joe's the person buying the house. He'll enjoy the property as much as we did." I leaned in closer, kissed him back and got out of the truck. I watched him back out of Frank's driveway before waving hello to my dear friend.

Frank opened the door. "Good afternoon, young lady."

I gave him a quick peck on the cheek. "Ahhh, the man in my life with Southern syrup in his voice. Burr, it's cold out today." I set the envelope down on the hall table. Frank helped me off with my coat. After he hung it up on the coat rack, I handed him the envelope. "Erin also wrote about a few other events that might help her case."

"Good. If anyone can do this, it's Judge Abrams. Let's sit in the dining room."

Frank popped his head through the swinging door. "Ally, Julie's here."

Ally was Frank's house manager. She shopped, cooked, cleaned, did his laundry and ironed his clothes.

"Ally, how are you?" I asked, as she came into the dining room.

"I'm wonderful. It's nice to see you. Enjoy." She set the tureen down in front of Frank. When he lifted the lid on the Royal Blue Aves, I could smell what was inside.

"I haven't had chicken and dumplings in… forever." Frank said as he filled our bowls.

"It looks delicious." I looked up from my bowl and noticed a broken candelabra in the center of the china cabinet. "Frank, is that a menorah?"

Frank raised his eyes. "My secret is out. I'm a Black Southern Jewish man." He continued to eat.

I looked around the room and saw many items. All blue and white. "Ha, ha, ha! I love it!"

"What part do you love? My being Jewish. Or that I was a man so deeply and passionately in love, I would have done anything to make my wife happy? Including letting her decorate."

"No wonder why *you* are the most respected figure in my life."

"I'm honored." He stood up. "Come sit with me by the fire."

I followed him to his study. On the table, between two brown leather chairs, was a warm pot of tea, and a small dish of shortbread cookies.

Frank handed me a cup. "How's Erin these days?"

"She's better every day. Although Dan saw her crying yesterday. Frank, she has no family. I can't let her go back to that man. He kept her in the basement, for God's sake."

"Is there anything I can do?" I could feel his gaze traveling across my face. "Name it."

"What you're doing is wonderful." I looked into his eyes. "I just hope the judge can make sure Erin is never found guilty of kidnapping."

Frank went to take a bite, but pulled the cookie back out from his mouth. "You don't worry about that. Judge Abrams might be retired, but he's still the smartest judge I ever met."

I felt better knowing that. "Frank, will you spend Christmas with us?"

"I wouldn't miss it for the world." We heard Dan's voice in the foyer. "Sounds like your husband's here."

Dan joined us for a cup of tea as we chatted about Chanukah and Christmas.

Chapter 18

I hugged Frank goodbye, thanked him for a wonderful lunch, and for helping us with Erin.

"Next time you'll have to join us for lunch," Frank hinted to Dan as they shook hands.

"Sounds good," Dan, replied. "Hey, thanks again for doing whatever you can for Erin."

"No problem," Frank said as he waved goodbye to us.

Dan was backing down the driveway. "Did you have a good time?"

"I did." I was still looking at Frank's house, remembering the menorah. "Dan, will you take me Christmas shopping?"

"I just… sure. Where do you want to go?"

"To the gift store on Sand Hill Cove. But not now, tomorrow. I need to make my list."

When we got back, we both went to the inn. Dan was looking for Jesse, and I needed to see Kourtnee.

"It's quiet around here with no guest," Dan remarked, before turning back around and adding, "Stay out of the truck."

"Anything you say." I went down the hall, smiling to myself. I could hear Kourtnee singing a lullaby to Delilah. I stood in the doorway for a moment.

Kourtnee waved me in. "She's out like a rock."

I peeked into the playpen. "I like how she raises her butt up in the air."

"Kevin's mother told me he used to do the same thing. What's up?"

I sat down in the chair. "How much cash do we have in the safe?"

Kourtnee made a clicking noise with her tongue. "How much do you need? Mr. Duncan paid for his daughter Kiersten's entire wedding, in *cash*. I didn't ask where the money came from. But I have to warn you, it smells musty." She opened the safe, snapped her fingers, and asked me, "How much?"

I whispered back, "Two-thousand."

She handed me the money and then handed me an invitation.

"Bea told us about Kelly's new restaurant." I looked at the date again. "It's New Year's Eve… send her a nice floral arrangement with a note congratulating her. During the year we'll all go. But—"

"Don't worry about it. I'll take care of it. I didn't know she was Irish. Did you?"

"With a name like Kelly?" I smiled. "Did you know Frank is Jewish?"

"Get out of town." Delilah turned her head to the other cheek. Kourtnee looked at her. "Don't worry about her, she can sleep at a carnival."

I waved the money. "Phew. I'll see you later."

I stopped by the kitchen for a cup of tea before searching for Erin. I found her sitting in the library, reading.

"I found you." When I set my teacup down on the end table, I looked out the window and saw Dan and Jesse taking packages from the back seat of the truck.

Sitting down, I asked Erin for her and Kyle's sizes.

"I look like a vagabond, don't I?"

"No, but I'm sure you're not comfortable wearing Kourtnee's maternity clothes."

"Actually, they're quite comfortable. Julie, I insist you let me work for my clothes. It doesn't feel right. You doing all this for me. I asked Kourtnee if I could help her, but she said whatever Julie says goes. I just…" Her body shifted. She started fidgeting with her sleeve.

I glanced around the room. A voice whispered in my head. *Pride.* "I'll tell you what. When we open the inn in January, you can chose to assist me in the dining room or help Kourtnee with the books." I pointed to her. "But right now, I want you to concentrate on Erin."

She set the book down on the table. "You got a deal."

"Good, now tell me your size."

Erin grinned. "I'm a twelve. I don't need a lot. I... I never did. Honestly."

She sounded just like me. I used to be the same way. "What book are you reading?" I asked.

She held up the book. "*Temptation.*"

"Ahh, Jude Deveraux, one of my favorites. I've read every book in this room. I call them my mini vacations."

Erin's eyes roamed the shelves. "I love to read, too."

"You're welcome to sign a library card and take one to your room." I picked up my cup and added, "I'm kidding. Oh yeah, I delivered your photos and letters to Frank today. He seems confident Judge Abrams can protect you, should Josh seek custody of Kyle. For the time being, I have to ask you not to go into town."

She drew in a deep breath. "I... umm, I would never leave the inn." Her bottom lip quivered. "I'm too scared to go."

I could see the panic on her face. "I'm sorry. I had to make sure. Erin, I can't protect you if you're not here."

She nodded. I felt like an idiot for upsetting her.

Dan walked past the door. "Where's Erin and Kyle?" he asked.

Teresa answered him. "Erin's in the library with Julie and Kevin took Kyle in the kitchen for something to eat."

"Erin, the moment you ran away from Josh, you proved to him you were strong enough to survive without him. What size did you say Kyle wears?"

She smiled warmly at me. "Five. Maybe you should get him six. He's been eating a lot more since we got here."

I smiled back at her. "Sounds good. By the way, I've put on ten pounds since Dan's been here."

"You look great," she said. "My mother was in great shape, like you."

"I wish I could have met your parents. They sound like good people."

Her eyes were damp. I knew she missed her mother.

"My father was a skeleton man, always smelled of fish and tobacco. He used to read to me all the time. Mostly, he made up stories, blurred by his cigarette smoke."

"And mom? What did she like to do?"

"She loved to bake. Every Sunday, she would bake her Irish soda bread. I used to take a piece to school with me. That and a can of ginger ale were my lunch. Other than that, Mom never did too much. She barely left the house. Dad would bring home whatever groceries he could carry."

"What did you do as a family?" I asked, hoping to learn a little more about her.

Erin glanced up at the photo of Dan and Lady. A framed five by seven I had taken of the two of them down by the pond. "Not much. We didn't have a camera, so we never did things like hang pictures or put photos in scrapbooks. My mother never told stories or spoke of the past. She was more concerned about my future." Then Erin spoke so softly I barely heard her. She picked up the book and opened it.

I knew the memory had touched a nerve. It was obvious she missed her parents, especially her mother. When she glanced down at the book, I decided to leave her to her reading. "Don't you just love how a good book can take you to a better place?" I said.

She nodded.

"Okay, sunshine." I leaned over and kissed her on the top of her head. "I need to check my list. Twice. Ho, ho, ho!"

Chapter 19

As I headed down to the cottage, I was so excited about making my list. I loved Christmas! I began to laugh, but then a feeling of dread rolled up my spine. My heart jumped into my throat. Was I holding Erin hostage? As much as I wanted to protect her, I couldn't let her leave the inn. Right? That didn't feel good to me. I wanted her to be happy. Live the life she desired. Why did she have to live like this and for how long? I wondered if Judge Abrams could serve an order of protection.

At four o'clock, the temperature was already at freezing. By the time I reached the front door, I was frozen.

I stepped inside, hung my coat up on the hook and heard Dan say, "Dinner will be done in an hour." Grateful he had lit a fire. I sat on the floor with my back to the orange flames. Dan came over and sat down next to me.

I tapped his leg. "Burr, it's cold outside."

He laughed. "Why didn't you buy a place down south?"

"I don't know. Wait! You were the one who brought me to Rhode Island. It's your fault I fell in love with Point Judith." I thought for a second. "Maybe, I came here because it was a familiar place and it reminded me of you and our moment in time when we were both happy."

"I'm happy wherever I am as long as I am with you," he said.

"And you make me happy, Dan!"

"What was the first thing you did when you arrived?"

"I checked into Sal's Bed and Breakfast and slept. The next day, I saw the old farmhouse. I'll admit, I was infatuated with the building. Anybody would be. It was a huge old house with lots of rooms."

He rested his head on the palm of his hand. "Weren't you lonely?"

"I had books. Some nights when the moon was full and the breeze felt inviting, I would wander down here by the pond. Sit for hours, reading. When my flashlight went dim, I'd walk back up to the house."

He blew out a breath. "You created a life. You could live without me. I wasn't so lucky."

"Dan, I missed you. Every day." I almost cried. I could feel his pain. I never meant for my leaving to hurt him. "Being without you... wasn't living. I cried for you every day."

Dan gave me one of his heart-stopping smiles. Still as handsome as ever. I thought he was going to kiss me, but he pulled me to my feet. For a moment, he looked like he wanted to say something. He stepped into the kitchen, opened the oven door, looked back, and motioned to me. "Dinner's done."

I inhaled, knowing exactly what was in the oven. It smelled delicious. His venison stew was one of my favorites. I poured the iced tea as Dan set our plates down. "Mmmm." I closed my eyes as I inhaled its aroma once more.

Dan pointed his fork at my plate. "I'm glad you like it. I miss cooking alongside you, cooking for you, showering together. I especially miss hiking *with* you, talking about our day. I've missed you so much."

I put down my fork, reached over and touched his hand. "What's wrong?"

"We used to do everything together. It used to be just the two of us." He took his first bite.

"Tomorrow, you and I are going Christmas shopping. In the spring, we'll create a new hiking path. Dan, we have two-hundred and thirty acres. There's a lot of things we can do together." I raised my eyebrows. "If we had a swimming pool..."

"Yeah, Frank told me. We'll see. I'll make you a deal, you design a bigger shower and I'll put in a swimming pool."

I clapped my hands. "I have to have a pool. I'm an Aquarius, you know!"

"Yeah, yeah, did you talk to Erin? What does she need?"

"Clothes."

"It's Christmas." Dan put *his* fork down. "I'll think of something fun to get her." He leaned back in his chair. "What do you want for Christmas?"

"You." I leaned over and whispered in his ear. "All I want for Christmas is you."

We cleared the table, washed the dishes together, and sat by the fire until we both fell asleep.

The next morning, I made a mental note to do something fun with only Dan in the next few days.

"Knock, knock. I heard we're going Christmas shopping," Jesse said as he closed the door. "Baby, it's cold out there."

"Take your coat off. Dan's getting dressed. Do you want a cup of coffee?" I turned around and held up my cup, letting him know it was still fresh. "It's still hot."

"Nah. What did he say about Kyle?"

"Who?" I shut the coffee maker off. "Dan?"

"Yes, Dan. Did he tell you we're getting him an iPad for Christmas?"

Dan walked into the room. "Amanda says he's more than ready for one."

"Great idea. Guess what I ordered for Erin?" They were both staring at me when I said, "Ancestry."

"What the…?" Jesse shook his head.

"Oh," Dan said, "Ancestry dot com. Julie and I took the test. The program to search for your relatives." He came to where I was standing and kissed me on the cheek. "Smart. I like your idea. Jesse and I were thinking about buying her school supplies."

"Well, that's a great idea, too." I grabbed my coat.

Dan looked at Jesse. "Ready?"

"It's hot in here."

"Only because you have your coat on." Dan slapped him on his shoulder. "Let's go."

Dan opened the front door and we stepped out into the frigid December air. The morning *was* crisp and the frost crunched beneath our feet.

Dan put his arm around me. "I think you might get your wish." He pointed to the sky. It had taken on the color of gray. "It's going to snow soon."

A moment later, Dan started the truck and asked, "Where to?"

"I'd like to go to the Polka Dot Panda, it's a children's boutique."

Fifteen minutes later we heard, "I need to eat." Jesse leaned forward in his seat. "When is Michael coming back?"

I laughed. "They'll be back the first week in January. Right there, it's on the right."

Dan pulled the truck up to the front door, and we all got out.

I picked out underwear, socks, pants, and shirts. Dan gathered all of the winter gear: leggings, jacket, hat and gloves.

Jesse opted to wait by the door. He said Kyle would hate everything. When we stepped outside, Jesse insisted we go to a toy store. "He's a kid. He needs toys, not damn underwear! It's Christmas. Think like a kid."

"Fine. Where to?" Dan asked.

"There's a Walmart in Kingston," I said. "Let me see your phone, I'll look up the directions." Dan handed me his phone.

"Now you're talking. We were back in the car heading to Walmart when Jesse shouted, "Wait, stop! Pull the truck over. I want to go in there." He pointed to a store on the right.

We all got back out of the truck. I read the window display: "Deb's Devine Love. Love, Light and Inspiration. Angelic readings. Spiritual guidance and healing." I looked at Dan. "Is he kidding?"

Dan pointed to the woman behind the glass. She was setting up her window display. Inside, a different woman greeted us.

"Welcome," she said, holding a basket full of stones.

"Hello!" Jesse said to both women.

"If you need any help, my name is Debi; I'll be right over there." She pointed to a small round table.

"Thank you," we all said at the same time.

Dan and I looked around. I bought a pink shell necklace and a stone with the inscription "Believe" on it. Dan, on the other hand, bought nearly twenty stones. Each stone individualized. "Don't look," he said.

I raised my hand. "I'm going out to the truck."

I was almost to the door when I heard the woman, Debi, telling Jesse, "You have to believe. The best things in life are unseen. That's why we close our eyes when we kiss, laugh and dream." I turned around and saw her hand him his shopping bag.

"Merry Christmas," Jesse said to Debi. "Merry Christmas," to the woman smiling back at him.

I didn't see that one coming. I got in the truck and looked back at Jesse. He was staring at the storefront. "Are you okay, big guy?"

"Leave him alone," Dan teased. "He's in love."

"With who?" I inquired. "The owner or the *woman* in the front window?"

Dan look in the rear-view mirror, then at me. "Where am I going?" He pointed to his cell phone.

"Make a right at the next light. Then it's about ten or fifteen minutes."

While Dan and Jesse went into Walmart, I went into a few of the smaller stores. I found the perfect menorah, the cutest teapot for Teresa and a few learning toys for Kyle. In the bookstore, I bought colorful and realistic plush farm animals for Delilah and Brin. I bought all three of the boys a Noah's Ark-that included two animals of every kind. I also picked up books on tape, coloring books, and plenty of books for Kyle to read.

By the time I reached the truck, there was no room for my packages. "What did you buy?" I blurted out, scanning the backseat.

Even the back of the truck was full of boxes. I saw garland, lights, and wreaths popping from several bags.

"Come on," Dan said as he took my packages and set them on a massive pile on the backseat. "Get in. We've got a lot to do."

I looked back at Jesse. He was grinning from ear to ear, pointing at Dan. "He's insane. I'm never going shopping with him again."

Dan started the truck. "Hey, some women like diamonds. Mine loves Christmas."

"Yeah, okay," Jesse, said, laughing. "Can we please get something to eat?"

"Ooohh, I'm sorry. Let's go to Kelly's new restaurant. It's on our way home." I looked at Dan's cell phone for the address. "Mulligan's Irish Pub. It's on the left, past Moo Moo's Ice Cream Parlor."

"Okay, and then after we drop you off, we have to come back and pick up the Christmas trees."

"Trees?" I rolled my eyes.

Kelly met us at the door and said, "Julie!"

"Congratulations!" I replied and hugged her.

"Thank you so much for the beautiful floral arrangement," she said to me and then told the man holding a stack of menus, "I'll seat them." Kelly sat us at a large corner table next to the fireplace. "Drinks are on me."

Dan and Jesse ordered beer, and I ordered water with a twist of lemon.

"Take your time. I'll be right back with your drinks."

The décor was not what I expected. Not one anchor, sailor or rope. Kelly opted for a more rustic atmosphere. The tables were hand-carved pieces of wood. If I had to guess, I'd say four or five inches thick. Brown leather chairs. Tin ceiling and wide plank floors. Over the bar, she had a huge flat screen television, and above the fireplace, a picture of a woman playing a ukulele.

I looked at my menu, and my mouth watered. "I'm having the cheeseburger."

"Sounds good," Dan echoed.

"I'm buying," Jesse said. "Who wants bacon on their burger? I'm doing the burger with cheddar and bacon."

"I got it, Jesse," Dan said, adding, "Bacon sounds good. Julie?"

"Yes, and avocado for me, please."

After Kelly brought our drinks and took our orders, Dan suggested Erin talk to Rose. "I think maybe Rose can help her with everything that's going on in her life right now."

"I agree," Jesse said.

I had to admit I agreed with them. "I'll talk to her right after Christmas."

A server brought our burgers and asked if there would be anything else.

"No, thanks. It looks delicious. I think we're good," Dan replied, and then took a big bite. "Oh, my God... this *is* good!"

We left Kelly a nice tip and promised we would all be back soon.

When we got to the inn, Dan and Jesse both told me to leave the packages to them.

An hour later, Erin, Teresa and I were in the kitchen baking Christmas cookies. Erin was telling us about how she met her husband and how he had taken her to every deli, diner and restaurant in Point Judith. "After we got married, he said it was time I learned to cook." She shook her head.

"What?" I stopped mixing and looked at her.

"Nothing..."

"You don't shake your head over nothing," I said to her.

Erin stepped back from the counter. "I was just wondering what kind of woman I could have become." She moved closer and began cutting her cookies out. "Yesterday, we walked for nearly two hours. I was remembering my parents the entire time, hoping they knew where I was and that I was safe. We returned to the inn just as the sun had fallen. I love the light of an early evening."

"We?" Teresa asked.

Erin smiled. "Kourtnee made Kevin go with me."

I looked at Teresa and winked.

"Kevin talked about his wife and daughter with such love in his heart."

Teresa laughed. "They remind me of Tim and Faith McGraw. You know, the country duo."

"Someone else said that as well," I said.

"I wished my parents talked to me more. I remember one day, we were all sitting in the living room listening to the radio. I think I was ten. I made the mistake of asking my parents about my adoption. My mother snapped. 'We traveled all the way to Ireland to bring you home. That's all you need to know!'"

I asked her, "Erin, how did you find out you were adopted?"

"Ever since I was a little girl, I knew. My father would tell me they adopted me because I was the most beautiful little girl in the world. Or, in one of his stories, about finding the perfect child to live with them. Traveling to Ireland to meet his little girl. I laughed so hard when he told me I belonged to an Irish setter who had too many pups. My mother never spoke of my birth or commented when my dad was telling his stories."

"Because she was so protective, right?" I said.

"I suppose. Every day, they both told me they loved me. We had little money. Anyway, my mom cried, and I felt bad. I told her I was sorry for upsetting her. That's when my father got up from his broken-down chair, touched my mom's shoulder and said, 'Not one day goes by that I don't thank God for providing me with the extra work to bring you home. Every day, I am glad we brought you here to live with us.' His hand was still on my mother's shoulder until she got up and went into the kitchen. That night when they came into my room to say goodnight, I apologized again. I can still remember how long my mother's lips stayed on my forehead. I knew she had forgiven me. After that, I never asked about my adoption. I felt horrible for making her cry."

"Wow, they really wanted you." Teresa went around me and patted Erin on her back. "That's love."

Erin flashed a smile. "I can only hope to be as good a parent to Kyle. They…" Her gaze drifted for a moment. "They were the most loving parents." She became silent.

"Erin, thank you for sharing your memories with us." She was opening up to us more and more. I felt good inside. Grateful the Lord put her in Jesse's path that morning.

Teresa snapped her fingers. "We need music. Christmas music."

Just then, we heard a loud noise coming from the lobby. "Don't look," I said aloud as Teresa ran toward the lobby. "Dan told me not to peek. I have my instructions."

We went back to our baking. Erin made Irish shortbread cookies in the shape of Christmas trees, Teresa made her cream cheese cookies with fig preserves, and I made my Italian cookies with anisette frosting. When it was time to frost the cookies, we called over to the daycare and invited Amanda and Kyle to join in the fun.

"Julie!" I heard Dan holler. "Julie!"

I walked out to the lobby and almost fell over.

"Yes. Oh, my…!" By six o'clock that evening, Dan and Jesse had a Christmas tree in every room on the main floor. I was standing in the lobby when I heard beep, beep, beep, coming from the driveway. "This looks incredible," I said as I turned to Dan. "Our manger." He had removed the large bowl from the lobby table and replaced it with our nativity scene. "It looks wonderful there."

Dan pointed to the driveway. "Your chairs are here."

I clapped my hands. "Yay."

Opening the front door, I stood there amazed. They had lights going up the porch columns. Every door and window adorned by a wreath. Each decorated with big velvet burgundy bows, pinecones, and berries. On the railing, garland decorated with birds: many small owls, cardinals, finches and seagulls.

I asked the driver to put the rocking chairs in the library. When I stepped inside the library, my heart lit up. In the corner was a twelve-foot Christmas tree with *our* angel on the top. I turned around. Dan and Jesse were both smiling like Cheshire cats.

"Get out of the way," Jesse teased. "We have stockings to hang."

Chapter 20

Tuesday morning, I received a call from Frank. He wanted to see Erin and me. He said it would be better if I was there when he told her what the judge's instructions were.

Outside, snow had fallen. The fruit trees stood dormant next to snow-covered bushes. I hoped they would survive their first winter in Rhode Island. By the time I reached the inn, my boots were sinking into the ankle deep snow. It was so cold the snow was sticking to the ground as if it had plans on staying. Once again, I felt chilled to the bone.

When I opened the front door, the wind pushed it out of my hand.

"Oh, my! Are you okay?" Teresa called out to me.

"Holy moly!" I stomped my feet on the doormat and took off my coat, scarf, gloves and boots. "Is Frank here?"

"No." Teresa shook her head. "But I put the coffee on. Hey, when is Lynnae arriving?"

"Tomorrow." Holding my hands in prayer, hoping the snow didn't stop their arrival.

"Okay. Erin asked me when they were coming, but I didn't know. She wants to help you get Lynnae's room ready. Erin's such a sweet young lady," Teresa said with love in her voice.

I nodded, rubbing my hands together. "I know she is. Right after we meet with Frank, Erin and I will set up their room. I can't believe it, I still have to wrap presents."

"Me, too. Let's wrap them together. We can listen to Christmas music and drink tea."

"Sounds good," I replied. Ever since Dan and Lady arrived, I had been spending all my evenings down at the cottage.

"What time is good for you?" she asked.

"Whatever time you say," I replied.

"Good morning," Erin said on her way downstairs.

I looked up at her. "Good morning."

"Morning!" Teresa turned back to me. "I'm so excited about tea time that I'm going to make us some gingerbread biscotti."

"Ooo, that's sound good," Erin said and smiled at Teresa. "I would love to help you."

"Okay, I'll start the batter, but I'll wait for you to bake them. They smell so good and they make the entire kitchen feel festive," Teresa said as she headed for the kitchen.

"Erin, you look so much better today." I motioned for her to follow me. "Let's get some coffee and wait for Frank in the kitchen. He's never late."

Erin and I followed Teresa into the kitchen. When we walked in, Dan and Jesse were sitting at the counter, eating their breakfast.

"What's going on?" Jesse asked, as he squinted, blocking the sun with his left hand.

"There's plenty of oatmeal if you ladies trust my cooking," Dan teased.

I shook my head. "Dan is a splendid cook! Don't let him fool you."

Teresa went over to the pot on the stove. "Geez, Dan, you cooked for an army. I'll eat it. It looks yummy." She turned to Erin and me. "Want me to bowl you up some?"

We both nodded. I poured two cups of coffee and one cup of tea for Teresa, then I asked, "Dan and Jesse, can I refill your cups?"

"I'm good," Jesse said as he stood.

"No, thanks. We're going shopping." Dan held up his thumb toward Jesse. "Someone still has presents to buy." Dan kissed me on the lips. "Love you."

"Love you, too."

Dan tapped Erin on the back of her arm. "I told Julie, Kevin plans to be in the daycare all day building bookshelves. So..."

"Sounds good." Erin turned slightly toward the men and added, "Dan... thank you."

Teresa set the bowls of oatmeal down and I watched her put cinnamon, raisins, walnuts, and butter on her oatmeal.

After Dan and Jesse left, Erin came over and sat down at the table. "That looks good."

I agreed, and we both put cinnamon on our oatmeal.

"You must be excited." Teresa raised her eyebrows at me. "Lynnae's staying for a week, right?"

I looked over at her. "Eleven days. They're not going back until January 3rd."

"Umm, how long is Jesse staying?" Erin asked between bites.

"He moved here. He sold his bucket truck, chipper and the business to his nephew."

"What?" Teresa shouted. "I'll bet Dan's happy. They seem close."

"We're both happy. Jesse is a good friend to both of us." I drank my coffee and ate my breakfast, remembering when our Rottweiler died. Jesse came to the house and helped Dan bury her. Afterwards, he went around to the back of the barn and cried as if she were *his* fur baby. That night he showed up with dinner.

"I like Jesse."

Teresa and I both almost snapped our necks looking at her.

Erin quickly threw up her right hand and held it out like a stop sign. "Not like that!"

"Thank God," I said, "because he's old enough to be your father."

"What?" Teresa blurted out. "How old is he? He doesn't look a day over forty."

"Huh, he turned fifty in June."

"Huh!" Teresa echoed.

Erin took a sip of her coffee. Swirled her oatmeal and then set her spoon down. "Every time I look at Jesse, I keep thinking about that morning when Kyle and I fell asleep under the tree. I heard this voice. When I opened my eyes, I didn't know what to do. He was so big. But his voice was low, tender, sweet, and raspy. He was looking at me and I could see kindness in his eyes. He got down on his knees, looked at Kyle and said, 'My name is Jesse, what's yours?' Then he asked Kyle if I was his mom." Erin bit down hard on her lip. "He asked Kyle for permission to pick me up." Her eyes were wet. She swallowed. "He put his arms out and said, 'I'm going to pick you up and take you to my friend, Julie.' Erin's lip quivered. "He held me close to his body and set me down on the front seat of his truck. When he buckled me in, I noticed he had tears in his eyes. He reached down and picked Kyle up. I watched him carry him to the driver's side. Jesse set him down on the front seat between us. When he buckled Kyle in, he told him everything was going to be okay. Then he looked at me and asked me what my name was. I don't remember if I answered him. I was still half-asleep. Yet, I felt safe with him. The next thing I knew you were running toward us."

When I heard someone clear their throat, my eyes rose from Erin.

Frank was standing in the doorway. "Sorry I'm late."

I used my napkin to wipe my nose. "Good morning, handsome. Can I get you a cup of coffee?"

"I would love a cup." Frank moved closer to Erin. "You're going to be just fine, young lady."

Through falling tears, Teresa said, "We have oatmeal. Dan made it. Would you care for a bowl?"

"No thanks, just coffee."

I looked at Frank. Something was wrong. My insides were flipping. He didn't have good news. I handed Frank his coffee. "Let's sit in the library." I looked back at Erin. "Ready?"

"I'll see you all later," Teresa said as we left the kitchen.

I sat on the sofa while Frank and Erin sat down next to each other on the wingback chairs. Frank opened the file and said, "Judge Abrams was able to get a signed order of protection. As far as your ex-husband's concerned, you, young lady, are at a safe house and he is not to come within—"

"Josh was served papers?"

"Yes. By two local sheriffs. In order for the temporary restraining order to be effective, you have to sign a sworn affidavit."

"What do you mean temporary?" I was quick to ask.

"As soon as Erin signs the affidavit, her order of protection will be for five years."

Erin blew out a long breath. "How am I protected? Because Josh doesn't care about papers."

"Erin, if your husband calls you or comes near you, he'll be in contempt of court. He'll go to jail." Frank looked at me. "Judge Abrams knows what he's doing. Judge Klingner put a rush on this order because of Abrams. Most women are granted a temporary stay. Considering your husband's past record, and aggravating circumstances, Klingner sought maximum protection." Frank leaned over and asked Erin if she enjoyed living in Connecticut. "Because that's where Josh was told you and your son would be until further notice."

At first, neither one of us caught on to what he was asking. "Oh!" I nodded. "Wait... what do you mean past record?"

"Judge Klingner's clerk remembered a case involving Josh and a previous girlfriend." Frank looked at me and shook his head. I decided to let it go.

Erin got up and put her arms around Frank's neck. When she kissed him on the cheek, she told him, "Thank you. Please tell Judge Abrams and Judge Klingner I said thank you for protecting my son and me."

Frank hugged her tight. A minute later, we all stood up. "You're in good hands. They don't come any better." Frank put his hand on my back. Then I heard him say, "Here she comes." He stuck his head out the door. "We're in here."

"How's it going?" Gina Marie came into the library, holding a file and a small box.

"Gina Marie, it's so nice to see you." I hugged her.

Gina Marie set the file and box down before taking off her coat, then she nodded toward Erin. "You're going to be fine. Don't worry. If anyone can make this happen it's Frank. Come sit with me. You have to sign these papers in front of me." Gina Marie flipped one paper after another. "One more. Sign here." With every signature, she used her rubber stamp. "You're all set."

Erin hugged her and said, "Thank you so much."

Gina Marie nodded. "Frank, I'll take these documents directly over to the courthouse. Erin, be good. Julie, I'll see you soon."

"Well, my dear ladies, I have a few things to do before the twenty-fifth," Frank said as he followed Gina Marie to the front door.

Chapter 21

Christmas Eve morning. "Ahh, that shower felt invigorating. Come on. Get up, lazy bones," Dan teased. "Let's go. Lynnae will be here in an hour."

I jumped out of bed. "I need a shower." Wearing only my panties, I bolted across the room, caught a glimpse in the mirror and saw a woman. Me. Happy. Feeling loved. After my shower, I asked Dan if we could have breakfast up at the inn, and if we could sleep up there.

"You read my mind." He shut the lights; made sure the fire was completely out, turned to me and said, "I can't wait for tomorrow morning."

"Me either," I replied.

We literally ran up to the inn. Not sure if it was the cold or our own excitement. I would have been on my derriere if not for Dan holding my hand the entire time.

"I'm glad it's not supposed to snow until tomorrow morning." I looked up. "I wouldn't want Barry driving in the middle of a snowstorm."

"He'll be fine. He drives a Suburban. They're pretty good in inclement weather." Dan opened the door, and I stepped inside. The lobby was dark. Usually Teresa turns on the table lamps.

"I'm starving this morning." Dan rubbed his hands together. "I'll start breakfast right after I light a fire."

"Okay, I'm going to turn on a few lights. Turn the coffee pot on and then I'll help you cook."

Dan and I turned all the lamps on in the lobby, including the one at the front desk, before going into the library. A door slammed shut. I looked up and waited for Teresa to come downstairs and catch me doing her job. "Oh, Erin. Good morning. I thought you were Teresa."

On his way to the kitchen Dan said, "Good morning."

"Good morning." Erin yawned. Then began wrapping her hair up into a ponytail. "Gosh, I can't wait for warmer weather."

"You don't like the snow?" I asked.

"I do. But I'm so excited to get outside. The other day when Kevin and I went for a walk, I discovered so many beautiful things around here."

"Wait until the gardens are in bloom," I said, adding, "Dan and I were just about to get something to eat."

Erin covered her mouth as she yawned a second time. "Sorry."

Erin and I turned on a few more wall sconces and by the time we reached the kitchen, Dan had chopped the pepper, onion, and mushrooms. Cracked several eggs and was flipping his second omelet.

"Just in time," Dan said as he handed Erin a plate.

"Thank you," she replied. "Can I help?"

"Dan!" Kyle ran over to him, and Dan picked him up.

"Hey, little buddy. Are you hungry?"

Amanda took her coat off. "We were outside making a snowman and he saw Dan in the window."

I sat on the floor and hugged Lady. I whispered, "Merry Christmas" in her ear.

"Well, good-morning, everybody!" Teresa was wearing her pajama bottoms and a sweater two sizes too big for her. She rubbed her face. "I think I overslept this morning."

"I knew I smelled Dan's cooking." Jesse held his hands out, and Kyle ran over to him. Jesse hitched his chin toward Erin. "Morning, Momma."

"Ho! Ho! Ho!" Barry said, holding a ton of luggage in his arms.

Kyle jumped down and ran right past Barry. "Sam! Max!"

I was ready to burst. The kitchen was bright and warm. I followed Dan's gaze. I sensed that he was pleased. Dan loves a crowd, and he enjoys cooking for everyone.

"Merry Christmas," Lynnae said as she put her purse on the kitchen counter.

I hugged her. "Merry Christmas." Then I kissed Barry on the cheek and asked who wanted coffee.

"Step right up," Jesse said, as he poured himself a cup of fresh brewed coffee.

"I need my tea," Teresa chimed in over the noise.

I cracked more eggs, while Dan chopped more vegetables. An hour later, we were all full and ready to start the festivities.

Dan and Jesse helped Barry unload his vehicle. No presents were to go under the tree. They hid the gifts in the billiards room and in the front hall closet.

Lynnae, Teresa, Erin and I went for a stroll to walk off the enormous breakfast we'd just devoured. Dan, Jesse and Barry were going into town to pick up the fish for Christmas Eve dinner. Amanda asked if she could take the boys sleigh riding. Then she looked at the boys. "I want to have story time before we come back over for lunch."

Kyle began jumping up and down. "Wait 'til you hear my story!"

Amanda looked at Erin. "He wrote a Christmas story about..." She motioned with her head toward Lady.

I felt Dan's hand on the small of my back. "Are you happy?"

"Extremely." I gave him a kiss.

"We won't be late. I want to eat lunch by one and dinner by five," Dan said.

I whispered in his ear. "Okay, Santa."

"Everyone needs to be in their bed early tonight," Jesse hollered, and the boys' eyes widened with recognition.

Barry gave Lynnae a kiss, and I heard her say, "I can't wait to tell her."

I looked at Lynnae's belly.

"Leggings, scarves and mittens," Lynnae yelled.

It was a coat fest at the front door. Some were on the coat rack but most piled up on the floor.

"Okay, I'm ready," Teresa, yelled to us as she came down the stairs.

We waited for Teresa to put on her coat. I wanted to show Lynnae the orchard, but it was too slippery. So we walked down the driveway and back. We were almost at the inn and we could hear the boys laughing and playing in the snow. We stopped and watched as they ran to the top of the hill and slid down to the bottom. Lady yelped as she ran after them. She always loved the snow.

"It's so cold. Let's make hot cocoa." I cupped my hands over my mouth and shouted, "Amanda." I motioned to her. "Do you want hot cocoa?"

We laughed when we heard the boys yelling and laughing. "No!"

"Maybe later," Amanda hollered back to me.

The four of us went inside, made our cocoa, and rekindled the fire in the library. I was warming my hands when Lynnae said, "The inn looks amazing."

"Very festive," Erin said as she tied her long hair back up into a thick ponytail. "Did Julie tell you, I'm going to start classes in January? I want to be a teacher."

"No way," Lynnae said, and pointed her finger at Erin. Then giggled fetchingly. "You know what? I had a dream about that."

"Really?" Erin smiled.

"I'm hungry," Teresa chimed in and we all laughed aloud.

"Me, too," Erin agreed.

I turned around and saw Barry's Suburban pull up to the front porch. "You're in luck. Our chefs have arrived."

We all got up and greeted them at the front door.

Lynnae turned to Barry. "Hey, call the boys in."

"I'll text Amanda," I said and then I whispered over to Lynnae. "Did you have time to go to Harney and Sons?"

"Uh-huh. And I picked you up two new flavors, organic Bangkok and a box of Paris."

"Paris?" I said with joy in my heart.

"Yeah, that tea has black currant, caramel, and citrus." She nudged me. "Trust me, *you're* going to love them. Bangkok is a green tea with coconut, lemongrass, ginger and vanilla."

"Sounds good. You know I love vanilla."

For lunch, Dan and I made a big pot of shrimp bisque soup, homemade croutons, and for dessert, vanilla fudge. After lunch, we all gathered in the library to hear Kyle's story.

"The place looks great," I heard Barry say as he sat down on the sofa next to Lynnae.

"Doesn't it?" Lynnae agreed as she picked Max up and sat him down on her lap.

"Dan and Jesse decorated the entire place. Inside *and* out," Teresa told them.

I sat down on the floor near the Christmas tree. As soon as Lady rested her head on my lap, Kyle came over and sat next to us.

Amanda came in and handed a piece of paper to Kyle. I noticed she had the first word of every sentence in big bold letters.

Kyle looked at it and said, "Now?"

"Sure. Why not?" Amanda sat down on the end of the sofa.

"Read it, Kyle." Sam motioned to him. "Wait. Where's your mom?"

"I'm right here." Erin waved her arm. She was sitting on the floor next to one of the rocking chairs.

Everyone waited for Kyle to begin. At first, he smiled, shook his head, but then jumped to his feet.

"When I was in the forest with my dog we saw a bear. Lady bit my shirt, pulled me behind the tree and kept me safe. The bear was drinking water from the pond. Lady tugged on me again. She dragged me all the way home. We ran inside our big house and Momma made us lunch. She even gave my dog, Lady, a bowl of soup for keeping me safe. Before we go to sleep, Mommy puts a chair against the door to keep me and Lady safe in our new bedroom. I love my new dog and she loves me. Me and Mommy love our new home. Kyle 2010."

Better than the look on Kyle's face was the love in his heart. When he looked at Lady and teared up, my heart could have exploded.

Teresa had tears in her eyes. "Merry Christmas."

"Best Christmas story ever," Lynnae said as she handed Teresa a tissue.

I held my arms out to him. "Kyle, can I have a hug?"

"Sure," he replied as he put his arms around my neck.

I told him, "Kyle, that was beautiful."

He leaned back. "Did you like it?"

"I loved it!" I replied.

"Good job," Max shouted.

"Boys," Amanda called out. "Let's go back over to the daycare for a few more hours." She winked at Sam.

"Oh, yeah," Sam replied. Waving to the others. "Come on guys."

"Okay, but dinner is at five," Dan added.

"Amanda, wait." I stood up, grabbed the envelope from the tree, and handed it to her. "This is just one of your presents. My way of saying thank you." We hugged, and they were off to Neverland.

"I'm hungry," Jesse shouted.

"Again!" Everyone said.

"What? We had soup…" he exclaimed.

"Good, then you can help me," Dan said with his hand on Jesse's back. "Let's go to the kitchen."

We all followed Dan's lead. Teresa put Christmas music on. Lynnae grabbed an apron and handed it to Barry. "You know you want to help."

"What can we do?" I asked.

Dan pointed to the menu board. "Read it to me and tell me where you want me to start."

I read, "First course, baccala' with pasta—"

"Yikes! What's that?" Teresa inquired from the makeshift bar on the end of the counter.

I laughed, "Salted cod."

"Oh, I like cod. Okay."

I continued with the evening's menu. "Dan's deep fried calamari with pineapple dipping sauce, clams casino, shrimp cocktail, baked haddock, smoked trout and an antipasto salad."

"And my cheese tray," Lynnae added. "With olives. I'm craving cheese and olives."

I looked at Barry. Nothing. He was motionless. I couldn't wait. I want them to have a little girl.

"Jesse, can you open this?" Teresa handed him a bottle of wine.

"Sure." He opened it and asked if Barry wanted a beer.

"Grab me one too," Dan shouted. "And grab the clams while you're over there."

"I'll open the clams," Barry volunteered as he reached for the clam knife.

Suddenly, I looked up, and my heart started pounding. Erin was whiter than ever, sweating, and she looked like she was about to fall over backwards. I turned to see what she was staring at. A man was standing outside the kitchen window. I didn't recognize him. He was wearing dark clothing, and he had on a brown hat. Slowly, my eyes went back to Erin. She was within his sight of range. I moved to stand in front of her. My insides surged when I heard the door open. I heard Jesse say, "The UPS guy's here."

Dan took the small package from the man, handed him a twenty, and told him, "Merry Christmas."

I made Erin sit down. After my heart leveled, I got up and poured her a glass of water.

"My head is spinning," she said after taking a sip.

"It was a delivery man. You're okay. Sit here until you regain your composure," I said to her and handed her a napkin.

"He looked just like Josh," she said and then sipped her water.

A few minutes later, Teresa poured wine into our glasses. Erin stood up, brushed the sides of her arms and asked what she could do. I grabbed a few serving trays and Lynnae opened a box filled with miniature pastries. When she set them down at the end of the counter near the bottles of alcohol, Teresa looked at them and asked, "Yum! Can I have a cannoli?"

"Sure!" Lynnae replied.

Barry walked over to the bar, poured three shots, kissed Lynnae and said, "You be my glass of wine and I'll be your whiskey, honey."

"Barry, get away from those scandalous women and open the clams," Jesse teased him.

I looked at Barry. "Welcome to our loud, crazy, fun, happy home."

Barry handed Dan and Jesse each a shot glass and said, "Cheers!"

Teresa turned the music up a little louder. Banged her hip into Lynnae and said, "Crazy. She got that right."

Lynnae laughed. "You mean still crazy."

Everyone was moving to the sound of Amy Grant, "Rockin' Around the Christmas Tree."

"Whoa, what are those?" Teresa's eyes lit up.

Lynnae placed chocolates on a plate. "Chocolate caramel marshmallows." She raised her eyebrows. "Yes, I made sugar free ones, too."

I smiled and started to say, "I've missed—" but Lynnae popped a salted caramel one into my mouth.

"What the hell? Where's ours?" Jesse asked as he reached for one.

Lynnae handed him a small dish that also included three homemade soft pretzels on it. "Enjoy."

"Give me a bite," Dan said jokingly.

"I'm *not* sharing…" Jesse teased.

"We need to open another bottle," Teresa said as she tossed the empty wine bottle into the recycle bin.

"No more wine for you ladies." Dan winked at me. "I need my sous chef."

"I'm your huckleberry," I teased.

Dan laughed loudly. "Can you chop the onion and peppers?" Then he looked away and hollered, "And someone needs to fry the bacon."

"Okay, boss," Lynnae, hollered back at him.

"I said please," Dan said to her.

"No!" we all shouted.

"Okay, please chop the vegetables and someone needs to press the garlic."

"I'm definitely chopping," Teresa said, laughing.

When Teresa started singing, Breath of Heaven, I had goose bumps. She hit every note. For a moment, time stood still. No one moved. I placed my hands over my heart when she sang the words, "Breath of heaven. Hold me together. Be forever near me —"

Chapter 22

Christmas Eve had always been quite an affair for Dan and me. At the inn, we kept the tradition, an intimate gathering in the smaller dining room. The snug room called for a relaxing theme: baskets of juniper and lady apples. Homemade gingerbread cookies served as place cards. A green and tan plaid silk taffeta tablecloth, with matching napkins adorned the table set for twenty. On the buffet table were two potted paperwhite plants. The night before would always be about the children.

By four-thirty, we had consumed two bottles of wine. Set the table. Lit the candles, and turned on the music in the dining room. Dan set a bottle of 2010 Le Ragnaie Brunello in an ice bucket. The room was ready. All we had to do was serve the food.

"It's quarter to five. Where are the kids?" Dan asked as he took the tray of clams casino out of the oven.

When Mariah Carey started singing, "All I Want for Christmas is You", Teresa turned it way up, and we had to do it. Teresa, Erin, Lynnae, and I sang the entire song at the top of our lungs. We were pointing our fingers at the men, singing, "All I want for Christmas is you… baby." When we saw three wise men standing in the doorway. I heard Teresa holler, "Whoops!" then she ran over and turned the music down.

Sam held out his hands. He was holding gold coins. Max was beaming. "Mine smells like pine trees."

"Incense," Sam, corrected him. "Kyle's gift is oil. Can we put them under the tree?"

"How about we put your gifts near the manger," Dan said. "Come with me, my three wise men."

As soon as the boys saw how festive the dining room was, they all ran to find their seats. Kyle picked up his gingerbread cookie and asked if he could eat it.

Dan suggested he leave it for Santa.

"Aunt Julie," Sam asked, pointing to a quote I had framed. "Who is Ray Bradbury?"

I stood near the teacart and read the quote aloud: "We are cups, constantly and quietly being filled. The trick is, knowing how to tip ourselves over and let the beautiful stuff out."

"Did he make those tea cups?" Sam asked.

"No. My liking him has nothing to do with a teacup. I like him because he believed in himself. He was a forward thinker." I loved his backstory.

"I like," Lynnae said, "the big picture of Charles Dickens hanging in the daycare."

"Writer," Sam said. "Are they all writers?"

I smiled. "Most of them."

"Huh, I get it now," Barry said. "That's why H. G. Wells is hanging in the billiards room."

Several times during dinner, I caught Lynnae smiling at Barry. In between each course, I was hoping they would share the news, but seven courses later, not one word.

"Dinner was delicious! I'm stuffed!" Jesse leaned back and crossed his arms over his chest.

"Mommy, can we have cake?"

"Max. Who did we bake the cake for?"

"Jesus..."

"That's right. And when is His birthday?"

"Tonight?"

"Well, he's got a point," Barry said as he rubbed the top of Max's head.

Lynnae shook her head, and that's all it took for Barry to agree with her. "Tomorrow. Mommy says tomorrow's His birthday. Come on, you've had enough sweets for one night.

Let's go to the library, sit down by the tree and I'll read you a story."

Barry read *The Night Before Christmas*.

Afterwards, Erin told the story of how her mother used to put a thick candle in the largest window on Christmas Eve, as a welcoming light for Mary and Joseph.

Chapter 23

I could not believe my eyes when I looked at the clock. Dan didn't come to bed until almost two a.m. He said they ran out of room, so they moved the rockers to the billiards room and left Michael and Kevin's family presents in the closet until after the boys opened their gifts.

As soon as Dan snuggled up against me, he fell asleep. *Thank you, Lord, for this man, the arms wrapped around me and for watching over us. Amen.*

We both woke up excited. I looked out my window and saw snowflakes. "It's snowing." I clapped my hands. "Yay!"

"Shhhh!" Dan held his finger to his lips. "We need to set things up."

Downstairs, Dan stopped in the library just long enough to turn on the Christmas tree lights and to light the candle in one of the front windows. Then he turned his attention to the fireplace.

Thanks to Lynnae, we had muffins, croissants and mini egg frittatas ready to go. While I warmed breakfast up, Dan placed decanters of juice and coffee on the serving cart. At six-thirty, he rolled everything out to the lobby. We sat outside the library, waiting for everyone to come downstairs.

"It's seven o'clock. Where are they?" Dan said to me.

"Stop! You're like a big kid," I replied.

A few minutes later, Jesse called down to us. "Are the boys up yet?"

I laughed. "Grab some coffee and sit down. Geez, Jesse, you're as bad as Dan."

Jesse poured himself a cup of coffee and took a blueberry muffin. "Did she go in?"

"No!" Dan slapped me on my leg. "No one goes in the library until the boys go in."

And with that said, Jesse yelled, "Santa's here!"

First Erin, Kyle and Lady. Then Teresa, followed by Barry, Lynnae, Sam and Max.

They were all on their way down the stairs when Santa walked through the lobby. He came from the library and headed straight for the front door. It wasn't Dan, Jesse or Barry. I didn't know *who* it could have been.

I looked up, and the boys were in awe. Max was holding onto Barry's hand.

"Ho! Ho! Ho! Merry Christmas," Santa said on his way out the front door.

And everyone came running down the stairs.

Even I was amazed at the amount of presents under the tree. Of course, all three boys found their own Moto Tec Mini Quads. "Go ahead. Give 'em a test drive," Dan said as he pointed to the lobby. Dan picked Kyle up and sat him down on his quad. It took Dan no time at all to show Kyle where the go peddle was and the brake. A second later, Kyle was on his way. The boys rode their quads for a few minutes and the adults inhaled caffeine.

A few seconds later, Dan approached me from behind. "Merry Christmas, my love."

I leaned back, resting my head on his chest. "Merry Christmas, sweetheart."

"Well, what have we here?" Frank shouted to the boys.

"Frank and Sal are here!" Sam hollered from the lobby. "They're in there."

"Merry Christmas, everyone." Sal raised his head up to Dan.

I met them at the door. "Merry Christmas. Thank you for coming."

"Can I get the two of you some breakfast?" Teresa asked, as she greeted them.

Sal gave her kiss. "Still drinking your tea, I see."

"Oh, yeah!" Teresa started to pour their coffee.

"Just coffee for now. Thank you." Frank took the cup from Teresa.

"Come sit with me," Teresa said as she approached the library. Teresa, Sal, and Frank sat on the sofa together.

"I'd like to go first," Dan said as he picked up two packages. "Frank, I can't thank you enough."

I noticed Dan had placed everyone's personalized stone in the center of each of their bows.

Dan bought Frank a Stetson hat. "I've always wanted one." Frank pointed his finger at Dan. "You saw my stack of magazines. Thank you." Frank read his stone aloud, "Mentor."

"Teresa," Dan said as he handed over her gifts.

First, she pulled the stone from the gold bow and read, "Tea Partner." Then she opened her other present. A variety of teas.

"Thank you." She hugged and kissed Dan.

"Lynnae and Barry, you're the best!" Dan handed them a medium size box. On the top were two stones. Friendship and Family. Lynnae opened the box and pulled out an envelope. "Seriously? Two nights at The Blue Dory Inn."

Barry looked at the note card. "December 30th and 31st."

Dan handed Jesse a bottle of brandy and an envelope. "A fishing trip on the Frances Fleet. You're kidding me, right?" Jesse laughed, then stood up and handed Dan an envelope.

Dan laughed as well. "Great minds think alike!"

"Yeah, but yours is whale watching, old man," Jesse teased him and there was a smattering of laughter.

"Erin, this is for you." Dan slid an enormous box over to her. "Go ahead, open it."

Erin pulled the ribbon and lifted the top off. "Thank you!" She smiled and hugged him. She looked at us and said, "School supplies."

"Julie." Dan held his hand out to me.

I reached for his hand, and he pulled me to my feet. We walked over to the window. "Oh, my, goodness!" Outside was a new gray Ford Explorer with a big white bow on it.

"No more driving Miss Julie!" He spun me around and kissed my lips. "Merry Christmas."

"Umm, may I go next?" Erin said in a low voice.

We all said, "Yes..."

Erin stood up, reached under the tree and pulled out several flat packages. She had one for every adult. "I promised myself I wouldn't cry." She wiped her eyes. "Like that's not going happen. I just want to say thank you for taking such good care of me and Kyle." She smiled and handed me a black-and-white photo of the inn.

"Oh, my word!" I said. "Erin, it's beautiful. I love it!"

"Kourtnee said I could use the camera and the printer in her office."

Dan stood up and hugged her. "This is great!" He showed us his photo. She had captured Lady and me down by the pond.

Jesse's was a photo of himself, Dan, and me. His was in a frame.

Teresa's was a photo of her and me from just the other day, enjoying a cup of tea together.

"Barry and Lynnae, I hope you don't mind I have two for you. I couldn't get the four of you together at the same time."

Lynnae held up a photo of the three boys playing outside. And a photo of Barry and Lynnae standing in the doorway, kissing.

"Frank, yours was the easiest to capture." She had taken a photo of him laughing at Kyle and Lady playing ball in the front yard.

I looked at Frank. "That is a great shot of you!" Then I asked Erin, "Can I get a copy of that?"

"Sure," Erin replied, "they're still in the camera."

I stood up and handed each of them their gifts. "Frank, I know Hanukkah ended on the 9th. What do you say, next year we light this together?"

He kissed my cheek and whispered in my ear, "Thank you!"

"My turn," Jesse said, as he handed Erin her gift.

"Oh, Jesse. An HP Pavilion." She cried when Jesse hugged her.

"I'll have none of that. It's Christmas, for heaven's sake. No excuses. Get your homework done," he teased her.

Erin laughed and wiped away her tears. "You got it!"

Dan handed her our gift. "We both want you to know that we're here for you," he said.

Teresa raised her teacup. "Here, here!"

Erin wiped away her tears. I knew she liked it when she held it to her chest. She got up and came over to hug me. "You're welcome," I said.

Lynnae asked, "What is it?"

"A program to help find my birth mother. Ancestry," Erin said, beaming from ear to ear.

"Ohhh," Jesse said.

In all the commotion, we almost forgot about the boys. "Dan, will you call the boys in?"

"Umm, let's eat something first," he said as he helped me to my feet and we all went out to the lobby. We could hear the boys roaring around in the kitchen, laughing and having a great time. Dan lifted the cover from the omelets and placed one on a plate for me.

"This looks delicious," I heard Frank say. "I'll have another cup of that coffee now."

Dan poured Frank a cup of coffee.

"Muffins are good. Who made them?" Jesse said jokingly.

Lynnae looked at Jesse. "Smartass! Who do you think?"

I rolled my eyes. "That's my girl!"

Barry went to the kitchen, and I heard him telling the boys that Santa left a few more presents under the tree for them, but first they had to get something to eat. "Park them in the lobby. Watch out!"

We took our plates and sat down in the library. Dan, Barry, and Jesse sat on the floor, Frank in one wingback and me in the other. Erin, Lynnae, and Teresa sat on the sofa together.

Jesse handed all three of the boys their iPads.

Dan handed Kyle, Sam and Max each a set of walkie-talkies.

An hour later, we had a mountain of wrapping paper, one Easy Bake Oven for Max, nine sets of Legos, six pairs of pajamas, a toybox for Kyle, three toboggans, tool boxes, tool belts, and one carpet from Sam and Max to Kyle, complete with its own construction site printed directly on it.

For the daycare, puzzles and board games for young imaginations. And my favorite, more books than any child could imagine.

It was an apple pie kind of morning!

Chapter 24

About a half-hour after lunch, Frank said his goodbyes. Said he was going to see his brother and Bea. "I'm real proud of my niece. Glad to see her excited about her education. You all have a pleasant afternoon." He tapped me on the nose. "I'll be seeing you soon."

Amanda had the week between Christmas and New Year's off. She was spending Christmas day with her family. And on the 27th, she was looking forward to spending four days of skiing with five of her friends at a ski resort in Exeter.

"We're taking the boys outside for a while." Dan bent down and picked up a small pair of snow pants. "We'll be back in time for dinner," he said as he helped Kyle step into his. "There you go, buddy. Hand me your coat."

"That sounds like fun." I gave Dan a kiss goodbye then yelled to Barry, "There's snow tubes big enough for adults in the daycare."

"Come on, old man, I'll race you for one," Jesse said as he ran out the door.

"Enjoy your afternoon, ladies," Barry said as he kissed Lynnae goodbye.

"Have fun!" Teresa shouted to them as they headed out.

I put my arm around her shoulders. "Tea time."

"Tea sounds good." Teresa pointed toward the library. "But what do you say we pick up the mess in the here first?"

Erin looked back and echoed Teresa's thoughts, "Good idea."

Lynnae, Erin, Teresa and I picked up crumpled wrapping paper, empty boxes and about a thousand sheets of tissue paper. "All clean," Erin said.

There was something different about Erin. She sounded like a new woman.

We were on our way to the kitchen when Lynnae asked Erin how she has been holding up.

"I'm much better, thank you. I'm learning to not be afraid."

"I can't believe you feared your own husband," Teresa said to her.

"I have a great idea, why don't you take pictures of the gardens this year and we'll have Kourtnee include them in the brochure for next year's garden tour," I said hoping to keep the mood upbeat.

"You offer tours of your gardens?" Lynnae asked as she turned the stove on.

"Yes. It started when a woman from the Ladies Auxiliary had lunch with someone who was staying here. She called and asked if she could host a meeting here and tour our gardens," Teresa replied as she handed Lynnae four cups. "Cool idea, right?"

"She's always had the most incredible gardens." A moment later, Lynnae turned around and added, "Water's hot." Then she filled our cups and brought them over to the table.

"Let's use my new tea box," Teresa said as she set it on the table and opened it.

I placed some cookies and pastries on a tray and set it on the table next to Teresa's tea collection. "I think I ate a few too many pastries earlier. I better not eat anything else."

"Thank God for Dan," Lynnae said as she looked at me. "What? He knows you better than you know yourself." She handed me a shortbread cookie. "No sugar, Sugar!"

Then Lynnae handed me a small box. I pulled the ribbon and opened it. Inside was a new teacup. I pulled it out and read: "Grandma" on the front.

"Seriously?"

"Yep, she'll be here the end of April. We haven't told the boys yet. I wanted to tell you first."

I hugged her, as did Erin and Teresa. We spoke about Barry and Lynnae building their new home, possible baby names and, how wonderful the boys were going to be with their little sister. Teresa spoke about our family growing every day. "Including you and Kyle," she said as she tapped Erin's hand.

Erin was holding the string on her tea bag, bouncing it up and down in her cup. "I don't mind telling you guys what happened." She looked at Teresa with sadness in her eyes. "I had just put Kyle to bed, taken my shower and went downstairs to see where my husband was. Josh asked me what was on my mind. He said, 'You've been quiet for the past few days.' I sat down in the oversized chair in the corner and told him I wanted to go collage as soon as Kyle started kindergarten..."

She swallowed. I saw her chest rise up and down. "He threw the bottle at the wall. Liquor was all over me, and the lampshade. I hollered his name. I didn't mean to scream so loud. I was afraid I had woken Kyle. I stood up and looked up toward the top of the stairs and the next thing I knew Josh had ahold of my hair with one hand and the other was over my mouth. He dragged me down to the basement. Shoved me into the corner and told me I was an ungrateful bitch. Then he hit me so hard I fell over my desk. The last thing I felt was him kicking me." She looked at me. Reached over and held my hand for a moment.

"When I woke up, my clothes were torn. My arms and legs were weak. I looked around the room. Crawled back up the stairs. Josh was out cold in his chair and next to him was an empty bottle of Jack Daniels. I knew by his snoring that he was sound asleep." She let go of my hand and rubbed her neck. "That's when I went upstairs, grabbed my son and ran until I couldn't run anymore."

Silence. The only sound I heard was birds outside, feeding from the feeder.

We all took our first breath. Teresa was stoic. Lynnae was breathing heavily.

"You should have fucking shot the bastard," Lynnae said.

Teresa reached over and began rubbing Erin's back. "You did the right thing."

"I still say, shoot the prick and then run."

"Lynnae…!"

"What? Like you don't want to kill him?"

Teresa's lips grew into a flat line.

"Erin, would you be willing to talk to Dan's therapist? Dan thinks she's wonderful." I saw Lynnae raise her eyes as she looked at me. "Dan was never a fan of therapy until Lynnae suggested Barbara. And Barbara highly recommends Rose."

"If you… umm, if you think I should talk to her. Then I will."

"I do. I don't want you living in fear and I'm afraid with every trauma comes the fear of reliving," I said, and hugged her.

Chapter 25

Outside the kitchen window, I saw Lady covered in snow. I stood up and motioned to them to come inside, but no one noticed me. I opened the side door and hollered, "Come inside and get something hot to drink."

Dan waved to me. I noticed the boys all had red, runny noses.

"It's cold out there!" Barry said as he closed the door behind himself. "Man, that was fun!" After he hung his coat up, he picked up the boys coats as well. Then he walked over to Lynnae and hugged her.

She screamed, "You're frigging freezing!" as she pushed him away.

Barry bent down and picked her up again. "That's it! You're going outside." He put her down and said, "You promised. No more swearing."

"Sorry," she said and pouted her bottom lip.

Lady shook off and Dan opened the door for her. "Good girl."

"I'm hungry. When is Michael coming back?" Jesse asked.

Teresa handed Jesse the plate of cookies and pastries.

"Mommy, can we have Jesus' birthday cake now?" Max asked tugging on Lynnae's arm.

"Sure." Lynnae got up and brought the large box over to the table. She lifted the top and placed the sheet cake in the center of the table. "Who wants a slice?"

"Me, me!" Kyle shouted as Erin pulled his boots off.

"I'll put the teakettle back on," Erin said as she stood up. "Hang on, young man." She wiped his nose and patted him on his bottom. "Okay."

"Before we sing happy birthday, it's Kandoo time!" Lynnae said to the boys.

Kyle tugged on Sam's sleeve. "What's can do?"

Sam took Kyle by his hand and brought him over to the vegetable sink. He held up a container of moisturizing hand wash. "You'll like it. It smells like grapes. Just don't lick your fingers."

"I did that once," Max said, and then stuck his tongue out. "It doesn't taste like grape."

Everyone sang happy birthday and enjoyed a piece of Lynnae's marble cake.

"What time *is* dinner?" Teresa asked as she reached for a second piece of cake.

"What time does everyone want to eat?" I replied.

"Let's go into the billiards room for a while," Dan suggested. "Then it's make your own pizzas!"

"Pizza! Yum," Sam said, raising his eyebrows.

"Yeah, let's watch Dan run the table," Jesse said jokingly and then added, "you all know he's a pool shark, right?"

Ding-dong. My cell phone chimed. I picked it up and read Michael's message. "Teresa, when is our first guest arriving?"

"January seventh. Four couples."

"Umm, Michael said Christine isn't feeling well and they won't be here until Monday."

"The third or the tenth?" Teresa inquired.

"The tenth," I replied. "I hope she's okay. I better call him."

I went to the office and texted Michael to see if he was available to speak to me.

My cell phone rang before I could read his reply. "Merry Christmas. How is Christine? Okay, we love you too." I left the office feeling deflated. I couldn't do anything for him. Michael sounded devastated on the phone.

Everyone had moved to the billiards room. Dan, Jesse, Barry and Lynnae were playing pool. Erin and Teresa were setting up the Monopoly board, and the boys were laughing and joking about who was going to be hit in the face first. Lynnae thought it would be funny to watch them play the game Pie Face.

"Did you call Michael?" Teresa asked as I stood in the doorway.

"Yeah, he didn't say much. Just that Christine isn't feeling like herself. He thinks it's best they stay at her parent's house for another week."

Lynnae turned around and asked, "Is the baby okay?"

"Brin is fine." I glanced out the window and then added, "Michael promised me he'll be back on the tenth."

"Come sit down and play with Erin and me." Teresa motioned for me to sit next to her.

I saw Dan looking at me. Frequently, he would smile and wink at me. He was resting his chin on his pool stick when I heard him say, "I thought I'd try my new twenty-two out tomorrow. Anyone care to join me in a little squirrel hunting?"

"When'd you get a new gun? I didn't see you unwrap a gun," Jesse said, before taking his shot.

"Julie bought it for me for my birthday."

"When is your birthday?" Teresa asked as she rolled the dice.

"It was in November."

"Seriously?" Teresa shouted.

I saw Lynnae look at me. "She doesn't have a birthday calendar?"

I looked at Teresa. "I'm sorry. I–"

Teresa put her hand on mine. "We totally understand. Believe me. I know why you were so private. But that's all changed now. Right, Dan!"

Dan looked over at us, but said nothing.

I nodded my head to him. "As soon as Kourtnee gets back, I'll start one," I promised.

Dan shouted, "Starting with January. Julie's birthday is on the twenty-ninth."

Abrupt laughter came from the boys' table. Sam was the first to receive whip cream in his face. I looked at him. He was such a great kid. "Sam, how old are you now?"

"I'll be twelve soon," he replied and I just smiled at him.

"Are you okay?" Teresa asked as she tapped my hand. "It's your turn."

I looked over at her. "I'm worried about Christine. I hope she's okay."

"Julie, maybe Christine is suffering from anxiety, fear, and despair after childbirth. When I had Kyle, I was so depressed. My doctor wanted to prescribe antidepressants but as soon as I told him I was breastfeeding, he told me to try yoga. Believe me, it helped. He also suggested I cut back on my sugar intake."

"That's it! You've won every damn game." Jesse put his pool stick back on the cue rack. "I'm hungry. Who wants pizza?"

"I do! I do!" the boys hollered.

No surprise. Jesse made his pizza first.

"Are Dan and Jesse really going squirrel hunting tomorrow?" Teresa asked as she placed basil on her mini pizza.

I looked over at the two men. "Dan enjoys hunting. He hunts for food. Jesse only pulls his gun out for mercy. A wounded deer alongside the road, a rabbit hopelessly caught in a fence. One year, Jesse sat for twenty-four hours with a lost fawn, crying in fear of not finding its mother."

"Umm, what does he do with the dead animals?" Erin asked as she set four pizzas on a baking sheet.

"Well, the last time he brought home a couple of squirrels, he put them in a spaghetti sauce."

"Are you serious? You're kidding, right?" Teresa almost choked on her seltzer.

"No, Teresa, I'm not. Actually, squirrel tastes just like the dark meat on a chicken."

"I am not eating it! Does it really taste like chicken?" Teresa shrugged her shoulders. "Maybe, I'll try it."

"Mommy, can I go with Dan tomorrow?"

Erin was walking toward the ovens, but stopped. "I think you should wait until you're a little older."

"Kyle, Mommy's correct. A couple more years, you'll be old enough to learn about gun safety and how to hold a gun." Dan looked at Kyle. "Whatever your mother says goes."

Jesse smiled and said, "Hot damn, that looks good!"

I looked up and saw Dan and Jesse looking at Erin, bent over in front of the oven.

After dinner, Lynnae told the boys to head upstairs. "Pajamas and then it's story time in the library."

I stood up and said, "I'm going into the office for a few minutes. I want to go over Michael's menu and iron out a few details before our next meeting."

Dan put his hands on my shoulders. "I'll come with you. I want to ask you something."

We both sat down in the chairs in front of Kourtnee's desk. I looked at him.

"Julie, I saw you look at me earlier. Maybe Jesse was looking at Erin's ass. I assure you, I was looking at the four pizzas coming out of the oven. In fact, I can tell you, mine was not in her hands. Three pepperoni and one with peppers and onion." Dan sat back. Crossed his feet and laced his fingers. "Promise me, if I ever make you feel uncomfortable, you'll tell me about how you're feeling."

"Dan, I looked at you because I was worried about Christine. I wondered if we were ready to cook for a large number of people. I know you weren't looking at her derriere. Wait, was Jesse really looking at her ass?"

Dan sat up. "You *wish* he was looking at her like that." He scratched the back of his neck. "Remember the woman in the window at the gift shop?"

I looked at him. "No way."

Dan nodded. "Her name is Sherry."

"She had a ring on every finger. For heaven's sake, she's a married."

"No, she's not. She told Jesse to call her any time."

"She still could—!"

"Let it go." Dan pointed his finger at me. "She's not married."
I laughed.

"I followed you in here because I wanted to tell you something. Jesse said if we build a new house, he wants to build one, too. But I was thinking, if we cut back a little we could build houses for *all* the employees."

"Seriously? Oh, my goodness, I could use the rooms upstairs as corporate rooms."

"What?"

"Think about it. There's already a conference room up there. I'll bet I could get big corporations to book the entire floor. Oh, Dan, it's a wonderful idea."

He reached over and touched my cheek. "Say nothing to no one before we go over the plans."

I jumped up and kissed him. "I love you…"

"I love you too. Tell me, how much money do *you* have?"

"I don't know." I looked at him. "Seriously. With my spending habits?" I laughed. "Kourtnee controls the money." I reached over and grabbed the ledger from the top drawer of her desk. I looked down and back at Dan. "A lot!"

Dan and I looked over the numbers. I read Kourtnee's note. "In 2010 we had sixteen weddings with approximately one-hundred guests. Two with two-hundred and fifty guests. We took in a profit of, $766,500."

"In wedding business?"

"Trust me, we enjoy catering weddings."

"We won't touch that money. Unless we need it. Let me talk to Frank and–"

"Dan, if the staff aren't living at the inn, we'll make more–"

"Julie?"

"Okay. Fine." I was grateful beyond words. Dan was not only good with money; he was great at making it, too. "Wait, talk to Gina Marie, she's the budget master in the building industry."

Chapter 26

December 30th, Lynnae and Barry left for a nice long weekend away. To go along with our gift of two nights at the Blue Dory Inn on Block Island, Dan had given them a gift certificate for dinner at Eli's Restaurant. I had planned to take the boys down to the cottage; however, Erin asked if they could stay with her and Kyle.

"Hello! Is anybody home?" Kevin said as he arrived.

"Kevin and Kourtnee are home!" I shouted, jumped up and ran to greet them.

"Welcome home." I took Delilah from Kourtnee. "Merry Christmas, sunshine." I kissed her on her cheek and for the first time, she smiled at me. "Aww."

"What's going on?" Jesse asked. "Here, let me help you with that."

"Thanks," Kevin replied. "Dan, Merry Christmas." He shook his hand.

"Merry Christmas. Happy New Year!" Dan grabbed Delilah's diaper bag and portable playpen.

Kourtnee took off her coat. "Ahh, it's good to be home."

I saw Dan smile.

"So, what's been going on?" she asked.

"Plenty," Teresa replied. "Lynnae and Barry just left for a romantic weekend. Michael and Christine aren't coming back until the tenth."

"Never mind all that," I said. "It's Christmas. Get settled in. I want you to open your presents."

"Presents?" Kourtnee stood there staring at me. "Oh, I get it. Dan's here. I should have known. Sorry, we didn't buy…"

"Birthdays," Dan said. "We're celebrating them, too."

I stood by the doorway leading into the library. I wanted her to see her new rocking chair.

"Um, how did you miss all the decorations?" Teresa said, shaking her head.

"I saw the ones outside before we left for vacation. Oh, my…" Kourtnee turned toward me. "I love it! Delilah is going to flip." She picked up the bow and began rocking. I put Delilah down and she immediately ran over to her Momma.

Kevin stepped inside and said, "Thank you." He kissed me on the cheek. "That's nice, too."

I looked up and saw he was holding his tickets for his fishing trip.

We all went into the kitchen for a bite to eat. I grabbed Michael's recipe binder and looked up his dinner plans for January 4th and 5th. "Is he kidding me, he wants to serve roast rack of lamb with a vinegar mint pan sauce," I said, laughing out loud.

"I'll cook the lamb," Dan shouted and laughed. "What else is on the menu?"

"Roasted red potatoes, steamed baby spinach and crab stuffed artichokes for the appetizer. Okay, I can handle that."

"What's for dessert?" Kourtnee asked.

I looked back at the menu and read, "Molten chocolate cakes with sugar-coated raspberries." I shifted on the stool. "I need to place my orders."

"How many people?" Dan asked.

"Six." Teresa's gaze connected with Dan's and she responded, "So far!"

"No problem," Dan said.

The next day, I met with Kourtnee in her office. "Good morning, it's nice to have you back. How was your vacation?"

"It was nice. Delilah says Dada over and over until he picks her up."

"Aww, where is she?"

"With Kevin. She's definitely a daddy's girl."

I noticed a new photo of Delilah and asked, "Did Erin take that picture?"

"Yes," Kourtnee said. "Did you like the one she took of the inn?"

"Are you kidding me? Everyone loved their pictures. That was so sweet of her."

"Oh," Kourtnee said as she jerked up straighter, grabbing her notepad. "I want to tell you what Erin said to me the day she used the camera. At first, she hesitated but then said, 'By the way, this year you can deduct up to ten-thousand dollars' worth of office supplies.'"

"Seriously?"

"Yeah!" Kourtnee nodded. "I looked it up, and she was right. I'm making a list of everything I bought for the office and giving it to the accountant."

"Geez, I was hoping she would help me in the dining room, but maybe she should help you with the books," I blurted.

"She's asked before but I told her whatever you say goes. Honestly, Julie, now that I have Delilah, I would love the help. Especially during wedding season."

"You got it! Umm, how many weddings do we have booked so far?" I asked.

Kourtnee opened the hard copy of the calendar, looked up and said, "Thirty-six." She sounded exhausted when she added, "Six in July."

"We're going to need help. Especially with Bea gone," I said as I blew out a long breath.

Kourtnee got up and closed her door. When she sat down next to me, I knew she was about to tell me something important.

"Molly spoke to me before she left for vacation. Her father's not doing well."

"Oh, no!"

"I know. She had to put him into a nursing home. She goes to see him every day. They're taking good care of him, but it's expensive. She didn't know how to tell you, but she got offered a new position. A fantastic one!"

My heart sank. I loved Molly. She brought so much happiness to my life. "Does she need more money?"

Kourtnee shook her head. "No. This job is good for her career. A developer in Newport offered her a job as interior designer for *all* of his condominiums and townhouse projects. Her first job starts with the Silo Golf Course project." Kourtnee stood up. "We can't hold her back. It's that good!"

"Why didn't she come to me?" I blew out another breath. "I'm going to miss her."

"I'll run an ad the end of January," Kourtnee said.

"Kourtnee, I don't know where I would have been these past few years without you. You're happy here, right?"

She smiled. "I'm not done watching over you... yet!"

"Thank you. We had better schedule a meeting. I'll call Amanda and Cathy myself." I held my hand to my mouth, looked around and said, "Can you get everyone's date of birth for me?"

"Umm, I have them in a file. Why?"

"Dan would like for me to start a birthday calendar."

"A birthday calendar?" she said, holding her hands up.

"Yes. We are going to celebrate a lot more around here," I said, and headed out the door.

Chapter 27

Our first weekend without a chef went off without any problems. We went from six guests to twenty-four. I could not have done it without Erin. She was amazing. She helped me in the dining room, assisted Dan in the kitchen, and had all the laundry done before I could strip a single bed.

"Julie," Erin said from behind me. "I made an appointment with Rose."

I turned around. "I'm glad to hear that. When is it?" I asked, wondering how I would get her there.

"Tuesday at ten a.m."

"*Tomorrow?* Oh, okay. I'm sure Dan can take you." I felt bad suggesting Dan instead of myself, but I wanted to spend as much time as I could with Lynnae and the boys before they left on Wednesday.

"Well, if you don't need me for a while, I'd like to install the Ancestry program on my computer."

I gave her a hug. "Erin." I stepped back. "I'm so proud of you. My heart smiles, knowing you are taking care of yourself. Good luck! Hey, don't forget to do your homework," I added, sounding more and more like a fairy godmother.

She grinned. "Yes, Ma'am."

I heard Dan's voice coming from the kitchen. I could also smell cinnamon. Barry, Kevin, Jesse and Dan, all seated at the counter eating something. I looked over at the workspace and noticed four or five baking trays filled with Lynnae's hot cross buns. "You made my favorite!" I said and Lynnae turned around and handed me one. I took a bite and closed my eyes. When I opened them, everyone was staring at me. "What?"

"If you groaned any louder, I would have thought you were having sex with that bun." Lynnae said jokingly as she placed six in a box.

"Who are they for?" I asked.

"Frank. Dan's meeting with him later and wanted to bring him something."

"Aww, that's so nice of you." I sat down next to Dan. "Can you give Erin a ride to her appointment?"

Dan looked at me. "Appointment?"

"She's meeting with Rose tomorrow," I explained, reaching for a napkin. I looked back at him. "Can you?"

"Um, Barry," Dan said, "When are you going to the tackle shop?"

"Tomorrow morning," Barry replied.

"Can you give her a ride?" Dan asked.

"Sure," Barry said, and then got up. "What time?"

"At ten," I replied.

"No problem," Barry said.

"Thank you," I said and then looked at my cell phone. "Cathy and Amanda are on their way over. I have to meet with them and then I want to spend some time with you." I pointed to Lynnae, and she teased me with another hot cross bun. I mouthed the words, "Love you."

Teresa was sitting at the front desk reading when the phone rang. She pointed to the library as she picked up the phone. "The Inn in Rhode Island, may I help you?"

When I peeked in, I saw Cathy and Amanda looking out the window. "Nice ride." Amanda turned and said to me.

"Thanks, you can drive it any time. It has two video monitors in the back of the driver and passenger headrest. Kourtnee registered it to the inn, so you're already covered on the insurance," I said.

"Ooo, I can take the kiddos for ice cream this summer," Amanda announced, smiling.

"Does anyone want coffee or tea?" I asked, before sitting down.

Cathy held up her cup. "I grabbed a cup from the spa before coming over. Thanks."

"I'm good." Amanda pointed to a bottle of water.

"We're thinking about staying open all year and I wanted to hear your thoughts."

"I'm fine with that," Cathy said. "One question. Where are we going to host weddings in the winter?"

"Good question. I haven't figured that out yet."

"Hey, we can put a big tent on the terrace. At the ski resort they had four propane heaters." Amanda held up her finger. "Hang on." She showed me her cell phone. "Look. Fire Sense commercial patio heaters. Plenty of heat. It will be fantastic! Count me in."

"Great! Let me talk to Kourtnee. I'll have her create a calendar. Everyone can put in for his or her vacation. How does one week paid vacation sound?"

"Wow, that sounds fantastic," Cathy, said.

Chapter 28

Yesterday, I watched Erin take the boys and Lady to daycare. She made everyone breakfast, and she completed her first assignment for school. All before I had my first cup of coffee. *I wish I could bottle her energy.*

"Are you ready to head up to the inn?" Dan asked me.

I turned my reading light off. "Dan, can I ask you a question?"

He looked at me. "Anything!"

"Why didn't you want to take Erin this morning?"

"Come over here for a minute." Dan sat on the edge of the bed and I sat down next to him. "I never want to make you suspicious. The last thing I want is for you to wonder where I am." He inhaled. "Or who I am with."

"I'm —"

"Julie, you can't imagine how bad my life was. I messed up. I won't make that mistake again. I'm not putting myself in a position where you have to wonder. It's as simple as that. I knew Barry was going into town. And if he wasn't, I would have suggested Jesse."

"Oh, Dan," I said, feeling good in the moment, and grateful.

"I know it's going to take time for you to trust me. I'm going to do *whatever* it takes. For as long as it takes." He put his hand on my back. "I know you love me as much as I love you. Julie, I want you to trust me."

"Okay."

He kissed me. "I'm meeting with Kevin to go over your plans. He's the only person who knows we're planning on building the houses. He's so excited. Kevin really knows the property. You realize we're old enough to be their parents. I like Michael and Kevin a lot." He smiled warmly. "Yes, I like the women." Then he kissed me.

"I do, too!" I said.

"I was thinking I'd treat everyone to a celebration at George's for your birthday?"

"I haven't been there since our last vacation together," I said.

"You've been in Rhode Island for almost three years and haven't gone to Georges of Galilee?" He shook his head.

"Oh, wait. Teresa and I stopped in for a quick dirty martini the day you arrived," I said jokingly.

"What do you want for your birthday?"

"You." In my most seductive voice, then added, "All of you."

Dan kissed me, and I melted in his arms. A half hour later, we took another shower and headed up to the inn. With his long strides, he reached the front porch step first. When he opened the door, Teresa was sobbing. We ran to her. "What? What's the matter?" Dan asked, trying to help her to her feet.

"Erin's at South County. They were in an accident. Barry's…"

From behind me, I heard breaking glass. Then a loud thump. Lynnae was lying on the floor. "Oh, my God!" I screamed as we ran over to her.

Dan picked her up. Her head was dangling from his arm. He sat her down on the chair and told me to grab a cold cloth. "Julie. Go!" he shouted.

By the time I got back to the lobby, Lynnae's eyes were open. She sprang to her feet, crying and screaming, "Barry!"

Dan held her close to him. But when we reached the front door, Lynnae's legs must have crumbled, because she fell to the floor and hit her head on the door frame. Dan picked her up, carried her, and set her down in the backseat of my Explorer. I climbed in and held her in my arms. No one thought to grab a coat. It was freezing in the car. Dan reached back, fidgeting for something, and I asked him what he was trying to do.

"Open the heater vents," he said.

I reached over Lynnae, and pushed it all the way up. Dan handed me his cell phone. "What hospital did Teresa say?" he asked, and I saw him looking at me in the rearview mirror. "Stay calm Julie. Are you okay?"

I was shaking, but I answered him. "South County." When I spoke the words, Lynnae opened her eyes. I held her in my arms and rocked her. It took Dan fourteen minutes to reach the hospital.

He pulled up to the emergency room door, jumped out and opened Lynnae's door. Holding her in his embrace, he helped her inside. We were standing at the registration desk, asking where Barry and Erin were. When the nurse looked down at the chart, Dan turned around and asked a man sitting in the waiting room if he could park the gray Explorer.

"You got it!" the man replied.

"Thank you," Dan said to him as he ran out the door.

The nurse looked up at us and motioned to an attendant to bring a wheelchair over for Lynnae. "The woman is in room number two, on your left, behind the curtain." She looked up from her papers and said, "Mr. Woodland is on his way to ICU." Then she glanced up at Dan and pointed to Lynnae. "Mrs. Woodland, I presume?"

Dan nodded.

"Go down the corridor, make a right. There's a waiting room on your left, I'll let the doctor know you're in there."

I looked at Lynnae; she was white as a ghost. Dan assisted the orderly and made Lynnae sit down in a wheelchair. I kissed her on the cheek. "I'll check on Erin and be right back."

Dan made his way toward the corridor.

I moved the curtain and found Erin. She appeared fine. The moment she saw me, she put her arms out to me. I sat on the edge of the bed and held her.

Erin started to cry. "I'm so sorry." Voicing the unfairness of the situation.

"Shh," I whispered. "It's okay. Everything is going to be just fine. Are you okay?"

The nurse said, "Thank God for seatbelts."

I turned toward her. Barry always insisted the boys and Lynnae wear their seatbelts. "The driver, Barry, he had his seatbelt on as well, right?"

The nurse shrugged her shoulders.

Like a needle stuck on an old stereo, the letters. 'ICU' kept playing in my head.

"Yes," Erin said. "He had his seatbelt fastened but... it didn't matter."

"What happened? Do you remember?" I asked pleadingly.

Erin looked down. "Someone drove right into Barry's side of the truck. I overheard one of the paramedics say the man appeared to have suffered a heart attack."

"Is he okay?" I asked.

The nurse shrugged again, offering a deep sigh and thoughtful expression.

"I remember I had my hands out in front of me, stretching my arms toward the windshield. The next thing I knew, the air bag had deployed. I pushed it out of my face. Barry was covered in blood. I screamed for help. As they were putting me in the ambulance, I saw them carry Barry out of the truck. Julie..." she cried.

I hugged her and told her Barry's tough. "He's a big man, strong, he'll be okay. Don't you worry," I said as I noticed her new bruises.

Chapter 29

I kissed Erin and told her I needed to check on Barry. She insisted she come with me. The nurse said she would have to get clearance. "I'll bring her to the waiting room near ICU as soon as Dr. Shannon comes back with her x-ray results." The nurse looked down at Erin. "I promise."

I touched the nurse's hand. "Will you stay with her?"

"For as long as I can." She raised her eyebrows for me to leave.

I walked in and found Lynnae sobbing in Dan's arms. For a minute, it looked like Lynnae might crumble into a thousand pieces. Gone was her radiant smile. When she saw me, she stood up and held out her arms. She turned slowly, wobbled, and almost fell to the floor.

All three of us sat down on the small sofa. Dan on one side and me on the other. Three hours later, Dr. Shannon walked into the waiting room. He placed his hand on Lynnae's shoulder. "Mrs. Woodland?" Lynnae's eyes met his. "I'm sorry it's taken me so long to get to you. Your husband has suffered a concussion. He took a terrible blow to his head. Looking at the CAT scan, I don't see any broken bones or fractures. Right now, I am concerned with his loss of consciousness. We are waiting for the result of one more test before we move forward. Questions?"

"Can I see him?" Lynnae pleaded.

"Only for a few minutes."

"Based on the CAT scan, can you tell us his prognosis?" I asked.

Dr. Shannon looked at me and then at Dan.

Lynnae sat up straight. "These are my parents. Julie and Dan Holliday."

He nodded. "It is very difficult to make an accurate prognosis at this time. Let's see what happens in the next few hours." Before he left the room, he put his hand on Lynnae's shoulder again adding, "I'll check on Barry in an hour. You stay strong, now," he said looking directly at Lynnae.

"Thank you." Lynnae's voice was soft. She turned to Dan and he helped her to her feet.

Dr. Shannon held the door open for us. "Down the hall on the left. They're expecting you."

Dan and I held her in our arms. A nurse pointed to Barry's room. No door. Only a curtain pulled back.

It was worse than I expected. There were lines everywhere. Barry was on a breathing machine. The left side of his face covered in red marks and slashes. His head was wrapped in gauze.

Lynnae reached out and touched his hand. Dan pushed a chair up to her. Then he sat her down. Dan stood behind her. His hands never left her shoulders. Tears were running down his face. When our eyes met, I inhaled and shook my head. I hated to see a man cry. I took a deep breath. I had to be strong for Lynnae.

I stood at the foot of his bed, listening to his monitors. Looking at Lynnae remembering the day she walked into my bakery. From, that lanky young girl who had dreamed of becoming a baker to a serious and composed woman.

Her dreams of marrying the *right* guy – Barry.

When Lynnae put her head on the side of Barry's bedrail, Dan let go of her. I could hear her begging him to fight. "I love you," she whispered over and over.

A nurse came in. Moved about the room. Stood in front of the monitors, writing her findings down on her chart. Before she left the room, she gently touched Barry on his forehead. She flashed a grin at Lynnae. "We're all praying for him."

"Thank you so much," Lynnae whispered back to her.

I found her words comforting. I was glad Lynnae had acknowledged her.

Lynnae sucked in a breath. "Wake up. Please, wake up." Tears were streaming down her face. "I need you."

When Lynnae moved her head and rested it on Barry's chest, Dan looked at me and motioned for us to leave the room. Dan and I met everyone in the waiting room with sad eyes. When Jesse's eyes filled with tears, I went back into the room, closing the curtain behind me, and sat at the foot of Barry's bed. Lynnae was like a sister to Jesse.

"He's a healthy man with a will to live. Barry's going to pull out of this," I said to Lynnae, hoping she believed me.

Lynnae sat there for a minute. She reached down and touched his hand. "Talk to me, Barry. Tell me, 'I got this.'"

A moment later, two doctors came into the room. Dr. Shannon said, "This is Dr. Plimpton, she's Barry's neurologist."

Dr. Plimpton held out her hand. "Mrs. Woodland, I am going to do everything in my power to help your husband." She placed her hands on the foot of the bed. "He's very weak. Now we wait and see if there is any more swelling during the night."

I looked at her. "Dr. Shannon said he was waiting for one more test. Has that test come back yet?"

Dr. Plimpton looked at me and then at Lynnae. "The test Dr. Shannon was referring to is the test of time."

Chapter 30

Dan came into the room and told us they were keeping Erin overnight. They want to observe her for the next twenty-four hours. Lynnae looked up. "Oh, my. That poor baby. How is *she*?"

"Her neck hurts her, and that's why they want to keep her. They just want to make sure she doesn't have any spinal issues down the road," Dan said.

Lynnae's entire body was shaking. Her hands were trembling. "I had forgotten about her being in the truck." Tears filled her eyes, but she refused to let them fall.

I hugged her.

Dan walked over to us. "I'm going to get you something to eat. I'll bring you back anything you'd like," he said to us.

Lynnae looked at me. "He's right, you should eat."

I was too upset to think about food. "Can you bring saltines and ginger ale?" I looked back at Lynnae, "Lynnae?"

She didn't answer me. She just nodded.

Dan kissed us both. "I'll be right back."

People with long white jackets moved in and out of the room.

By evening, a low-grade headache had settled on my right temple. Lynnae reached over and tapped me on my leg. "Tell me one of your stories." She rested her head on my shoulder. I began stroking her hair. Lynnae let out a tired sigh, when a nurse came in holding a cup of water and a handful of oral swabs.

"This will help to keep his lips moistened," the nurse said.

I reached up and took the cup and swabs from her. "I'll do it." We both stood up. Lynnae busied herself by fluffing Barry's pillows and by moving his tissue box from one night table to the next and back again.

She touched the side of Barry's face. "I love you," she whispered, leaned down and kissed his forehead.

Nighttime surrounded us. The only light in the room was from Barry's monitors. Dan sent me a text message. He was sitting in the corridor with Jesse outside Erin's room. I texted him back, "I'll see you in the morning. Thank you for the soda and crackers."

Lynnae made a sobbing sound. "Wake up!"

I felt the sting of tears. *This is not how it was supposed to be.*

"I can't take this crap," Lynnae said in a raspy voice. She meandered around the room and then let out a sigh.

At one a.m. I heard Lynnae say, "Remember how long he made me wait? He wouldn't make love to me, unless it was special. Pissed me right off when he called me a girl. Now, I just want to hear him say, 'Girl, stop worrying. I got this!'"

Seconds turned to minutes and then into hours. By three-thirty, Lynnae had fallen asleep. All those months. Time lost. Precious moments that I never saw happen because of my tainted mind. I didn't care about the woman who had given birth to her. She was mine to take care of... to look after. I bent down and gently brushed the hair from her face. Then I remembered her news of having a little girl of her own.

I picked up the glass of water, dipped the swab, and moistened his lips. A lump formed in my throat. "You made me a promise. I'm holding you to it. Open your eyes, Barry, come back to your family. They need you." I kissed the side of his face. "She's waited all her life for you. You are the love of her life. Those boys need their daddy. Your baby girl is expecting you to be the first to hold her." I closed my eyes to the sound of the machines. Beep. Beep. Beep.

Chapter 31

Five a.m. three doctors, including Dr. Plimpton, came into the room. "Good morning," Dr. Plimpton said to us as Lynnae lifted her head up and opened her eyes.

Lynnae and I both stood to greet them and hear the news.

"Could you give us a moment?" One of the other doctors asked.

"Of course," I said. I looked at Lynnae. She wasn't moving. "Come on, sweetheart, we'll wait outside the room," I said to her and gently touched her elbow.

We were standing near the nurse's station when two men pushing a gurney stopped outside Barry's room. Dr. Plimpton came to us and the men wheeled the gurney inside. "We're sending Barry down for another MRI." She reached over and touched Lynnae's forearm. "This is normal procedure." She motioned for us to step out of the way. When they rolled by us, Lynnae sucked in a breath. I saw the doctor wince. "I'm sorry," she said to me. "What is your name?"

"Julie Holliday, I'm Lynnae's—"

"Mother," Lynnae said. "This is my mother."

She put her hand out, and I shook it. "Please come with me." We followed her to her office. She closed the door and held out a chair for Lynnae. I sat in the one next to her.

"Let me tell you what I know." She sat down and opened a file folder. "At the accident site, at first, Barry was unresponsive. Then he would make movements, but they made little sense. He would move body parts that weren't an appropriate action given the stimulant he received." She stood up and walked over to us, holding an iPad in her hands. Dr. Plimpton grabbed a chair and pushed it between ours. "When Barry's truck got struck, the impact caused him to hit his head in a manner that may have jarred or shaken his brain." She scrolled to the top of the iPad. Tapped on the screen and said, "We believe Barry has suffered a contusion of bruise on the left side of the brain, when the skull slammed and the brain was displaced, sort of like Jell-O if you dropped your container on the floor. Allowing it to become injured during the shakeup."

She pointed to the iPad. "Bleeding over the left surface of the brain. Um, that would be the left occipital lobe from this bruise. The same as if someone hit you very hard in the arm with a baseball bat. The damaged tissue would make it bleed."

I liked her. She was phrasing her words positively to make Lynnae feel better.

"Looking at this diagram." She motioned with her hand from the neck to the top of the head. "We can see one tiny white spot in the left occipital region. That is a small spot of blood." She pointed to an even smaller one at the top and said, "Here's another one in the right frontal cortex. We call those hemorrhagic contusions. Small spots of blood that show damage to the underlining brain tissue."

Lynnae's breathing was erratic. I looked at her. So much for calming and reassuring. She appeared terrified. I wasn't sure who would hit the floor first, her or me. I asked, "How do you treat this kind of injury?"

"Unlike those injuries that you may have heard about called epidermal or subdermal hemorrhages bleeds on the outside of the brain. Those can be surgically evacuated, relieving the pressure on the brain. Where these are located, there is no surgical treatment for this. The treatment revolves around keeping pressure inside the skull as low as possible by medical means."

We heard someone knock on the door. Dr. Plimpton turned around. "Yes."

A woman wearing a blue shirt and matching pants handed Dr. Plimpton a file. "Mr. Woodland's latest MRI."

Dr. Plimpton reached up. "Thank you." She looked at it and took a deep breath. "Good news." She pointed to the same photo we had just looked at. Then she pointed to the new MRI delivered to her. "There's no further damage. Barry has not developed any *more* spots of blood."

"What's next?" Lynnae asked with barely a breath left in her.

"We wait. Your husband needs to fight." She looked at Lynnae. "Is he a fighter?"

"With all his heart," Lynnae replied.

Chapter 32

At eleven o'clock that morning, the emergency room physician told Erin she could go home. Dan insisted on staying at the hospital with Lynnae and me, but I begged him to go home and take care of the boys. Someone had to explain to the boys where their mother and father were. Dan suggested telling them Lynnae and Barry went back to Block Island. Lynnae told him that would be fine. She gulped. "Sam will not take this lightly."

"But Sam knows school starts tomorrow," I said.

"Julie, please!" Lynnae snapped at me.

"I'm sorry. Lynnae," I said, trying to apologize.

"I can't deal with anything other than my husband." Lynnae crawled onto the foot of his bed. Wrapped her arms around his feet. "Wake the fuck up," she said, rubbing his legs.

Dan kissed me and promised me he would return with clothes for the two of us.

"Wake up. Please wake up. I need you. Your sons need you." An hour later, she drifted off to sleep.

I quietly moved my chair next to Barry's head and sat down. The room would have been silent if not for the monitors. When a nurse made an entrance in the room, I held my finger to my lips. "Shh." Then I pointed to Lynnae, and the nurse nodded.

A minute later, she came in with blankets and pillows. She bent down next to me. "I'll have the orderly switch the chairs for reclining ones." She flashed me a smile. "We believe in positive energy. Don't be afraid to talk to him." Before she left, she turned around and said, "I'll send two dinners in at four o'clock." Then she pointed to the sign above the nurse's station: "South County a *Friendly* Hospital."

I stood up and moistened Barry's lips with another swab, then I whispered in his ear, "Okay, the staff is extremely nice and friendly. Please, can we leave now?" Nothing.

By day three, I had to admit I was getting worried. With every passing hour, Barry seemed to drift away from us. Lynnae refused to eat any more than she had to. Stressed, her stomach couldn't handle any food. Her face, drawn. We saw Dr. Plimpton again. Each time, she assured us, Barry was stable and we needed to give him time. If I hear the word 'time' one more time, *I'm* going to explode.

Two a.m. Lynnae closed her eyes. I tucked a blanket over her. I sat in the corner with my cell phone and looked up symptoms of a head injury that included unconsciousness. When I read, "After traumatic brain injury (TBI), the deepest level of true coma lasts two to four weeks. If the person does not wake from the coma, they enter semi-comatose state, called vigil coma or vegetable state that include sleep/wake cycles."

My heart started racing. I needed a glass of water. I wanted Dan. Lynnae groaned. That's when I got up. Grabbed a cool cloth, and wiped Barry's forehead. I moistened his lips and begged him to wake up. Nothing except that damn beep, beep, beeping sound.

I stood at the window. I never saw the snow come down. The entire parking lot was covered in snow. It was beautiful, magical. I looked up at the sky. I saw Him. Four gray lines. His stance was firm. His arms stretched out. I closed my eyes and pleaded, "Dear Heavenly Father, please place Your healing hands upon him. Wake him up. Bring him back to his wife and children. Lord, I am begging You. In Jesus' name, I pray. Thank You." I opened my eyes. "Amen."

"That was beautiful," Lynnae whispered.

I sat down next to her. Held her in my arms. Perhaps she was holding me. We both fell asleep.

I woke up during the night. Jumped out of the chair and felt a chill go through my body. I looked at Barry, his lips were dry, so I moistened them with the swab. Then I whispered in his ear, "You promised me. You told me that you would take care of her. Barry, I trusted you. I believed you when you said you loved her with all your heart. You told me those boys would never have to put a damn thing back. You have a daughter coming soon. Wake the hell up! You have a family to take care of."

My tears touched his face. I turned around and grabbed a tissue.

"Where are my boys?" Barry asked in a raspy voice.

I looked at him. His eyes were on Lynnae.

I turned around. Lynnae was sitting up in the chair with the look of surprise and joy on her face. Tears streamed down her cheeks. I stepped back.

Lynnae stood up. Held her hands over her heart. She whispered, "Thank You." When she moved closer to him, three nurses and Dr. Plimpton came in.

"Welcome back!" Dr. Plimpton chorused. Then she motioned for all of us to leave the room. "He'll be fine. Let's give him and his wife a moment. It's their time together."

I had a new revelation about the word "time". I liked it!

Chapter 33

It was Barry's last day in the ICU unit. They were moving him to a private room. A room with an actual door. When Dr. Plimpton and the orderlies arrived, we left the room. It was time I made a few calls. Lynnae went to the nurse's station to thank everyone. Nurse Meilleur told Lynnae their prayers were answered.

"Thank you. Thank you so much. Honestly." Lynnae hugged her. "I appreciate everything, your prayers, the pillows, blankets *and* the reclining chairs. It made my time here more comfortable."

I put my cell phone back in my pocket. Lynnae and I waited together for them to prep Barry for transport. Twenty minutes later, they wheeled Barry out of ICU and to his room upstairs. We followed them down the corridor. I put my arm around her. "I ordered a fruit basket for the nurse's station and a gourmet basket to be delivered to Dr. Plimpton from The Fruit Company.

"I swear you are the best fairy godmother in the world!" She kissed me on the cheek. "Thank you."

"You're welcome." I thought. *Every little girl deserves a fairy godmother.*

An orderly pointed to the elevator on the right. "Second floor, room 209. We'll see you upstairs."

"Wait!" Lynnae kissed Barry on the lips. "I'm right behind you."

He smiled at her. "I know that."

I looked at Lynnae. She raised her hand to her mouth. "He's back!" she mumbled.

We stepped into the elevator. Lynnae pushed the button. "You have no idea how that used to drive me crazy."

"What?"

"Barry, always saying, 'I know that.' Oh, Julie, he remembers." The elevator door opened, and we got off on the second floor.

I pointed to the sign above the nurse's station and laughed. "Welcome to Recovery! You're One Step Closer to going HOME." Instead of the letter O there was a red heart.

Dr. Plimpton was standing outside room 209 as they wheeled Barry inside. "Ladies, can you give me five minutes alone with this handsome man? I have some instructions to go over with him."

Barry raised his eyebrows at Lynnae.

We stood outside the door and heard her introducing Barry to his speech and physical therapists, and to his dietician. "I want liquids for one more day. I know you're starving. I need that throat of yours to heal. Ooo, tomorrow you can have pudding."

Barry chuckled.

"He's going to be just fine!" Lynnae looked at me. "He loves pudding."

After everyone left the room, Dr. Plimpton told us to come in. "He's in skilled hands. Trust me; you can go home for a while."

"I'm not leaving him," Lynnae said in a stern voice.

Dr. Plimpton smiled. "I didn't think so." She pointed to the bathroom. "You're welcome to use the shower." Then she put her hand on the chair. "It reclines. I'll be back tomorrow." She touched Barry's arm. "I'd like to get some sleep now."

"Doctor Plimpton," Barry said, sounding extremely raspy. "Thank you."

She winked at him. "You're welcome!"

Lynnae climbed onto the bed and sat down next to his buttocks. "I just realized something. She checked on you every few hours. I don't think she ever left the hospital."

"By the looks of the two of you," Barry said, sounding tired.

Lynnae bent down, resting her head on his chest. Barry put his hand on the small of her back. At that moment, my heart settled.

"I'll bring you a change of clothes in a few hours," I told Lynnae.

When Lynnae didn't answer me, I said to Barry, "Shhh."

He mouthed the words, "Love you." Kissed the top of her head and closed his eyes.

I stepped out into the corridor. Closed my eyes and held my hands high above my head. "Thank You!" Then I called Dan and asked him to come get me. "So much better. Yes. Okay, I'll wait for you at the main entrance. I love you too."

Chapter 34

I stood outside, and breathed in the crisp, fresh air. It was a new dawn. A better day. I was thankful for the miracle that saved Barry's life. Dan pulled up to the front door of the hospital, got out, and held up my winter coat. Once again, I was grateful for the man smiling back at me.

"Your cheeks are rosy. How long have you been standing there?" he said to me.

"I don't know." I got in the car and kissed his cheek. "I don't even know what day it is."

"Saturday, January ninth."

I blew out a breath. "Michael will be home tomorrow."

Dan pulled out onto the road. "They're back. Teresa called him and told him what was going on. I'll tell you what, she's some feisty when she has to be. She's the first one up and the last person to go to bed at night. One more thing, the inn is full. Jesse and I have been sleeping at the cottage."

I glanced over at him. "Seriously?"

"Apparently there's a winter festival going on somewhere." Dan handed me a small bottle of water and an egg sandwich. "Eat it while it's hot," he said.

I grabbed it with both hands. "Have you seen Christine?"

Dan almost snapped his neck, looking at me. "Something's going on with her."

"What do you mean?" I asked, pulling the bottle of water back out of my mouth.

"To start, nah, I'll let you see for yourself."

Start over.

I was still looking at him when he continued, "The inn is fine. By the way, Erin has been a tremendous help. Kourtnee told me she fits right in."

When Dan put his signal on for Mallard Way, every ounce of me felt relieved.

He reached over. "You're home and I'm guessing by the looks of that hair, you're going to want a shower."

"I wish I could take a quick shower at the inn," I said.

"How well Teresa knows you. Your clothes are already in her room."

Dan parked the car. Waived to four couples as they walked by our vehicle. "Come on, I'll bring you up a pot of tea," he said as he turned off the engine.

Dan went to open the door and my heart raced. I was home and he… was with me. We were home!

Chapter 35

Dan and I stood in the lobby. It began with an aroma. The air smelled of baking loaves. "Ahh!" I inhaled as Dan held out his hand for my coat.

Teresa ran from behind the front desk. "I am so happy to see you." She looked at me. "I have so much to tell you, but not now," she laughed. "Go take your shower."

"I'll be right back." I stopped on the bottom step. "Teresa. Thank you!"

When she smiled up at me, I noticed she had tears in her eyes.

Teresa's room was immaculate. She had one Bible on the chair next to the window and one on the nightstand. I liked her room. White cotton nightgown draped perfectly across the bottom of the bed. White lace doilies everywhere. "Comfortable with a touch of country," I said.

When I went into the bathroom, I saw a pink terry robe hanging next to the shower and to the left, matching slippers. A warm smile came over my face when I noticed a note on the edge of the bathtub. I recognized his handwriting. I flipped the note open and read, "I love you with all my heart. I hope you enjoy the new jar of vanilla bath salts. Love, Dan."

I turned on the water, poured a handful of salt crystals in, and inhaled. The aroma was calming, and it made the water even more inviting. Slowly, I sank into the warmth of my surroundings. I knew if I closed my eyes, I would not wake up for days. When the water turned cold, I jumped into the shower long enough to wash my hair. I washed Teresa's tub and left her the jar of bath salts to try, along with a note thanking her for everything.

Standing in the lobby, I could hear Michael and Christine. They were in the billiards room. "You haven't baked in weeks. Never mind, you won't even look at me. Let alone let me touch you. It's bread." I heard Michael say to her.

"Baguettes," Christine yelled at him. "She baked baguettes!"

Oh, dear. I decided to leave them be for the time being.

No one was in the lobby, and I wondered where everyone was. Then I heard voices coming from the kitchen. I stepped in as Erin handed Dan a baguette. He took the crusty item from her, smelled it, and took a bite of it.

I was standing behind Teresa. We both watched him eat the entire piece in three bites. "Guess you're not sharing," Erin teased.

Teresa moved in closer and reached for one. "They smell so good. I want my own, too."

A half-hour had passed. The mixer was still moving extremely slowly not to allow the dough to become dry. Erin was still busy at the mixer when Christine entered the kitchen. Dressed entirely in black, her hair uncombed, and she had forgotten to put her signature red lips on. *This is not good.*

Christine paused, as if she was calculating her options. She snorted. Her stance was serious. Hands on her hips. Nostrils flaring. "What are you doing?"

At first, Erin didn't hear her. Then she shut the mixer off. "Oh, hi."

Christine held her hands out. "Are you the baker now?"

I stood back. I wanted Erin to defend herself. In front of her, a tin of warm popovers. "I baked." Her eyes narrowed. "I didn't mean to…"

I stepped alongside Christine. "I asked Erin to fill in for all of us. If you don't need her help in the kitchen, I'm more than happy to have her assist Kourtnee." I raised my eyebrows.

Inwardly, Christine appeared to be boiling. Yet she contained herself and pushed a cookbook toward Erin. After freeing up space on the counter, she went into the pantry. When she came out, she dropped a ten-pound bag of flour onto the counter, causing a white cloud. Christine began spreading flour on her workspace. When she dropped six eggs in the center, I knew what she was making – my favorite Italian cookies. A few minutes later, she started kneading dough as if it needed a beating. When she wiped her hands on her pants, I had to turn around. But I stopped when I heard Christine tell Erin, "You know popovers always go into a cold oven, right?"

"Of course. Otherwise, they won't rise. And don't peek, right?" Erin said in a questioning voice.

I left the kitchen to them, to sort it out for themselves, and headed over to the daycare. I wanted to see the boys, and I needed to hug my baby. As soon as I opened the door, Lady rushed over to see me. The boys, Sam and Max, seemed fine. Even Kyle appeared happy. I thanked Amanda and told her I had something I needed to take care of.

Something made me go back to the kitchen. This time, I saw Michael standing over the stove stirring what appeared to be a white sauce. He had one eye on the saucepan and the other on his wife. Christine was feeding Jesse something out of her palm. One glance from me, and Jesse knew to get up and move away from her.

I followed Jesse out to the lobby and scolded him like a schoolboy. "Jesse, are you serious? What the hell is wrong with you? Can't you see something is going on between Christine and Michael? Don't play into her hands."

Jesse curled his lip, shook his head, and bolted out the door.

Chapter 36

I went back into the kitchen to grab myself a bite to eat, and witnessed Michael trying to kiss Christine on the back of her neck, but she squirmed away from him. Tossed her apron onto the floor and went into the food pantry.

Michael put both his hands on the counter, bracing himself. Then he looked down and picked up her apron. When he looked up, our eyes met, I motioned for him to follow me. He held up one finger, indicating to give him a second.

As I approached the lobby, I saw one of my guests hiding behind a book. He was sitting in one of the wingback chairs. The lamp next to him was on. On the table, a stack of books, all classics. As I got closer to him, I noticed he was reading one of my favorites, *To Kill A Mockingbird*. Teresa hung up the phone and motioned for me to come closer to where she was.

"I told him it was okay to borrow some of your books." She looked at me, and her face tightened. "Is it?"

It's funny how sometimes you find a friend, in the most unlikely places, and almost immediately you find yourself talking to them about anything. Teresa was one of those people. "Of course." I flashed her a smile. "I'm waiting for Michael. I have to find out *what* is going on with Christine."

She studied me with shades of curiosity, as though something else was going on and she couldn't fathom it. Did she know something I did not?

I leaned in closer so she would be the only person to hear what I was about to say. "Michael tried kissing her, and she pulled away from him."

"You have got to be kidding me. The things you learn." Teresa looked at the man, reading, but he wasn't paying any attention to us. "Do you think?" she whispered.

"What?" I whispered back.

Teresa shook her head. "Nothing," she said and then added, "I have something I need to talk to you about, but not right now. I'm waiting for a few more guests to check in."

I glanced down. On the front desk, as small as it was, her nameplate held a story. She has always been so independent. Yet, I wondered what she needed to tell me.

"Oh, Julie, I'm sorry, truly sorry," Michael stammered, coming into the lobby, before he noticed the man sitting right next to where he was standing.

For some reason, the man laughed aloud, looked around to see if anyone noticed and continued reading.

I knew Michael carried his troubles within himself. There had always been something mysterious below his surface, and it kept him from being forthcoming with his feelings. But I was never one to press for all the details. Until now. I motioned for Michael to follow me into the library. However, there were two women reading in there. We went into the large dining room and sat down at the end of a table. I reached over and touched his hand. "I know it's none of my business, but…"

"Julie, you of all people have every right to know what is going on. Especially here." Michael took back his hand and rubbed his neck and shoulders. He leaned back and shook his head. "I wish I knew. Julie, I love my wife. And God knows I love Brin with all my heart. But ever since the baby, Christine's different. She only picks the baby up to feed her. Even I know that's not right. She's just… I don't know anymore. I'm so sorry about the way she treated Erin. I'm embarrassed."

I winced. "Oh, gosh, I'm sorry. I had no idea." I reached over and held his hand in my own. "I'm here for you and for Christine. Let me do some research on Christine's behavior. In the meantime, do you remember what you told me on your wedding day?"

Michael set his other hand on top of mine. Blinked, his eyes remembering. "Yes…"

"Good. Now take care of your family. Your wife needs you. Michael?"

"Yes?"

"Tomorrow, why don't you to take Brin to Amanda."

"But?"

"Trust me. While I'm in town, I'll pick up a nursing pump for Christine, and I'll talk to the pharmacist about getting her some vitamins."

"How do you know so much about babies?"

I stood up. "I only know how to love them." I caressed his cheek. "You can never have enough children in your life."

Michael went to find Christine. I informed Teresa that I would be down at the cottage in case anyone needed me.

"Wait," she said. "Dan called me a minute ago. I told him you were having a little talk with Michael. He said he was coming up to get you because you needed to get some sleep."

"Sleep, sounds good, but I have something I need to take care of first. Call me if you need *anything*."

I opened the front door, stepped outside, saw the lightning and ducked just as the thunder made a loud sound.

"Let's go!" Dan shouted to me.

Dan and Jesse held me by my elbows and practically carried me down to the cottage. When we stepped inside, I noticed a makeshift bed on the couch. The fireplace was roaring and dinner was on the table. After we ate, Dan ordered me to go to bed. I was happy to oblige. I made myself cozy under the covers, hoping Christine would be okay, wondering if something more was going on with her. I thought about Dan and our own marriage. *I don't know many marriages where couples spend so much time together and still want more. We are best friends, and we adore each other. After all these years, he still loves to pinch my derriere, and I am a love struck schoolgirl every time he enters a room.* I closed my eyes, hoping Michael and Christine's marriage was strong enough to get through whatever it was tearing them apart.

Ten hours later, I woke up to the smell of bacon frying. I stretched my arms out.

"Coffee?" Dan asked, standing in the doorway.

"What time is it?" I asked, remembering I needed to go to the drugstore.

"Eight o'clock," he replied, smiling.

"Good. I have time. I'm taking Erin to see Rose at ten.

"I'm driving you," Jesse hollered from the kitchen.

I looked at Dan. "I can drive myself."

"Did you find your driver's license?" he asked, and then tossed my robe on the bed.

"Funny. I never lost it. I just tucked it away. Thank you. If it was lost, I could always pull my State Trooper CJ Miller's a friend of mine card out."

"Except that only works in New York."

I got up, put my robe on, and yawned. "Let me use the bathroom."

Dan set my coffee down on the nightstand. "Breakfast is on the table."

"I'll be out in two seconds," I replied. "I need to check on Barry." I texted Lynnae, washed my face, brushed my teeth and combed my hair before going to the kitchen.

"Well, you look better," Jesse said.

I bent down and kissed Jesse on the back of his head. "Good morning. How long did Teresa say you had to shack up down here?"

Jesse looked at Dan. "Yep, she's awake! Hey, I was thinking I'd bring my friend Sherry by for dinner." He kept his gaze to one side.

I rolled my eyes at him. "The woman from the little gift shop? You like her—"

"Not like that! You know I'm not the marrying type. Do you want to meet her or not?"

"Easy, Elvis!" I laughed at my own words. I haven't had to say that to him in a long time. "Tonight would be just fine. I'll." I thought for a second. "I'll need to let Michael know right now." I picked up my cell phone and sent him a text message. Instantly he replied, "You got it!"

My cell phone beeped. "Four o'clock. We have a full house."

"Michael says four—"

"She gets off at four," Jesse whined.

I took the fork out of my mouth. "Um, we either have to eat at four or after all the guests are served."

"I get it. I'll tell her another time." Jesse stood up, and I knew his feelings were hurt.

"Jesse, why don't you invite her to dinner on the twenty-ninth?" I looked at Dan. "Would you mind instead of us all going to George's of Galilee, we stay home?"

"If that's what you want." Dan reached over and took our plates to the sink.

"I would like that. Then everyone can meet her. In the meantime, how about you bring Sherry by tonight and the four of us will have a late dinner here."

Jesse's eyes lit up. "O-kay."

"Good, I'll grab whatever Michael is making and we'll have our own little party." When I texted Michael back to cancel the family style dinner, I read Lynnae's message, Barry's doing so much better. I'm in the cafeteria. He's with his speech therapist. Some hot chick! LOL! I think it's time to bring him home. NO LOL! Love you.

I texted her back: Love you more!

The phone rang. Dan picked it up. "Hello. Sure hang on a second." He motioned to me. "Teresa's on the phone."

"Good morning, is everything okay?"

"Fine. Do you want me to drive Erin to her appointment?"

"No, thanks. I'm on my way up," I said.

"Okay, because she's sitting in the lobby with her coat on."

"I'll see you in a bit." I hung up the phone and declared, "I need three more of me."

We all headed up to the inn together. Dan said he was meeting with Kevin this morning. Dan put his hand on my shoulder. "When's the next meeting?"

"In the spring," I replied.

"We'll need to go over these numbers before that," he said to me, looking very serious.

"Okay, when do you want to get together?" I asked, trying to keep up with the two of them.

"Next week, you, me, Jesse, Kevin and Kourtnee."

I thought for a second. "No, if I'm having a meeting it's with my entire staff. I have enough elephants in the room right now. I don't need any more problems or hurt feelings."

Dan put his arm around my shoulder. "You're right. Let us know what day. If we're going to do this, we need to file for the permits by February."

"Dan, have you spoken to Frank? He's more than willing to help and he knows all the right people," I said.

Dan and Jesse both stopped walking.

"What?" I pleaded.

"Nothing," Dan replied and continued toward the inn.

Chapter 37

Dan went in search of Kevin and I needed to get Erin to Rose's in the next few minutes.

On most days, the inn ran smoothly. Everyone worked in great harmony. Lately, though, it seemed like trouble was brewing everywhere.

"I'll start your vehicle," Jesse said to me as I peeked in the door, looking for Erin.

Teresa was smiling and speaking to three women about where to go shopping in Newport and about tonight's dinner menu. I didn't see Erin. Perhaps she was in the kitchen. When I walked past Kourtnee's office, she was on the phone. I heard her say, "June of 2012 is available. Great, as soon as we receive your deposit, I'll block the entire weekend off."

I entered the kitchen and found it to be empty. It didn't feel right. I looked around, wishing the walls could talk. Then I heard arguing. Christine and Michael were in the food pantry.

"I love you. I'm not giving up on you. Not now or ever," Michael's voice was loud and grumbling. Then I heard him say, "Christine, please."

"Yeah, well, right now, you're stressing me out," she hollered. "Baking gives me peace. I'll bake whatever the hell I want!"

My heart sank. I left the kitchen before they saw me, feeling bad for both of them. I was standing in the hallway, staring at the tan, green and cranberry oval rug – *I could not lose Michael...*

"I'm ready," Erin said as she waved her wet hand in front of me.

I glanced up at her. "Why are your hands wet?"

"Oh!" she wiped her hand on her pants. "Snowball fight with Jesse. I just came from the daycare. I told Kyle I was going into town with you and that I wouldn't be having lunch with him. That's when Jesse hit me with a snowball."

"So you fought back." I reached out and tapped her on her arm. "Good for you."

As soon as we stepped outside, we saw Jesse motioning to us to hurry.

"One day it's raining and then next it's freezing cold. I can't wait for spring," I said as I watched Erin get in the backseat.

"This is a beautiful car," Erin said as she rubbed her hands together. "Burr."

"Want me to turn the heat up?" Jesse asked her.

"No, I'll be fine in a minute," Erin told him.

"Thank God for Kevin. He's so good at salting the walkways. Otherwise we'd be on our derrieres," I said jokingly.

Jesse drove down the driveway, turned onto the main road, and asked Erin, "How's school coming along?"

"Great. My instructor seems to be happy with my work. Julie?" she cleared her throat. "I learned the name of my birth mother and father."

"Really? Erin, that's great!" I said, smiling.

She took a deep breath. "According to Ancestry, my birth mother's name is Margaret Murphy. My birth father's name was William McInerney. He died three years ago."

"Erin, I'm so sorry. Are you okay?" I said, glancing back at her, wishing I could give her a hug.

"Yeah. At least one of them is still alive," she said, pressing her lips together.

Jesse remained stopped at the traffic light, until the driver behind him blew her horn. "How'd you figure that out?" he asked her.

Erin answered him. "Julie gave me Ancestry for Christmas. Ancestry connects people. Both my mother and father were registered. They ranked over three-thousand. Meaning child/parent relationship. Julie, the woman who adopted me, her maiden name was Murphy."

Jesse pulled the car over about a block away from Rose's office, turned around and asked Erin, "Do you think?" He tilted his head.

"They were related?" she said as she sat up closer and rested her hands on the back of our seats. "They could be, right? I mean maybe that's not just a coincidence."

"Murphy is a very common name in Ireland," I said. "Erin, how did you learn about your father's death?"

"I Googled his name. Three men in Ireland died with the last name McInerney. William's obituary said he leaves behind his companion, Margaret Murphy. Both Margaret and William are a one-hundred percent match as my biological parents."

"Erin, I'm so proud of you for working on finding your real parents," Jesse said, as he pulled away from the curb. "Good job, woman!"

"Thank you," she replied, and sat back.

A minute later, Jesse parked the car and said, "I'll wait right here."

Erin and I walked into Rose's office. She was leaning against a desk in the reception room. "Come right in. Julie, it's nice to see you again." Rose extended her hand to me and then to Erin. "You must be Erin."

"Yes, ma'am."

Rose grinned as she said, "Julie, can you give us an hour?"

"Um, I want Julie to stay," Erin replied rather hesitantly.

I inhaled deeply. "Erin, Dan assures me you're in expert hands. I'll sit out here. I promise." I shook my head. "I won't leave."

Erin winced. "Please come in with me?"

Rose spoke up. "I don't see any problem with you coming in. If that's what Erin wants." Rose held her hand out and we both stepped into her office. She sat down across from us. "Julie, I'm glad you came today. I've been meaning to send you an invitation to speak with me."

I flipped my hair back. "Me?"

"Yes." Rose tilted her head. "I thought maybe you and I could speak about some of your old memories."

Erin turned to face me. I could feel her eyes on me.

I was staring directly at Rose. "What you call memories, I refer to as wounds. I'm good." I made a clicking noise with my tongue. A sign indicating, at least to me, I was pissed off. I hated her! And this was only our second encounter. It wasn't my normal way of handling things. But at that moment, I was stressed out to the max. "Thank you for your concern." My lips flattened into a thin line.

"That's fine. Perhaps in the future." Rose picked up her pen and held it to her chin.

I heard Erin clear her throat.

"Erin, why don't you tell me something about yourself." Rose glanced down and wrote something on her notepad.

"I was married for almost five years, but I left my husband because he beat me."

"How often did he hit you?" Rose asked, with deep concern.

"Just once," Erin replied as she fiddled with her sleeve.

Rose glanced up from her paper. "I'm so sorry," she said, shaking her head.

"He punched me in the face, kicked me between my legs and…" Erin stared down before continuing. "He beat me so bad I had to crawl up two flights of stairs to reach my son." She started to cry, but somehow continued. "When he was sleeping, I grabbed my four-year-old and ran."

I reached over and touched her arm. "It's okay," I whispered. "You can do this."

"Erin, you did the right thing," Rose said. "I commend you for getting the hell out when you did."

Erin reached over and took a tissue, wiping her nose and nodded.

"Can you tell me what happened next?" Rose asked as she set her pen down and leaned in closer toward us.

Erin shook, quivering in her seat. "It was the middle of the night. I believe one or two in the morning." She closed her eyes then opened them and cried, "I carried my son as far as I could…"

Rose picked up the pen. Her head moved from side to side as she wrote feverishly. Then she looked up from her writing. "How far did you have to run?"

Erin wiped her tears away. When she blew her nose, I answered Rose, "She ran from Scarborough Hills to the end of my driveway in Point Judith."

I felt Erin's eyes on me. She cleared her throat. "We took pictures of my bruises."

"Who? Very clever, by the way," Rose said, swallowing as if she had a rock-hard lump in her throat.

"Julie did."

I smiled at Erin; I was so proud of her.

"Julie's friend told us to take the pictures." Erin sat back in her chair.

"I asked a dear friend of mine, Frank Freeman, if he knew someone in the judicial system who could help us. I had to know if Josh could accuse Erin of kidnapping. Frank's friend, Judge Abrams, instructed us to take the photos."

Rose stopped biting the tip of her pen. "I know Frank. He couldn't have put you in better hands. Judge Abrams plays golf with my husband. Abram's tough, and best of all, he doesn't tolerate domestic violence."

Erin sat up. "I don't want to lose my son."

"Why do you think you'll lose your son? Do you have the means to take care of him?" Rose asked.

Erin bit her bottom lip and her chin began trembling.

I intervened and said, "Yes! She has a job, a home and a new family."

Erin's face lit up. A relaxed expression suddenly appeared.

Rose smiled at Erin. "As long as you can support your son, provide a good home for him and give him a proper education, I don't think you have much to worry about."

Behind Rose was a credenza. There must have been twenty photos on it. All family photos. When our eyes met, she picked up the one on her desk and handed it to me. "Taken Christmas morning."

Her children took after her. Her husband appeared to be much older. A good-looking man in his late fifties.

"You have a beautiful family," I said as I showed the photo to Erin and then set it back down.

"My husband's an attorney. He specializes in divorce. Most of all, he too despises domestic violence." Her eyes narrowed. "Erin, I wish more women reacted the way you did. I can't say it enough. I'm proud of you for making the decision to get away when you did."

Chapter 38

Erin and I said goodbye to Rose. When I opened her front door, I almost stepped on Jesse. He was sitting on the front step.

We got in the Explorer, and Jesse asked me, "Where are we going next?"

"I need to stop at the drugstore and pick up something for Christine. I'll only be a minute," I replied.

"I know where CVS is," Jesse said and drove down the road. Then he asked Erin if she was okay.

"I'm scared. What if something were to happen to me, who would take care of my son? Josh never even held Kyle. He didn't even pick him up when he was crying. He said babies made him nervous." She rubbed her hands together, tapping on the driver's headrest. "I don't want Kyle to be an orphan."

When I turned around, I noticed she was making eye contact with Jesse in the rearview mirror.

"He'll never be an orphan!" Jesse said aloud.

Erin smiled at him and rested her hands on her lap.

"I hope you're right," she said and looked out the window before adding, "Julie, thank you for saying I have a family."

"The Lord works wonders. All we have to do is recognize them. Erin, I'm glad you ran in my direction." I tapped Jesse on his leg. "I'm grateful Jesse found the two of you."

Jesse stopped the car in front of the drugstore.

Before I could get out of the vehicle, Erin suddenly ducked down in the backseat. "Oh, my god," she whispered. "That's one of Josh's clients!"

"I'll come back later," I said.

"No, go in. He doesn't even like Josh. He probably won't say anything," Erin said, keeping her head down.

"Are you sure?" I said.

"I'm sure," she replied.

Jesse spun around to face her. "Did you make eye contact with him?"

"I don't know," she replied, then added, "yes."

Jesse told me to wait until the man drove away. Then he looked back at Erin and said, "Relax, it's not like he knows Julie or her vehicle."

When I got back in the car with Christine's pump and vitamins, I said, "I pray he didn't see you."

We rode in silence for several miles.

Jesse put his blinker on for Mallard Way and we all breathed a sigh of relief.

"Julie?" I heard her say from the backseat. "Thank you for going in with me."

"You're welcome."

"Julie, do you think my mother didn't want me because she wasn't married?

"I don't know, sweetheart." I looked at Jesse, he was shaking his head and I thought I saw tears trickling down his face.

Chapter 39

Jesse parked the Explorer in the inn's employee parking lot and said, "What else does she have to deal with?"

I almost replied what do you mean, until I saw tears falling from behind his sunglasses and running down his cheeks.

As soon as we stepped inside, Kyle ran to Erin and Lady rushed past everyone and came to me. I bent down, gave her a hug, and told her I loved her. She must have missed me because she gave me more kisses than usual. I stood back up and greeted several people passing through the lobby. I loved it when the inn was overflowing with guests. I thanked God for keeping me busy.

"I'll be over at two for story time," Erin said as Amanda, Sam, Max and Kyle turned to leave.

"Wait a second." I bent down and held my arms out. "I need a hug."

First Sam, then Max, and Kyle. I stood up and gave Delilah and Brin each a kiss. Then I hugged my baby girl again. "Love you," I shouted. I smiled as I watched them argue over whose coat was whose. For so long, I was afraid to get close to babies and small children. I guess my heart just ached for my own. Now, I was grateful for every one of them.

Amanda took the children back to daycare. And Erin and I headed for the kitchen. The aroma was amazing. Erin turned to me declaring, "Something smells delicious."

When we popped into the kitchen, everyone was sitting at the table except Kevin. Michael immediately asked us if we were hungry. "Care for some soup?"

"What kind?" Erin asked.

I glanced down at Jesse's bowl. "Yes, please."

"Sweet potato and pear. I also made fresh croutons. Sit, I'll serve you."

"No." I waved Michael off. "We can get our own. Oh, my, this looks so good!"

Erin inhaled. "I smell brandy."

I turned to face her. "Can you still eat it?"

"Oh, yeah! Irish girl? Brandy? Julie?"

We sat down. "Where's Kevin?"

Kourtnee pounded her fists on the table. "You're the third person to ask me. He's doing Delilah's laundry. Don't worry, he ate."

Michael laughed. "He ate the last of the beef and vegetable soup."

Christine got up from the table. When she came back, she set a platter in the center of the table. "I made sugar cookies." She nodded at me. "A little brown sugar and lots of cinnamon, cloves, nutmeg and cayenne."

"Cayenne? Outstanding!" I reached over and took one. "You're the best." I put a few croutons on my soup and cooed, "I am surrounded by the best!"

Jesse helped himself to two cookies.

"Would you like some milk?" Christine asked in a voice that was new to me.

I raised my eyes up from my soup. You could have heard a feather drop.

"No! I can get my own," Jesse replied.

Kourtnee got up from the table and brought back a container of milk. "What? I like milk."

My cell phone rang. "Hello. Frank, how are you? Um, okay. That sounds great. See you then. Frank's coming to visit me," I said as if I was dating the king of the prom or the captain of the football team and I wanted all the girls to be envious. But then I looked at Dan.

Dan and Jesse were glaring at each other as if they knew the reason behind Frank's visit.

"Julie, can I see you before Frank gets here?" Teresa asked me.

"Sure." We got up and rinsed our bowls before placing them in the dishwasher.

I noticed everyone had moved away from the table except Dan and Jesse.

Teresa and I went into the library. "Sal asked me to marry him."

"Congratulations! Oh, Teresa, I'm so happy for you. What did you tell him?"

"I told him yes, but I'm not leaving you!"

Chapter 40

A moment later, we heard Frank say, "Hello."

We both stood up. I gave Teresa a hug and told her we needed to schedule a teatime.

I opened the door and Frank turned around. "There you are," he said, holding a box from Ferry Wharf Fish Market.

"IIow's my favorite person in the world?" I murmured, hugging him.

"Hi, Frank, it's nice to see you," Teresa said, smiling. "You know you always make our day a little brighter."

Frank put his hand on Teresa's shoulder. "Just seeing you gals brightens my day."

"Teresa, will you let the others know I'm visiting with Frank?" I said.

"Sure. Frank, can I get you something to drink?"

"Tea," he said to Teresa, then asked her, "Can you put this in the fridge for me? I bought smoked fish."

Teresa took the box, and I thanked her.

I closed the door behind us. Frank and I sat down on the small sofa. "I'm glad you called me. I've missed you. Tell me about Frank."

"It's been awhile since our last visit." He raised his eyebrows. "First tell me, how's that red-headed belle adjusting these days?"

"Erin? She's fine, thanks for asking. And thanks to you, she's in good hands. I took her to see Dan's therapist and Rose informs me that Judge Abrams is the best!"

"Rose? Oh, yes, I know her well. Her husband's an attorney, you know."

"She told us. Frank, you would be so proud of Erin."

"Knock, knock," Teresa said as she reentered the room. "Michael added a few slices of lemon and poppy seed pound cake and told me to tell you hello."

"Give my thanks and tell the lad I said hello." Frank took his cup from Teresa and set it down on the end table.

"Thanks, Teresa." I reached up first taking the plate, and then my cup.

Frank gave his cake a quick sniff. "I told Dan that I wanted to tell you this myself."

I sucked in a breath, remembering how many times I had noticed Dan and Jesse both acting peculiar.

"I'll need to go away for a few months."

"Go away? Where? When?"

"Apparently," Frank confessed, "the doctors think I have cancer."

My heart stopped. I tried to be strong. Trying to hold back my tears, I couldn't. I cried, "I'm so sorry."

"No crying now. I'm not done with you yet. I heard we have some more houses to build." Frank tapped me on my leg. "I went and told those crazy doctors all about you. Said I can't wait to watch you swim in your new pool."

"Frank, where do they want you to go?"

"I don't want you worrying about me. I'll be back for your next project. I promise." Frank licked his lip and then chewed on it for a minute, as if he were thinking about what to say next. He cleared his throat and said, "I'm only going away for a spell." He cleared his throat again. "The prostate is not as bad as the bone cancer and that's why–"

My eyes filled up fast. My heart was heavy. "Oh, Frank."

"Doc said I could go to a number of places. He suggested New York." Frank took several sips of his tea. "I hate the city. I'll be in Georgia for, oh, I'm guessing a few months. Don't you worry, my sister will look after me."

I got up and hugged him. "I love you with all my heart. I'll do whatever you need me to do. How can I help you?" I sat back down. "What can I do for you?"

He scrunched his nose at me. "I want you to be strong. Stand up for what's right. Protest against the whole world, if you have to. Women like you are rare. You have a big heart, and don't take no for an answer. Keep baking apple pies and building your dreams. Don't worry about what others think or say. You keep loving that man of yours."

His voice was authoritative and yet his demeanor calm. I knew he was more worried about me than himself.

I tried to hold myself together. But I couldn't. Behind my chair, the slow sound of the clock. *Tick. Tock. Tick.* Outside, I heard crunching on the gravel. Frank shifted in his chair. His hand had a slight tremor as he reached for the tissue box. "I'm going to beat this *or* die trying."

"You're not going to die. And you're *not* alone. Please say I can visit you…"

"I'll be home before you've had a chance to miss me. In the meantime, Gina Marie will be taking over my business." Frank raised his eyebrows. "She baked me a sweet potato pie. Mmm, mmm it was good. I told her there's just one thing. I get to keep you and your new house project."

I got up and kissed him on his cheek. "You'll always have *me*!"

Chapter 41

Frank and I could hear Teresa telling Dan and Jesse that I was in the library with my mashpia, Frank. "I'd like to see them before I go," Frank said to me.

I got up and opened the door. "Frank needs to see you guys." I motioned for them to come in.

Frank, Dan and Jesse talked about the two of them keeping an eye on Frank's house and garage.

"If you need to stay at my place." He reached into his pocket and pulled out two sets of keys, tossing one set to Jesse. "The house is yours." He gave Jesse a nod before adding, "Hands off my house manager, Romeo. She's married. And Mark is a big man!"

Jesse laughed. "Is she hot?"

Frank and I both gave him the same look.

"I'm kidding." Jesse stood up and shook Frank's hand. "I appreciate it. Don't you worry now, you hear me? Just get better and get home as soon as you can. We'll take care of your place."

Frank reached over and patted Dan on his knee. "You're still coming to see me tomorrow?"

"Absolutely. At eight, right?"

"Yes." Frank stood up. "I better be going. I need to pack a few more things." He put his arms out.

I let out a heavy sigh. "Please call me when you get to Georgia." I leaned back. "Promise me."

I felt Dan's hand on the small of my back.

"I promise," Frank said softly, and then walked out of the library. "I'll see you again, Teresa," he said, and I thought *Dear Lord, I hope so.*

"Bye, Frank. See you soon," Teresa replied.

When I heard the front door close, I collapsed into the chair.

Dan and Jesse stood in the doorway. I told them, "If it weren't for Frank, I would have crumbled a long time ago. I would not be sitting in this chair, if not for that man." I shook my head. "You have no idea how many times his sweet southern voice pulled me back in. Dan, why didn't you warn me?"

Dan turned toward Jesse and then back at me. "You would have cried before the first word came out of his mouth. Who are you kidding?"

Jesse sat down next to me. "Don't feel bad, Dan and I cried, too. Frank's a good guy. Salt—"

"I have to meet with him tomorrow," Dan said. "He wants to go over a few things with me and then I'm taking him to the airport." Dan shook his head. "He specifically said that you are not to come along. And I agree."

"It's hard enough on the old guy," Jesse said to me as he lifted my chin with his hand. "Are ya okay?"

"No! My heart aches." I glanced back over at Dan. "I need to schedule a meeting. I promised Frank I would keep moving forward." I turned to Jesse. "Did you pick your building lot out yet?"

Jesse scratched the side of his face.

Dan blew out a loud breath. "Tell her."

"I'm the gatekeeper. Bodyguard to all women. I want to build a gatehouse at the beginning of the driveway."

"Okay, bodyguard," Dan said jokingly. "Now tell her *what* you want to build."

"Oh, a log cabin."

I glared up at Dan. "You *told* him."

"No, I did not!"

I stood up, but then sat back down. "I'm dizzy."

Jesse immediately got up and Dan sat down beside me.

"You have got to stop. Julie, you need to slow down," Dan said. "Hire someone and I mean soon. I'm not complaining, but guess who changed all the beds, again this week?"

I took a sip of my now lukewarm tea and then asked him, "Who?"

"Erin, Jesse and me. That's who!"

I almost spit the tea out. "I wish I could have seen that. Please tell me Erin folded the sheets back at the top."

Dan laughed. "Erin showed us how. You should give *her* a raise. She's been running her tail off for the past few days."

"Dan, I was at the hospital with Lynnae and Barry. I couldn't leave her. Help me up. We need to go and see Kourtnee."

Jesse came back with Michael and Teresa. "What the hell?" Michael shouted.

Erin came running in. "What's going on? Is anyone hurt?"

"No one is hurt," Dan told her. "Julie's sugar dropped."

"Oh," Erin said, as she stood in the doorway next to Jesse.

"Did you get your homework done?" he asked, teasing her as he put his arm around her, squeezing her tight. "I've got my eye on you."

Teresa shook her head at Jesse before going back to the front desk to answer the phone. Dan and I headed for Kourtnee's office. I turned back around to get the empty teacups and plates and noticed Jesse standing in the doorway, as if he were holding up the doorframe. Erin was still in the library, looking up at Jesse.

I heard Jesse say, "Your clothes were torn. The indignity of it all. Your eyes never left mine. You said nothing, yet everything to me. That's when I knew it was okay to pick you up. Erin, you don't need to keep thanking me. It's all good."

Dan nudged me. "Come on."

We knocked on Kourtnee's door and asked her if she had a minute.

She waved us in and pointed to the seats in front of her desk.

She was flipping through the calendar at the year ahead when she said, "Good timing. I was just about to call you."

We sat down. "I need to schedule a meeting, and Dan wants to ask you a few questions. But first, tell us what's on your mind."

Kourtnee reached back and took hold of a manila folder. "Take a look at this." She handed the folder to me.

"Table and chairs?" I handed the file to Dan.

"Julie, we have enough weddings to support my idea."

I reached over and placed my hand on Dan's leg. For me, it felt like old times. Bad times. My out of control spending. Dan coming to my rescue. I wanted everything. All of it. The inn, a new swimming pool, a bigger home for Dan and me. I wanted to build the cottages for them. But I was scared to death. I couldn't risk it. Not again. Over the years, I've learned some hard lessons. I don't want to be that spendaholic. *I have to be strong enough...*

"Kourtnee, before I hear or agree to your idea." I took back my hand, rubbing my neck. "I want you both to hear me out. Not so long ago I almost lost everything. And by that I mean my bakery, my husband, our home and my little girl." I glanced over at Dan. "You have no idea, how hard it was for me to leave."

He closed the folder and gave me a gentle smile.

"I wanted to take Lady with me. Some people have children. I have my little girl." I folded my hands in my lap, sat back and continued. "Instead of talking to Dan about my suspicions, I began to self-destruct. I stopped baking, stopped caring about my business. I even stopped paying my bills. I didn't care about anything. Not even my walk with God."

Dan reached over and put his hand on my shoulder. Kourtnee folded her hands and rested her chin on them. I sat there thinking, *please Kourtnee don't ever leave me. I need you more than you will ever know.*

"I was days away from losing my bakery and my commercial property." I looked over at Dan. "We were sitting in the living room, when a commercial came on about refinancing. I'm not sure if you knew it or not, but you saved me."

Dan tapped his hand on my shoulder. "I remember. I asked you what your mortgage rate was."

"Yes, you did. And when I told you twelve percent, you offered to pay the entire mortgage. Did you know I was in foreclosure?"

"No. I knew something was wrong. But I had no idea how bad things were." Dan took his hand back and scratched the side of his face. "I hated the idea of the bank getting all that interest. You were falling apart, more and more and I knew it was my fault." Dan shook his head, reached over and took my hand in his. "Julie, from now on, I want you to come to me. I don't care what it is. If you suspect me of something, cheating on you, anything."

He stood up and went around the desk. Kourtnee moved her chair back making room for him. He reached out to her, but instead put his hand on the corner of the desk. "If for any reason you need money." He blew out a long breath. "Kourtnee, I want you to come to me."

She patted Dan on his hand. "Relax. Both of you. The inn is not in any financial trouble. In fact," she paused, as if waiting for Dan to take his seat, "we are about to have our best year ever!"

Dan bent down and gave her a hug. I laughed when she said, "Okay! All righty then. You can sit down now."

Dan smiled and sat down next to me. "I'm glad to hear that," he said, pursing his lips while nodding. "She's good!"

I was beaming with pride. "I told you."

"Julie, if you didn't tell me yourself, I never would have guessed that about you. Dan, she has put every cent into this place. I can honestly say she did not spend one penny foolishly." Kourtnee pointed her finger at me. "You didn't have to say much. I knew you were hurting. But that's all in the past. So listen up. With Erin's help, I think we can do this."

I stopped her. "I'm glad you found a position for Erin." I felt better, and I trusted both of them. "Kourtnee, can Dan and I tell you why we came to see you?"

Dan sat up in his chair. "No." He held his hand out. "Let her tell us what she's thinking and then we'll explain what we'd like to do."

"Thank you, Dan. Okay, so you know how we rent the tents, tables and chairs for weddings with more than seventy-five guests?" She opened the file and took out a spreadsheet. "I'm proposing we spend thirty-nine thousand dollars and buy our own tent, tables and chairs. And..." She held up a finger. "That price includes twenty-five café tables and one-hundred patio chairs for the terrace."

I thought about her idea. She was very good at her job. Kourtnee would not have proposed her idea if she didn't have a game plan. "Okay," I said. "Tell me how long it will take to make that kind of money back."

"One." She held up the same finger. "One wedding will pay for everything." She handed me the file. "The tent has clear plastic windows and doors. We can host a wedding in the rain." She turned around and pointed to the photo hanging behind her desk. "Two-hundred and fifty people and it's all paid for."

"Umm. How much do we charge per wedding?" Dan asked.

"Ahh, not per wedding," she said. "Per person. We used to charge three hundred twenty-five dollars. Starting *this* year, we're charging three seventy-five per person."

I could see Dan's wheels spinning.

"How many weddings are scheduled that—"

"That have two-hundred and fifty guests?" Kourtnee raised her eyebrows. "Seven!"

"Seriously? Julie, that's amazing." He smiled at me. "I want you to hire more people."

"I have four people coming in next week. I'll interview them first, and if I think they're suited and trustworthy, I'll schedule an interview with Julie. Oh, Dan, do you want to meet with them?" she asked before pulling her hand out for the folder.

"No, no," Dan replied.

I liked her idea. I held up a picture. "What's with the linens?"

"Everything that you're looking at is included in the price."

I glanced at the pictures again. Crisp white linens enhanced by gorgeous floral arrangements. One smaller tent, a rollaway bar, café tables and chairs for cocktail hour. A bigger tent, tables and chairs. And she even thought about the cake table and gift table. "Wow, you thought of everything," I said with joy in my heart.

"I wanted to use cash, but Erin said that raises red flags with the IRS. Even though I report it as income. So I'd like to take the money out of the money market account."

Dan sat back in his chair. "How much cash do you guys have?"

"I don't know. Ask her, she's the bookkeeper," I said jokingly but meant it.

Kourtnee smiled. "Hmm, *that* was my first clue. She told me never to let her know how much cash we had. I'm kidding. Almost three-hundred thousand. Okay, two-hundred and seventy-one. To be exact."

I was grinning from ear to ear.

"What does it take to run the place? Down to the penny," Dan asked.

Dan was not only good at making money, he's even better at saving it.

Kourtnee handed him a different spreadsheet. Dan read it several times. I watched as she twisted her mouth in anticipation of his findings.

"Can I have a piece of paper and a pencil? Please," Dan said to her as he extended his hand.

I knew what Dan was doing. "I'm going to get a pot of tea. What can I get the two of you?" I stood up and put my hand on Dan's back.

"Tea for me," Kourtnee replied.

"Yeah," Dan said, and I knew better than to interrupt him, but I also knew he would not drink the tea.

I rolled my eyes. "Yeah, what?"

"Water. Get me a water, please."

When I got back to Kourtnee's office, Dan was still crunching the numbers. I put his glass on the desk and poured two cups of tea. Kourtnee and I each took a sip.

I almost choked when he shouted, "Hell, yeah! Okay, this is how we're going to do it. Rent the cottage out as a bridal suite for five twenty-five per night. The five rooms on the second floor for four seventy-five and the twenty suites for three twenty-five. And the upstairs corporate rooms for five-fifty a night."

"Dan?" Kourtnee was shaking her head. "One question. Where are *we* going to sleep?"

Dan handed the paper to her and glanced over at me. "Julie?"

"Kourtnee, Dan and I have sold our home and our property in New York. Dan owns the equipment we need to build—"

"Yeah, I got that, but where are we supposed to sleep. I have a baby."

"Kourtnee, Julie and I would like to reward the staff with their own cottages."

"Bigger than the one Frank built," I chimed in. "What do you think?"

"Are you serious?" She got up. "You guys…"

"You're important to us." I hugged her. "You're family."

Kourtnee laughed.

Dan and I were both smiling at her. "What?" I asked.

"You have no idea how difficult it is to make love with an eleven-month-old baby in the same room."

"I'm sorry about that. That's my fault," Dan said to her.

I looked at Dan, wondering why he thought it would be *his* fault. "Oh, because Jesse's in Delilah's room?" I said, looking at Kourtnee. "He can go back to sleeping on the sofa at the cottage."

"No. Stop. He's fine. Oh, my God, Kevin is going to be thrilled. Seriously. Every time Delilah wakes up and catches me on top, Kevin yells over to her mommy's riding a horse."

Dan and I both laughed.

"What...?" Kourtnee snapped her neck to the right.

I coughed. "I'm not saying a word. Okay, so I think we all agree, we need to schedule a meeting. Go ahead and place your order. Oh, wait. What about Erin?"

Dan reached for his glass. "What about her?"

"How many hours a day will she be working with you?" I asked.

"I need her two hours in the morning and two in the afternoon."

I nodded. "Good, that's exactly what I was thinking."

"Kourtnee, can you hire someone to help Julie with all that she does?"

She chuckled. "Yeah, right? Actually, I was thinking of hiring two people for the dining room, and two more to take over all of the laundry, and one extra person just for cleaning." She waved us off. "Don't worry about wedding season, Michael has his own crew he likes to bring onboard."

"One more question." Dan pointed toward her. "How much of a bonus did everyone receive last time?" He shrugged his shoulders and scratched his head. "It was blank on the spreadsheet."

Kourtnee opened another file on her computer screen. "Total of a hundred and ten thousand, Julie paid us a percentage of the wedding business. I have a copy of the checks."

"No, no. I wanted to make sure I didn't overlook anything. Julie, you're going to be fine. Even with the new houses."

"Wait! What are my responsibilities?" I said, wondering what I was supposed to do now that someone else would be making beds, cleaning, dusting and serving dinner to my guests.

"I got it! Innkeeper." She took a sip of her tea. "At The Inn in Rhode Island. Are we done yet?"

"Eek," I screamed. My cell phone was on vibrate. "Hello. No, it's good. Oh, Lynnae, I'm so happy to hear that. You got it!" I raised my eyebrows. "I'm with Kourtnee and Dan. Yes. I will. See you in an hour." I tapped on my phone. "Lynnae said the boys can go see their father." I stood up. "She said, hi, by the way. We're good?"

"Get going. I got this. Guys, thanks."

I blew her a kiss.

Chapter 42

Dan and I headed over to the daycare to get the boys. When we reached the lobby, Teresa and Erin were discussing upcoming events. "Sorry for the interruption but we have fantastic news! Lynnae just called me. The doctor said Barry is well enough to see the boys. Dan and I are going over to the daycare to pick them up and take them to see their father."

"Oh, Julie, that's great. That means he'll be coming home soon." Teresa put her hands together, and I knew she was saying a quick prayer.

Erin picked up her notepad. "I'll come with you, so Kyle isn't upset, when you take the boys and not him."

All of a sudden, I noticed all our Christmas decorations were still up. Normally, we take them down right after the New Year. "When I get back, let's all work on taking the decorations down," I said.

"Good idea, considering tomorrow is Martin Luther King Day." Teresa held up a picture Kyle had made in daycare, celebrating the day.

"That's adorable," I said before asking Erin, "How has Lady been? Because if she's any problem at all, we can take her down to the cottage with us." I was hoping she would say that she thought Lady missed Dan and me.

We were in front of the day spa when Erin said, "Kyle's not the only person to have fallen in love with your dog. I enjoy her company, especially when Kyle falls asleep at night. She's very smart. Kyle gets a kick out of her when she gives me the correct paw. I like how she stands guard at the bathroom door. Lady is very well mannered. I can't believe she doesn't get up on the furniture. And it's almost like she feels bad when she has to go outside. Geez, if you take her away, how will I know when to get up?"

Dan opened the door to the daycare. "No one is taking her away," he said.

"I'm glad you enjoy her as much as we do," I said, as I followed Erin inside.

The children were all napping. Amanda waived to us. First, I peeked in on Brin. Her lips were moving as if she was nursing. Delilah's tushie was straight up in the air. The boys were in their own individual daybeds. Kyle was hugging his new therapy cat Amanda had bought him for Christmas. I whispered over to Erin. "I forgot about his cat."

Erin whispered in my ear. "He loves when it purrs."

I heard Dan ask Amanda to call us when they woke up. "We'll buy them lunch on our way to the hospital."

"You got it," Amanda replied, smiling.

Before we left, I bent down and told Lady that Lynnae was coming home soon. I knew she understood, because she waggled her eyebrows. "I love you, baby girl." I kissed her goodbye. I knew she was content when she rested her head on her paws.

Erin, Dan and I were on our way back to the inn when I suggested, "I think we should hire a security guard."

Dan stopped walking. I turned toward him. "What?"

He held his hands out. "What about Jesse and me? Jesse used to be a bouncer. That's not enough?"

"Dan, I think Julie's saying this because I came face to face with one of Josh's customers. It's my fault, I'm sorry."

I felt bad. "That's not why I suggested it. I'm thinking about all the children."

"When did this happen?" Dan shouted, hands out in front of him, palms up, staring at me.

"The other day, when I took Erin to see Rose. Dan, we have children on the property. In a few weeks, you, Jesse and Kevin will be off building one house after another and—"

"Once again, you're right. I think it's a great idea. But?"

"Please?"

"I said it's a good idea. Especially if it means the children will all be safer."

Chapter 43

By eleven-thirty, Dan and I had taken the ornaments off the tree in the library, put away our angel, and packed up Erin's candle. Because of pure neglect, I had to toss out the paper whites. Dan asked if he should take down the garland on the mantle. "It still smells good." He shrugged his shoulders before adding, "What do you think?"

"Nah, take it down. Before we blink Valentine's Day will be here and no one will have the time to deal with it," I said.

"Michael and I just cleaned up both dining rooms. Where do you want to put these?" Christine was standing in the doorway, holding up the new silver candlesticks.

The vitamins offered by the pharmacist for Christine's postpartum depression seemed to be working. She appeared to be her old self. "Let's store them in the big pantry," I said. "We can use them on special occasions."

"Valentine's Day?" She asked, then rolled her eyes and said, "It must be lunchtime."

I smiled as soon as I heard Brin crying. Amanda and the children dropped into the lobby. "The boys are back, let's go," I said as I motioned to Dan.

"Mommy!" Kyle shouted as he ran over to Erin. She picked him up, winked at me, and headed for the kitchen.

I gave Lady a hug and told her to go with Kyle. Dan picked Max up.

"What's going on in here?" Jesse was back from visiting his new girlfriend. "Just in time for lunch. Something smells good."

"Actually." Dan put his hand on Sam's head. "Aunt Julie and I were just about to take these guys to see their father."

"Daddy?" Max inquired.

"We're going to see my mom and dad?" Sam reached over and tugged on my hand. "Really?"

"I think so," I said, smiling back at him.

"Are they on Block Island?" Sam asked.

"No–" I started to explain.

Jesse interrupted me by saying, "I'll go. I'll sit in the back with the boys." Then he picked Sam up, but Sam fussed.

"I'm too big!" he shouted as he squirmed.

Jesse kissed him on his cheek. "Never!" Then he put him down.

"I'm going to grab some lunch, before the gang returns from skiing," Teresa said to us as she checked her watch. "I'll see you guys when you get back. Give Lynnae and Barry my love."

Jesse shook his head. "What gang?"

"Guests."

"Oh! Why didn't she just say that?"

I reached past him and grabbed my coat. "Let's go see Daddy!"

Dan put Max in his car seat, buckled him in and asked Sam, "Where do you think you're going, Buddy?"

"In the back," Sam replied as he sat in the third row.

Jesse turned to Sam. "Why don't you want to sit next to me?"

I moved Jesse to the side. "I'll sit with the boys. Sit in the front." When I turned toward Sam, he already had his seatbelt on.

"I'm old enough," he said, looking out the side window.

"Hmm, and how old is enough?" I asked.

Silence.

"Julie, he's fine. Right Sam?"

"Thanks, Uncle Dan."

I tapped Max on his foot. "We're checking his birth records, when we get back."

"Mine, too?" Max asked, because he had to do everything his big brother did.

"Yep. Are you excited about seeing your mother and father?"

Max's eyes opened wide. Sam grumbled from the third row. Then we heard him say, "Mom and Dad aren't on Block Island are they?"

"No, Sam. Sam, your father was in an accident," Dan said to him.

"Was it bad?" Sam asked under his breath.

Dan drove onto the main road before answering him. "Sam, your father was in a minor car accident. But he's okay."

"Did he almost die?" Sam asked.

I turned to face Sam. "No, sweetheart. Daddy did not almost die. He just needed to stay in the hospital for a few days."

"Sam." Dan called back to him.

"Yeah, Uncle Dan."

"You're old enough to know the truth."

"Me, too?" Max said, sounding confused.

Dan pulled the car to the side of the road. Opened his door and then opened my door. He leaned in and said, "Let me in."

I got out of the car and Dan climbed into the back. "One of you can drive," he insisted.

It was musical chairs. Jesse sat in the driver's seat and I got out and sat in the passenger seat while Dan sat next to Max.

Jesse put the car in drive and drove to the hospital. I sat quietly and listened to Dan as he explained to the boys what had happened.

"I don't want you to be upset with your mother. She loves you very much. It was better for her to stay with your father. He needed her."

"You're right. Uncle Dan, I understand. Max and I had you and Aunt Julie."

"And Jesse," Max added.

"That's right, little buddy." Jesse turned around and smiled at Sam. "I love you guys."

Sam nodded his head. "Love you, too, Uncle Jesse."

I glanced back at them and then over at Jesse. Sam appeared better, and Jesse was beaming.

"We're here," Jesse said as he put the Explorer in park.

"Remember, we're in a hospital. So no loud noises," I said before adding, "okay?"

Dan unbuckled Max. Then he helped Sam out of the backseat.

We stopped at the front desk and waited for our nametags. Five minutes later, Dan was standing in Barry's doorway. I watched as both boys reached up and took hold of Dan's hands. Lynnae was reading to Barry. When she looked up and saw the boys, she motioned to Barry.

Lynnae stood up, and Max ran into her arms.

Sam was still holding Dan's hand. Dan told him to go see his father. When Sam didn't let go of his hand, he picked Sam up and hugged him. "It's okay. Oh, Sam…"

Sam buried his face on Dan's shoulder. His long legs, dangling, hitting Dan in his shins.

Lynnae gently set Max down on the bed next to Barry, came over and took Sam from Dan's embrace. "Oh, sweetheart." She held Sam's face in her hands. "Sam, your dad is right here." Lynnae picked him up and set him down on the bed next to Max.

Sam collapsed onto his father's chest. Barry hugged him. "I love you more than anything in the world." He kissed the boys on top of their heads. "I've missed you, too," he said.

Dan, Jesse, and I left the room. We went to the cafeteria and bought drinks for everyone. Lynnae said the doctor told her no more than thirty minutes. Dr. Plimpton wanted Barry to save his voice for a few more days. By the time we got back up to the room, Sam was telling Barry about his dream of becoming a news anchor. "I want to travel all over the world," Sam said, his face serious.

Barry nodded. "That's great, son." His voice was still raspy. He reached out, and I took his hand. "Thank you," he said with the biggest smile on his face.

I leaned over and kissed the side of his face. "We love you so much."

Lynnae picked Max up and tapped Sam on the shoulder. "Dad needs his rest. Sam, I promise we'll be home in a few days."

In a voice we were all surprised to hear, stern and grown up, Sam said, "Mom, don't worry about us. Max and I are fine. We're even doing our schoolwork. Dad needs you more than we do. Aunt Julie, Uncle Dan." Sam turned around and smiled at Jesse. "And Uncle Jesse are taking good care of us."

"And Kyle. And Lady," Max added, as our tears turned to laughter.

Lynnae kissed him on his cheek. "You better be good to Lady. She's my sister."

Max pulled back. "Huh?"

I kissed Lynnae and Barry goodbye. Dan and Jesse shook Barry's hand and told him they would see him in a couple of days.

Sam reached for Max. "Come on, Max, Dad needs his rest. Mom, take care of our dad for us."

Lynnae sniffled and waved goodbye, then mouthed. "Love you," to all of us.

We stopped at Aunt Carrie's Seafood Restaurant for lunch. When the server brought over a high wooden chair for Max, Max told her he was too big for highchairs. Jesse grabbed his hands and spun him around in a full circle. "That's right, you tell her." Then he sat him down on the chair next to his.

Our server set a menu down in front of each of us and asked if we wanted anything to drink.

We all ordered the homebrewed iced tea.

"No sugar in mine, please," I said.

"Okay, I'll be right back with your drinks."

I tapped Max on the hand. "Are you hungry?"

"I'm hungry." Sam picked up his menu and added, "Max usually gets chicken fingers."

"They have chicken tenders." I smiled at Max and asked, "Is that what you want?"

"Uh-huh. And honey. Please," he said, rubbing his hands together.

"Okay, I'm having the chowder," I said. "Who else would like a bowl of chowder?"

Max raised his hand. "Me."

"Why don't you let him taste yours first and if he likes it, then we'll order him a cup," Dan suggested. "Does that sound good, Max?"

"We both like chowder," Sam told Dan. "Daddy makes it on fish night."

Dan laughed. "Two cups of chowder it is."

"How about coconut shrimp? I'm getting the shrimp *and* a bowl of chowder." Jesse reached over and poked Sam in his side. "What do you think about that?"

"Me, too." Sam replied and closed his menu. But then looked up at Dan and added, "Can I?"

"Of course you can," Dan said as he reached for everyone's menus.

The server came back to the table and took our orders. "Excuse me," Dan called to the server. "Can we get a large order of fried calamari and French fries as appetizers?"

"Sure."

"And chocolate cream pie?" Max added.

We all laughed. I nodded to our server. "For dessert. Thank you."

"Aunt Julie, can we live here all the time?"

"Oh, Sam, I would love that."

As we waited for our meal, Max told us a story about dragons and butterflies. "I can draw them!" he said, smiling.

Sam inhaled and smiled. "When we get back, I'm going to ask Amanda to roll out the long paper so I can make a sign for my mom and dad." His eyes got big when our server set the appetizers on the table.

"Sam, I love that idea. In fact, I'll help you," I said right before I took a sip of my refreshing ice tea.

"I can sign it, right?" Jesse asked.

"Everybody can," Max said as he picked up his fork and stabbed another piece of calamari.

I tapped Dan's hand. "Thank you."

He flashed me a grin.

During our entire meal, both Sam and Max told one joyful story after another. "Aunt Julie, I like Amanda. She's the best teacher I ever had." Sam set his fork down. "Thanks for taking us to see our parents, and thanks for lunch. I'm full."

"Me, too," Jesse said, as he leaned back in his chair. "I'm sitting in the back so I can go to sleep."

After Jesse helped Max put on his coat, Max reached up for Jesse's hand. "Sit next to me."

Twenty minutes later, we arrived back at the inn. "Our guests must be back from their ski trip," I said as I noticed their license plate. "Hmm, they're from Rhode Island. Okay, let's go."

"We can walk over to the daycare by ourselves," Sam proclaimed. "We're old enough."

"No," Dan said loudly, "I'll walk you over."

"I'll take them," Jesse said as he held Max's hand up in the air. "Right?"

Max nodded. "Right!"

I blew them kisses, and told them, "I'll see you guys at four o'clock," then I watched Jesse race them to the daycare.

Dan and I had just stepped up onto the front porch when we heard a loud noise. People were shouting. Dan opened the door, and we heard, "I'll kill you and your fucking kid before I let you go!"

Bang! Bang!

Without thinking, Dan ran in and tackled the man. Teresa was standing behind the front desk, screaming. I could see Erin, Kyle and Lady. Kyle started crying hysterically. Erin dropped to her knees. Lady staggered and fell over onto her side.

I screamed, "Call nine-one-one! Somebody dial nine-one-one."

Chapter 44

Kyle bent down and hugged Lady. Dan wrestled the man's arms behind his back. To their right, I saw the gun. Just then, the front door swung open and slammed against the coat rack. Jesse came running in and immediately knelt down on the man's back. My eyes met Dan's. I ran over to Erin, Kyle and Lady. With one sweeping motion, I picked Kyle up and carried him down the hall.

By the time I reached Kourtnee's office, she was on the phone with the police. Christine took Kyle from me. Michael ran past me to the lobby. A chill came over me when I heard Dan scream! My knees gave out, and I dropped to the floor.

I took hold of the doorjamb, got up and went back to the lobby to pick up my little girl but Dan was standing there holding her in his arms. Blood was everywhere.

Teresa handed Jesse a piece of rope and ran over to Erin and me. Under her breath, I heard Teresa say, "Oh, my God, Erin, is that Josh?"

Erin gave us no warning. Before we knew it, she was flat on the floor. My heart started beating in my ears. I searched her entire body for gunshot wounds.

I couldn't find any.

As Josh lay face down, hands tied behind his back, Michael straddled him.

Jesse rushed over to us. "Julie, she passed out. That's all, thank God."

By this time, Kourtnee had entered the lobby. Jesse told her to grab a cold cloth and assist Teresa. "Teresa, let's go!" he shouted to her as he picked Erin up and carried her to the library.

Seven minutes passed before three police officers entered the inn. Guns drawn. Michael held his arms up and placed his foot on Josh's backside before he pointed to the gun.

An officer picked the gun up with a pen and put it in a plastic bag.

I saw Michael open the front door for Dan as he carried Lady outside. I saw him collapse on the first step. One of the police officers sat beside him. When Michael closed the door, another officer placed a set of handcuffs on Josh.

Two more police officers came inside, followed by several EMS workers and four men dressed in black suits.

Michael and I were standing together when Kevin came running inside. He stood with his hands on his hips, shaking his head. For a moment, I thought he was going to kick Josh in the head. Instead, he moved about as if he were checking every room. I heard him say, "She okay?" to Kourtnee and Teresa.

"Who are you?" one man wearing a black suit asked Kevin.

"I work here." Kevin pointed to me. "That's my boss."

The man held out his badge. "I'm detective Kohl." He nodded slowly. His tone was mild, but his eyes were steely.

I motioned to him with my hand. "Julie Holliday…" The next thing I knew the entire room went black.

Chapter 45

I opened my eyes and saw a female EMS worker taking my blood pressure. I read her nametag, *Mary M, Field Staff. Emergency Medical Services. Paramedic.* Jesse was sitting to my right, holding his head in his hands. I whispered, "Where is everyone?"

Jesse reached out a hand and helped me to my feet. "Come with me," he said, sounding tired and distraught.

As we entered the lobby, I could see drops of blood on the floor. My hand went to my mouth. "Oh, no." Jesse held me closer to him.

We stopped at the front door. He helped me with my coat. Outside, Lady was on the porch floor in a pool of blood. My heart crumbled, but I found the strength to sit beside her. Eight years cascaded down my face in the form of wet tears.

Dan's eyes widened, filling with tears. I felt his lips on my face. The entire world darkened when he said, "Say goodbye…"

I kissed her and before I could say a word, Dan, Jesse and Mary M carried her away.

A strange man helped me to my feet. Together we went back inside. I sat down in the chair near the picture of Eleanor Roosevelt. I sat there wondering which garden Dan would bury Lady in. I imagined Lady running in our field in New York.

Detective Kohl came over and sat down in the other chair. "I have to ask you a few questions."

I blew out a long breath. "I'll try my best."

Detective Kohl and I went into the library. Erin was crying in Teresa's arms. I sat down on the sofa next to them. "It's okay. You're both safe."

Erin's head fell into her hands and I heard her cry, "He shot Lady."

I hugged her. "It's not your fault."

"Oh, Julie, I'm so sorry."

Teresa stood up and said she was going to see Kourtnee. But I knew she was up to something.

"Before you leave the room, I need to get a statement from you."

Teresa nodded to him and sat back down, this time in one of the chairs.

"Okay. Who was in the room when Mr. Rhimes entered the building?"

Teresa motioned with her right hand. "I was. I'm the receptionist." She sat up and uncrossed her legs. "I greeted him and asked if I could help him." She shook her head. "He never answered me. He just looked around for a minute and then we both heard Kyle asking Erin when the boys would be back."

"Boys?" Kohl asked.

"Sam and Max. They go to daycare with Kyle." Teresa pointed to me. "They were both with Julie at the time—"

"I took them to see their father at the hospital," I said.

He pointed toward Teresa. "Go on. What happened next?"

Teresa swallowed. "The moment he saw Erin, his eyes hardened. He had this terrible expression on his face." Teresa's lip quivered. "I didn't see the gun until he shot it."

I handed her the box of tissues.

"At what point did Mr. Rhimes pull the trigger?"

"The second he saw Erin." Teresa cried. "I'm sorry. I should have warned them."

"Teresa, you had no idea who he was or what his intentions were." I waved my hand at the detective. "Can't this wait?"

Kohl shook his head. "Take me to the lobby." He stood up.

I helped Erin to her feet. Teresa and I followed him to the center of the room.

Kohl pointed to Teresa. "Show me where you were standing?"

Teresa walked behind the desk. "I was standing here when he started screaming, 'I'll f-in kill you.'"

"And where did you and your son enter the room?"

Erin and I moved to the other side of the lobby and stood near the hallway leading to the kitchen. I heard Erin suck in a loud breath. She bent down and ran her hand over the three bullet holes in the wood casing. Someone had circled them with a pen.

Detective Kohl walked over to Erin. "Please stand in the exact location."

Erin spoke up, "I was standing right here."

"Obviously, Mr. Rhimes is not a very good shot. Lucky for you, he missed every time."

Erin's eyes dropped to the floor and noticed there was still blood at her feet. She was trembling.

"And where was your son?" he asked.

Erin pointed to her right side.

I heard the detective inhale. "It appears Josh aimed for your son. But instead shot the dog."

I squinted my eyes at Kohl. "I'm taking her back to the library. You can finish in there," I told the detective as I led Erin away.

"I'll be back for everyone to sign their statements. In the meantime, no one is to leave."

"We'll be fine." I reached over and touched Kohl's elbow. But I don't think he appreciated me touching him, because he reached for his gun. "Sorry," I quickly said to him.

"Not a good idea," he told me.

I extended my hand to Kohl. "Please keep us posted."

He nodded to me. "Mrs. Rhimes, you're not to leave."

"I won't. I assure you." Erin reached for my hand.

"She's not going anywhere," I said.

I was thankful Detective Kohl told the other men to take down the crime scene tape.

We were in the library when I heard Jesse, Michael, and Kevin enter the lobby. I heard Jesse telling everyone we were all sleeping at the inn tonight. A moment later, Kourtnee, Christine and Kyle were asking Michael and Kevin what happened and where was everybody?

I called to them, "We're in here."

Kyle ran to Erin. "Mommy, Mommy!"

Erin reached out and hugged Kyle. My heart sank. When she closed her eyes, I could only image how she felt. I glanced over at Jesse, Michael, and Kevin. I was thankful for all of them. I felt blessed to have them in my life.

Dan entered the room without Lady and my heart sank deeper. He motioned to me and in a sad voice said, "Maybe you should take Kyle over to the daycare."

I stood up. "Erin, why don't you and I take Kyle to daycare? I'm sure Sam and Max will be happy to see him."

She nodded. "I could use some fresh air."

"I'll go with them," Jesse said to Dan as he reached for Kyle's hand. Jesse stopped in front of Dan long enough to say, "Why don't you come up with a game plan for the night."

Teresa stayed behind. As soon as Erin and I opened the door to the daycare, both Sam and Max ran to tell Kyle about their dad. Kourtnee picked Delilah up. Christine held Brin in her arms. Kourtnee and Christine sat in their rocking chairs. They both had tears in their eyes.

"We went to the hospital and saw our dad," Max said as he helped Kyle take off his coat. "Come over here, I'll show you what I drew."

"Yeah, you can sign our dad's card." Sam pointed to a piece of paper rolled out on the floor.

Kyle knelt down, picked up a marker, and wrote his name. You could have heard a feather drop. We were all waiting for him to tell the boys about seeing *his* father, but he told his favorite story about Pete the Cat.

Then Amanda read to the boys. *The Purple Pail* by Christine Ieronimo, a beautiful story about a pail that travels all over the world.

Chapter 46

I was standing outside the daycare when my cell phone rang. It was Lynnae calling to say they would be home the next day. I waited until dinnertime to tell the boys. I wanted to let things settle.

When I stepped inside, Teresa was on her knees, washing Lady's blood off the hardwood floor. I bent down next to her. "Thank you." Next thing I knew, Dan and Michael were using sandpaper on the wood trim. Two hours later, the trim was painted, and there was no sign that Josh had ever been at the inn.

Jesse had snuck in as quiet as a deer. He stood there pondering. "I'll sleep in the library," he said, as if that was a possibility.

"You can't sleep in the library," I quickly stated. "I have guests. Remember?"

My heart jumped in my chest when the front door opened. Kevin was wearing black from head to toe, his thick black hair hidden under his baseball cap. "I'll sit in the lobby tonight." He glared at me. "In case the asshole makes bail."

"I'll stay with you," Jesse said in a voice I'd never heard before.

"Seriously, I don't want to alarm the guests. They may be skiing now but, I—"

Kevin held up his hand. "Dan and I already discussed it. I'll be fine." He glanced over at Jesse. "*We'll*... be fine. Just for a few nights. We'll sit in the billiards room until the guests go to sleep. Let's make sure the doors and windows are locked."

I couldn't help but wonder. Was there a possibility of Josh being released? Would he come back? Although I own a handgun. I have never used it on a person. I was glad when Michael eased the tension in the room by saying it was time to think about dinner.

"Let's get something to eat," Michael announced as he rounded the corner out of sight.

"Good idea," Dan said as he reached down and picked up the pail of bloody water.

Jesse followed Michael's lead. His shoulders were so wide, I could hardly see who was in front of him.

Michael prepared grownup Sloppy Joe's for the children. "Julie." He turned to me. "What do you think about serving just the roasted chicken with red potatoes?"

"Sounds good. Do we know how many dinner reservations we have for tonight?"

Michael flipped up the first piece of paper hanging on the clipboard. "Sixteen."

"And what dinner choices did we offer?" I asked.

"Hmm, roasted chicken and vegan chili."

"I'll make the chili," Dan said from across the room. "For havens sake, let's keep things as normal as possible."

Michael turned around. "I'll do it."

"No, we'll help," Dan said as he reached for the recipe. "We're in this together."

Dan was correct. We *were* in it together. I stepped away. "I'll get the dining room ready."

Kevin put his hand on my shoulder. "Other than the front door, is every window and door locked?"

Teresa stood up. "The media room. We better check," she said, as they left the kitchen. "I opened it for the delivery man the other day." Teresa opened the door leading to the basement. Kevin stepped in front of her and she followed him downstairs.

I continued to make my way to the dining room. I stood alone in the dark room. *She's gone.* My baby was gone. To everyone else she was a dog. But to me, she would always be my little girl.

I touched the side table. The wine carafe and the stack of napkins, before I collapsed onto a chair. For ten minutes or so, I allowed myself to cry. Then I wiped my eyes, stood up and said a prayer.

In front of me was the repurposed dresser Teresa had made into a sideboard. She had four baskets on the bottom shelf and one basket in the center of the two top drawers. It was perfect. The bottom baskets were for tablecloths. In the two drawers, silverware. And in the middle, a basket full of cloth napkins. On the top shelf was the first item I purchased for the inn, Teresa's wine rack. I ran my hand over the two ceramic green artichokes sitting next to it. An hour and a half from now, I'd be serving dinner to our guests. Yet, it all felt so surreal to me.

Somehow, we got through the earlier part of the evening. Thankfully, I was never alone. Dan and Teresa assisted me in the dining room. Sitting at the large table for ten was a group of five women in their mid-to late-fifties. I could not get away from them.

"You should definitely check out the Newport mansions," one of them told me.

"Seriously," another said, "we started at The Breakers, and then went to Marble House, had lunch and then went to The Elms. But I have to tell you, the Chateau-sur-Mer was my absolute favorite."

"Huh!" One of the other women said. "You could have fooled me. You spent two hours in the gift store at The Breakers."

"Well, I can't help it," she pronounced. "They're pretty clever. They let you walk in the front door but lead you to the basement. Where all the gifts are!"

"I'll be sure to go. I'm so glad you all had a good time today." I motioned for Teresa to give me a second. "If you'll excuse me, I'm going to check on your desserts. Christine prepared a delicious apple puff pastry with almond ice cream and caramel sauce."

"Oh, my, that sounds delicious," said the silver-haired woman as she handed me her empty plate and then asked, "Can we take it into the library? I'm dying to sit by the fire."

"Of course you can. Whenever you're ready. I'll bring it to you. Would anyone care for some tea or coffee?"

"Tea, please."

"Yes," another woman replied.

Dan was chatting with an older couple about their day spent cross-country skiing. Teresa said I should spend a moment with the elderly couple sitting in the corner. Apparently, they arrived just moments after Josh had fired the gun. She put her hand on the small of my back. "I'll bring the ladies their tea and pastry."

"Thanks." I looked over at the couple and then took a very deep breath. "Good evening," I said as I approached their table. "Are you enjoying your stay?"

"Yes, very much." He set his napkin on the table. "Is everything okay?" He held his hand out. "I'm sure it is. I just want to make sure. Because if I can assist you in any way." He flashed me an NYPD badge.

I put my hand on his shoulder. "You're the best. Thank you. I assure you, we're fine and everyone is safe. The entire situation is under control."

"The officer told my husband that a man fired a weapon," his wife added without missing a beat.

"Sweetheart, just because some maniac discharged his weapon."

I looked at him. "He was here for less than fifteen minutes. My husband immediately took him down. And in as few as ten minutes, Rhode Island State Police, and the sheriff's department were here to take him away."

"See, honey, it's all good," he said.

"Thank you. Are you ready for some dessert?"

"We heard you telling those ladies about it. It sounds delicious," the wife said, sounding happier.

"Great. I'll be right back." When I turned around, both Dan and Teresa were gone. I went into the kitchen and set two dishes on a serving tray.

"How are you holding up?" Michael asked as he poured the warm caramel sauce.

"I'm heartbroken, confused and still in shock. Thanks for asking. Where are the children?"

"Kevin suggested a slumber party." Michael pointed to the basement. "They're in the media room setting up their sleeping bags."

"I love him." I took the couple their puff pastry and asked if there was anything else I could get for them.

"No, thanks. We're good. My wife has challenged me to a game of pool." He winked. "I might let her win, if she allows me a cigar."

"Or I might beat the pants off him," she laughed.

"Like she usually does," he admitted.

"Have a wonderful evening. Enjoy your game. And help yourselves to the brandy."

When I stepped out into the lobby, Teresa gave me thumbs up. I stopped to tell her about the slumber party downstairs.

"I'll stay up here until everyone goes upstairs." I felt her hand on my elbow. "Are you okay?"

I smiled. "I'm glad we have guests."

By nine-thirty, the children, Kourtnee, and Erin were sound asleep. I felt relieved knowing Kevin and Jesse were together. Dan and I tiptoed upstairs. We were in the lobby when I heard him crying. Without a word, I reached for his hand and together we climbed the stairs to our room. Neither of us got undressed. We held each other in our own silence. I have no idea what time we fell asleep.

Chapter 47

When I woke up, I remembered Barry was being released from the hospital. "Are you awake?"

"Yeah," Dan replied.

I rolled over and rested my head on his chest. His cellphone rang, so I moved out of the way.

Dan reached over and brought his cellphone to his ear. "Hello"

I felt Dan's hand in my own. He squeezed it several times. "Mary, oh, Mary, that's wonderful. Bless your heart. Yes, of course. Thank you," he said and then jumped out of the bed.

"What?" I said, and I too got up.

Dan pulled me in closer. "I'm sorry. I felt like I was going to pass out. My hands started shaking, and I thought I was going to vomit."

"I'm testing your sugar." I shook my head and looked into his eyes. "I think you have *low* blood sugar."

"Never mind my sugar," he said. "Julie that was Mary, the paramedic. Jesse and I were both so distraught; Mary took Lady from us. She took her to her veterinarian, Dr. McGhee, and together, they were able to treat Lady's gunshot wounds."

I heard him, but I wasn't sure I heard him correctly. "Lady's alive?" I shouted.

"Yes," Dan said. "Mary said her daughter, Madeline, is a veterinarian. When she took Lady from me, I thought there was no hope, but she did it. She saved her."

I dropped to my knees. "Thank you, thank you, thank you," I cried.

Dan bent down in front of me, held me in his arms, and cried, "Our little girl is coming home."

I leaned back. "When?"

"Mary said Lady's heavily sedated but we can go see her the day after tomorrow and in a week she should be able to come home."

I was so happy, I hugged him and we both fell over.

Dan laughed. "I'm headed for the shower."

"I'm right behind you," I said, getting up, catching a glimpse of myself in the mirror.

I let Dan step in first. I joined him. When I kissed the center of his back, Dan reached up as if he were holding up the shower wall. Water trickled down his back. I lathered his entire backside. Dan spun around, kissed me on the lips and said, "Now you turn around."

One by one, we rinsed off, towel dried our bodies, dressed and headed downstairs. Dan closed our door. "I need a cup of coffee so bad."

"Morning," Kourtnee said as she stepped out into the hallway.

"Good morning," Dan replied.

"Morning. Where's Dalilah?" I asked.

"Kevin took her to daycare early. He said something about going into town for a new security system for the daycare. He wants a security keypad on both doors. I have to stop in the office for a second. I'll meet you in the kitchen in a few minutes."

"Okay, we'll see you in a bit," Dan said.

"Good morning," Teresa said as we came down the stairs.

"Morning," Dan and I both said in unison.

"Hello, sunshine." I motioned to her. "Did you have your tea yet?"

Teresa held up a cup. "Jesse's in the kitchen. I told him I'd holler if I needed him." She rolled her eyes. "He locked the front door. Told me not to unlock it until he came back." She shook her head. "I have to stay here because the couple in the Jamestown suite are checking out by nine."

"Gotcha," I said.

We were in the hallway and we could smell cinnamon and something buttery-sweet baking. Dan stopped at the door to the basement. "I'll check in on the kids and be right in. I want to tell Kyle that Lady is coming home."

Tuesday morning, Dan and I drove to the vet's office to pick up our baby girl. Except for the bandage wrapped around her belly, she appeared fine. I cried when she ran to us, licking our faces, wagging her tail, ready to go see her little buddy Kyle.

Dan and Jesse moved Erin and Kyle to a room on the first floor as soon as we learned Lady was coming home.

Lady knew she was home the minute Dan turned onto Mallard Way. She couldn't get to the daycare fast enough. I laughed, telling Dan, "And you thought she couldn't go up the stairs."

We left Lady in the daycare with Kyle. Dan headed down to check on Kevin and Jesse, while I went over to the inn.

Christine was in the kitchen alone. The counter was covered with fresh baked goods. I stood in the doorway, inhaled the scent of warm cinnamon buns and thought, *My baker is back!*

Michael entered from the side door, holding several bags of groceries. "What's all this?"

"Mmm," I murmured, to encourage him.

"I'm baking," Christine replied, flashing him a smile. "Your favorite. Frozen mint mousse in a frosty chocolate shell, and apple strudel, German style, just the way you like it. Buttery. Oh, and cinnamon donuts for the kids."

"Wow," he said, amazed, looking around the kitchen at all of her accomplishments.

"I'm sorry," Christine whispered in Michael's ear but loud enough for me to hear her.

"Why, Christine?" He set the bags down on the counter, leaned back and added, "Why couldn't you just talk to me? Baking?"

"I thought you liked my baking?" she said to him as she picked up a tray of donuts.

"You mean, you thought I wouldn't be sympathetic? Christine, you had a child. A lot of women go through what you were experiencing."

She set the tray down. "I know, sweetheart." She looked over at me. "Julie, last night he whimpered in his sleep. Yesterday, I held our baby and for the first time, I realized exactly *what* I have." She moved closer to Michael and said, "I haven't been the same since giving birth to our beautiful daughter. I promise you, I will make up for my behavior."

Michael held his arms out to her. I heard him say, "I love you so much."

I left them alone. I was standing in the hallway, thanking God, when I heard, "Aunt Julie, guess what?"

I smiled at Max. "What, sweetheart?"

"Mommy and Daddy are coming home today and Uncle Dan said we can decorate the front porch."

"After breakfast," Dan said, coming down the hall.

I followed Dan, Max, Sam and Kyle back to the kitchen.

"Okay, who wants chocolate chip pancakes?" Christine waved a spatula in the air. "To the dining room, all pirates, sailors and superheroes."

At that moment, I knew my chef wasn't going anywhere, or my baker!

I took my coffee and headed for the large dining room. I was saying goodbye to the group of women when my cellphone vibrated. "Thank you so much," they all said.

I looked at my phone and immediately called Lynnae back. "Hey, sorry, I was saying goodbye to my guests. Oh, Lynnae, I'm so happy to hear this. Yes, yes, yes! Okay, sweetheart, we'll see you both in an hour." I put the phone in my back pocket and ran to the other dining room. I whispered in Dan's ear, "You have one hour."

Dan stood up. "Okay, breakfast is over, let's go!"

Jesse shoveled his last three bites into his mouth.

After spending almost two weeks in the hospital, on January 14th, Barry was finally strong enough to come home. It was a good day for everyone. I stopped at the front desk and asked Teresa about the number of guests checking in for the weekend.

"Hmm," she said, and then glanced at the register. "Twenty-two rooms, most with double occupancy." She looked up at me. "I'm putting Lynnae and Barry in Dreamscape. Dan said to keep Barry on the main floor."

"That's a great room. Plenty of room to move around in and it has a view of the daycare. Barry can sit in the window and watch the boys play in the snow." I smiled at Teresa. "Good job!"

Teresa and I both ran to open the front door. Jesse, Dan, and all three boys were carrying an armload of signs. "Outside, to the right, and down the side porch," Dan told the boys.

Kevin entered the lobby from the hallway holding a large Welcome Home basket. He smiled. "Frank heard Barry was coming home today, he sends his best."

Frank. I needed to hear his voice. I asked Kevin to put it in their room. Then I peeked in the library, I was relieved when I saw no one was in there. I called the number Bea had given to me, but he didn't answer. I left him a voicemail telling him I loved him, missed him, and I was praying for him. "I'm calling you back later because you and I both know I need to hear your voice."

I slipped away and went directly to the rose garden. No blooming English roses, no viburnum, not even a climbing rose bush, but there was the comfort of the resting bench. I opened the gate, and found Michael pondering something. He glanced up and patted the seat next to him. I sat down and asked him if he was okay.

"Julie, I'm so confused. I don't know what to do. One minute, she's looking at me with hatred in her eyes and the next, she's talking to me like nothing wrong has happened." He shook his head. "I had to get out of the kitchen."

"I'll do whatever you need—"

"I'll figure it out. She'll come around one of these days."

He kissed my cheek and said, "I better get back to work."

"Michael, I thought she was fine a minute ago."

"Yeah, and right after you left, she flipped me the bird and hollered I can't do anything right in your book."

"Michael, Christine just started taking the vitamins, let's give her some time."

We both got up and went on with our day.

It was almost noontime when the Suburban pulled up to the front porch. Lynnae only had to beep the horn once for Jesse and Dan to go running. Lynnae hugged them before opening the back hatch. Jesse reached in and set the wheelchair on the ground. Dan opened Barry's door. When he took Barry's hand in his own and held it to his chest, my heart started beating.

No tears! I told myself.

I stood on the porch and watched as Dan grabbed the handles and Jesse lifted the chair from the front. In three easy pulls, Barry was on the front porch. I bent down and gave him a kiss. "Show off," I said aloud.

He smiled at me. "It's good to be home." Then he pointed toward the front door and reached his hand out. I turned around and saw Erin standing in the doorway.

She stepped closer, and they hugged. Erin looked up at Lynnae. "Can I help?"

Lynnae smiled and handed her two bags.

Noontime, Michael and Christine delivered Lynnae and Barry their lunch. At one-thirty, we let the boys visit with their father for a while.

"Daddy, did you like your sign?"

"Max, I love my signs."

It was a hero's welcome home.

Chapter 48

Monday morning by eight a.m. I was ready to face anything, even Rose. I had become used to her comments and requests. For the sake of Erin, I ignored all of them. Especially her suggestions that the two of us become friends and go kayaking and jogging together. Who is she kidding, she wants my side of the story.

I was standing in the kitchen when Kevin came in for breakfast. "Morning," he said as he poured himself a cup of coffee. "Refill?" He reached over and helped himself to a chocolate croissant and a raisin bran muffin. He held the muffin up and said, "For later."

I nodded. "Good idea."

"Good morning," Erin said to him as he left.

"Morning," Kevin replied to her. "Croissants are good and hot."

Erin forced a smile. "Thanks, I'm not really hungry. Then she asked me, "Julie, does it bother you when Rose tries to talk to you? Because—"

"Not at all!" I lied and sipped my coffee. Both our eyes opened wide when Michael and Christine came out of the pantry giggling. Christine's hair was a mess.

Michael smiled in surprise and called out, "Good… morning, early birds."

"Morning, Michael. Good morning, Christine," I replied, wondering what they could have been doing in there for so long.

"Morning, Julie and Erin," Christine said, both cheeks glowing hot pink, with an appearance that could only mean one thing.

"Good morning," Erin replied and then told me she would wait for me in the library because she wanted to go over her assignments.

Dan and Jesse came out of the small dining room, and Lynnae popped in through the side door. I rinsed my cup, set it in the dishwasher and told Dan that I would be back in a few hours.

Kourtnee came out of her office and asked, "What's going on?"

I shook my head. "I'm off to see Rose." Before leaving, I reached over and tapped Michael on his hand. "I've missed your smile."

In the lobby, I glanced over at the grandfather clock and noticed it was already eight-thirty.

Teresa hung up the phone and said, "That was Detective Kohl. He said Erin could go to her house and get her stuff. The police will have to go with her and record everything she takes."

Both Teresa and I heard a loud noise come from the library. Erin was standing near the window and her backpack was on the floor, next to a book.

"I never want to go back to that house," Erin said, and then sat down on the sofa.

"I'll go with you," Teresa said with an expression of doubt on her face.

"I have to use the bathroom," Erin sprang to her feet and left the room.

Teresa followed her out as far as the front desk.

I sat down in a chair. On the mantel was a cast iron bust of Albert Einstein. I bought it because of the quote Lynnae had read to me a long time ago. In the center of the bookcase where the TV used to be was another one of my favorite quotes. That one was by Charlaine Harris, "Here's to books, the cheapest vacation you can buy."

"Julie…" Erin inhaled as she closed the door behind her.

I turned to her. I was thinking *her vacation is over. Her reality is about to begin.*

"I'm scared. I don't want to go. I especially don't want to go into the basement for Kyle's books and toys. Julie, I." She began to cry. "I have no desire to go back to that house. Not even if the police are there."

I wished Frank were here. I knew Dan, Jesse, Kevin and Michael are strong but it's Frank's wisdom that I missed during times like this.

At that instant, the door swung open. "Hey, are ya ready? Let's go!" Jesse waved us out of the room.

"Are you coming with us?" Erin asked, sounding pleased.

"Um, yeah!" Jesse held up his coffee. "Dan and Kevin are going to the day care until I get back."

I was relieved. Not for security reasons, but for the mere fact that I wouldn't have to listen to Rose. When we got in my Explorer, Erin told Jesse about being able to get her belongings.

"Teresa told me," he said as he started the engine.

"I don't want to go…" Erin cried.

"That's fine. You don't have to. Make me a list and I'll go," Jesse told her.

"Not alone!" I said louder than I should have.

He smirked. "Like Dan's going to let me. Man, he's overprotective." Jesse shot me a look. "Worse than you!"

"Erin, you don't have to go if you don't want to," I said.

We rode in silence until Jesse turned the radio on.

Jesse pulled up to Rose's office, jumped out and stood near the front door with his hands behind his back. *If that doesn't scream bodyguard, nothing does.* His stance was a clear sign of strength and confidence. This time, I made Jesse come inside with us.

I opened the door, and Erin stepped inside. Jesse and I sat down in the waiting room. I was thankful Erin didn't tell me to follow her in when Rose opened the door. We introduced Rose to

Jesse. The receptionist asked us if we cared for something to drink. We both told her, "No, thank you."

An hour later, Rose opened the door. We could hear her telling Erin, "Not all abuse is physical. The need to control is another kind of ill treatment."

In the car, Erin shared Rose's recommendation for Kyle to speak to a child psychologist. "But, I want to wait," Erin said. "I don't want him to leave the inn. Not yet."

When we got back to the inn, a few of the guests were still eating breakfast in the large dining room. I thought about how small the room appeared. Erin, Jesse and I helped ourselves to something to drink and sat in the kitchen at the counter. A moment later, Dan and Kevin came in from the side door.

"Michael's reading to the kids." Dan held his right hand up. "Amanda locked the door. Good news, right?" he said as he poured two glasses of his iced tea.

"Erin, are you excited to get your stuff?" Kevin asked as he took a glass from Dan.

"Dan?" Jesse raised his hand, pointing to the door leading down the hall with his thumb. "Erin's going make us a list, why don't you and I discuss a good time to go."

Silence.

I glanced over at Erin. "Stop. You're fine." Tears streaming down her cheeks, she had one hand on her mouth, and the other drumming the table.

"Oh," Jesse said to her. "Don't start that. You're not going." Then he sat down next to her. "Look at me. That bastard is never getting out of jail. He's going straight to prison."

Dan put his hand on the counter in front of Erin. "Make us a list and we'll get your belongings. You can stay here and help Julie."

"Yeah, and get your homework done, too," Jesse said jokingly.

Erin inhaled and wiped her eyes. "You're the best." She glanced up at Jesse and mouthed, "Thank you."

Jesse reached for an oatmeal cookie. "What?" shooting me that look.

I just smiled and shook my head.

Chapter 49

Thursday afternoon, Lynnae was singing and dancing in the kitchen. Christine, on the other hand, appeared puzzled. And for the first time, I don't think she knew what to do or say. She never moved her head, only her eyes. But every time Lynnae did a spin, Christine scrunched her nose. Barry was still under doctor's orders. Although he was eager to get outdoors, he remained in his room.

The inn was full. Every room booked. Knowing Josh was in jail awaiting his trial date, Jesse spent the night in Point Judith at his girlfriend's apartment. Dan and I went back to the cottage.

I woke up Friday morning terrified, knowing Dan, Jesse, and Kevin were meeting the police at Erin's house. She didn't want or need any furniture. She only asked for their personal belongings. In fact, she purposely requested they grab nothing that would remind her of that place.

Dan nudged me on my side. "Are you awake?"

"Yes." I stretched my arms up and yawned. "Thanks for making me a fire last night."

Dan sat up, and put on his pants. "I like curling up by a glowing fire with you." Then he pulled out a piece of paper and unfolded it. "Here." He handed the document to me.

"Erin's list?" I asked.

"No clothes? No shoes?" Dan got up and went into the bathroom. "What the hell did that man do to her?" I heard him say.

He stood in the doorway and then tossed the hand towel back in. "One of us could go."

"Kevin and Jesse want to go," I said, adding, "She doesn't want anything because Josh bought it for her."

Dan flopped back on the bed. "I hear you. Are you getting excited about our vacation?"

With everything and everyone around me, I had almost forgotten about our trip to Italy. "It will be nice to have a little peace and quiet for a change."

"I wish I had taken you sooner. From now on we're taking a vacation every year."

I sat up, slipped my feet into my slippers. "Next year, I'm taking you to Alaska."

"You got a deal," Dan said.

"Dan, I." I stood up. "You and I are going to have the time of our life in Italy."

Dan nodded. "Come on, let's go. You're making me hungry."

"Let me call Frank first."

Dan got dressed while I tried Frank's number.

I was so happy to hear his voice. He told me all about his treatments and about a nurse from Rhode Island. Frank and I spoke for several minutes. He was still Frank. Still capable of lifting my spirits. We only chatted about him. I didn't need to tell him anything, I just needed to hear his voice. I immediately felt better. Stronger than ever. I dressed, and we headed up to the inn with Dan swinging my hand, singing, "How Forever Feels".

We were almost to the front porch when we saw Jesse and Sherry getting out of his truck, and Dan's singing came to an abrupt.

I leaned in and gave her a kiss on her cheek. "Good morning, it's nice to see you again."

"You, too," she said, smiling shyly.

"Did you all get something to eat yet?" Dan asked.

"Not yet. Julie, Sherry's going to stay here while I go help Dan and Kevin."

I almost choked on my saliva. "Umm, okay." *Why?*

Everyone, including Barry, was in the kitchen. I hugged him.

I looked around the room and then at Sherry. "I'm sorry. Everyone, this is Sherry. Jesse's girlfriend."

Lynnae dropped her spoon. When it hit the floor, I thought the ceiling was coming down.

"Who wants breakfast?" Dan shouted.

For the next two hours, Sherry, Teresa, Kourtnee, Erin and I served breakfast to forty-two guests in the large dining room, two couples in the smaller dining room and somehow managed not to speak to one another.

We were all back in the kitchen when Kourtnee asked Sherry if she had a job.

I immediately thought, *bad idea.* Seriously, Jesse was not the marrying kind. I figured, *she'll be gone before she learns his middle name.* I was relieved when she said she loved where she worked. "Debi is the best boss in the world," but then she added, "I work there part time. We're only open Friday through Sunday."

Kourtnee raised her eyebrows several times. I motioned to her to leave the kitchen. A minute later, I met her in her office. "Are you out of your mind?"

She laughed, "What?"

"Tell me you ran the ad. You said you would take care of the staffing." I sat down. "What the hell is wrong with you?"

"Julie, she was good. No, she was great. Did you have to tell her anything? Because I didn't. She moved around that dining room like she owned it."

"I'm not saying she isn't good enough. What I'm worried about is Jesse. He–"

"Julie, Jesse asked me to interview her. She used to work as a waitress."

"Good to know. Send her to Kelly. Maybe she can work for her."

Kourtnee got up and closed the door. "Lynnae said you would react this way."

The door opened back up. "Did I hear my name?" Lynnae sat down next to me. "You're worried about Dan."

I inhaled, almost snapping my neck, to see her. "What? No! I don't know her."

"So you're planning to keep him locked up and away from everyone you don't know?" Kourtnee shook her head at me and then at Lynnae.

"Stop breathing like that, you'll figging hyperventilate," Lynnae said.

I shook my head. "Stop swearing," and then added, "her thong. By any chance did you all notice her under-garment hanging out?"

"So? Tell her she has to wear different pants," Kourtnee chuckled. "Not as tight and not so low."

"You don't know Jesse like I do. She'll be down the road—"

"Yeah, okay. Stop right there. He's been seeing her for a few months now. He's a big boy. Okay, a strapping bear of a man. He can handle it. Jesse likes her," Kourtnee said, smiling at me. "Jesse said Sherry's pretty, sweet, earnest, happy and she'll fit right in here."

I couldn't help thinking, *He likes her! Maybe she's the one?* My legs tingled and suddenly I had to pee. "Lynnae, mark my words." I pointed at Kourtnee. "Fine. Do whatever you want. I have to go to the bathroom."

Lynnae's cell phone rang. "It's my team." She swiped her phone. "What's going on?"

Kourtnee and I sat there in our own silence. I hated feeling this way. I had no idea why. I went to get up, but stopped myself.

"Oh, my God! Seriously?" Lynnae jumped up. "Yes, she's right here." Lynnae handed me the phone.

"Hello. Stephanie?" I listened to her tell me about their accomplishment. "I'm so proud of you. You're going to do great.

Good job! Of course, we'll all be watching. Okay, love you too. I will." I handed the phone back to Lynnae. Then I looked at Kourtnee and said, "Stephanie and Brooke won a contest. They're going to be on the show, Cake Boss, on March third."

"That's awesome!" Kourtnee said, smiling.

I stood up, hugged Lynnae and then gave her a high-five. "Good job!" Then I ran to the bathroom.

Before we knew it, it was time to serve lunch. Thankfully, only a few of our guests ever stay for lunch. Rhode Island is that beautiful. I watched as Sherry served more guests than Teresa, Kourtnee, and I combined. I thought about Jesse and how much he's given up for Dan and me. There wasn't anything we wouldn't do for him.

"Oh, thank you. Thank you so much!" I heard Erin telling someone.

I went to the lobby. The men were back with her belongings. Erin's eyes opened wide when Dan handed her a metal box. "We searched everywhere for the key."

Erin shook her head. "I never found the key." She shrugged her shoulders. "It was my mother's."

Dan put his hand on her shoulder. "Then I'm glad I was able to find it. If we missed anything, you let us know."

Jesse went back outside as Kevin came in carrying several boxes. Teresa went over and took a few of the smaller ones from him.

Erin touched Dan on his arm. "Can you open the lock?" He nodded, and she handed it back to him. "Thank you," she said, holding his gaze.

A little while later, everyone except Erin was in the kitchen. I sat there smiling as I listened to Lynnae telling them about Brooke and Stephanie.

"I'll make sure the media room is ready." Dan waved to Kevin and Jesse. "Let's go shopping."

I went back to the dining room to check on the number of bottles of wine. Sherry was sitting on the floor, folding napkins.

"Sherry?"

She stopped folding and held my gaze. "Teresa showed me where the laundry room was and these were sitting on the dryer. So I ironed them."

I sat in one of the chairs and asked her to join me. My heart sank when she added, "I'm in love with Jesse. I know it's soon, but I love him with all my heart. I just want be with him."

I seriously need to gain control of my emotions. I could have cried. "Jesse is a wonderful man. He's as good as they come," I said to her.

"He loves you guys. He said he's known you all his life."

"We both love him. Sherry, would you like to work here?"

Her eyes got big. "For real?"

"Let's see if Kourtnee has the paperwork ready."

We were standing in the hallway when I heard my name. "Can I see you for a minute?"

"Kevin." I held up one finger. "Give me one second." I told Kourtnee and Sherry that I would be right back.

"I want to show you my design." I followed him to the lobby. Kevin handed me a sketch.

It was beautiful. "Is that my?"

"Your bench? Yes. Julie." He rubbed his chin. "I wanted to create this garden for your parents." He put his hand on my arm. "And you."

"Thank you," I said, reaching for the diagram.

Kevin pointed to the center and then to the mound, the old streambed, and his version of the sky. "Mountains, water, sky for contemplating, not for growing. Karesansui, a formal garden meant for meditation."

I wiped my eyes and told him, "I love it. And I love you."

Chapter 50

Valentine's Day was less than a week away. I was so busy, I didn't even peek at the menu board. Lord knows the last time I had a cup of tea. People seem to move around as if they all had some place to go and something to do. No one stood still. I had no idea where Dan and I were able to get in a few early morning hikes. Last night, we sat in the Adirondack chairs discussing our new farmhouse, our plans to entertain during the holidays and enjoy our retirement, together. I kissed Dan and told him I would see him at lunch time. He was off to put the stakes in the ground for Michael and Christine's new cape and I needed to see Kourtnee. Dan and I decided on ten acres parcels.

I peeked into Kourtnee's office as she was about to hang up the phone. "Sounds good. I look forward to meeting you in person. Bye."

"Sorry to bother you. Can you tell me what day would be good for all of us to get together?"

Kourtnee made a clicking noise with her tongue. "You know Valentine's Day is this weekend, right?"

"Yes. On Sunday. How many guests do we have…?"

She glanced at her computer screen. "Tonight and tomorrow we have twenty rooms occupied. But on Wednesday we have fifteen rooms booked. Oh, wait. Yeah, that'll work. Wednesday is the best time to schedule a meeting. Thursday, we're back to a full house."

"I don't want to schedule a meeting. I want us to get together and hang out."

"Hang out? Did you just say?"

"Yep!"

Her phone rang. I went into the kitchen. Under Michael and Christine's note: *Gone Shopping! Be back by two,* I wrote my own note on the chalkboard: *Attention staff, meet me in the media room on Wednesday at 2 p.m. Thanks, Julie.*

Then I went over to the daycare for some construction paper. Cut each piece into a heart, and wrote the words: BUCKET LIST on the left side. And on the right I wrote, HEART'S DESIRE. On my way back to the inn, I noticed most of the snow had been washed away by the rain. When I reached the media room, Dan, Jesse, Sherry, Kevin and Barry were down there. Barry was holding one end of the measuring tape, and Jesse was at the other end. "Does Lynnae know you're out of bed?" I said, scaring Sherry half to death.

"Geez, you scared me," Sherry said, laughing.

Barry laughed at me, too. "Dr. Plimpton does. I'm good. I feel like a champion."

"He's fine," Dan said to me, and then asked me if I needed any help.

"No, but the room looks amazing. The boys are going to love it."

"What's that?" Dan pointed to my stack of hearts.

"It's time we all took a few minutes to unwind and do something fun."

I heard Lynnae say, "We're not coloring again, are we?"

"No, Lynnae, we're not. I didn't see you standing there."

Lynnae and Erin were holding several child-sized beanbag chairs in their hands. They dropped them on the floor and told Dan the truck was empty. "What are *you* up to?" Lynnae asked me.

"I was thinking we could all spend an hour together."

"Aww, you miss us." Lynnae took her sweater off. "Okay, Dan, what's next?"

Dan paced around the room. "Now we wait for the furniture to be delivered."

"What time did they say it would be here?" Erin asked.

Jesse was lying on the floor. He picked his head up. "Is your homework done?"

Sherry laughed.

From the top of the stairs, we could hear Teresa calling for Dan. "Your furniture's here."

Dan moved to the stairs and called back to her. "I'll open the cellar doors."

Jesse jumped to his feet. "I'll go upstairs and show them the entrance."

That afternoon, a timer clicked away in the kitchen. "One more person," Christine said as she took off her oven mitts.

"One more person what?" Lynnae asked her.

"Until you become my competition."

I stepped in a little closer.

"Christine." I heard Lynnae say.

I waited for Michael, hoping he would say something, but he held his tongue.

Christine ripped her apron off and threw it on the floor. *This was serious.* Pies were cooling in front of windows. Eclairs for dessert, still warm. A bowl of melted chocolate sat waiting to go on top. And I had a war on my hands.

Lynnae put her hands on her hips, stopping herself from swearing out loud, but of course we all heard her mumbling the words before she added. "I bake as an act of love. You are an artist. Trust me, I wish I could compete."

Gah! Did she really just say that? I shook my head at the thought.

At that instant, the side door swung open. "Julie," Erin said from the doorway. Her breath was shuddery, as if she finished a good cry. She was holding a letter in her hands. "I found this in my mother's box." She flashed it at me. "Dan got it open."

Lynnae and I both went to her.

Erin held up the letter. "It's from a woman named, Margaret." Her eyes lifted from the paper. "I think she's my birth mother."

Michael and Christine joined us, and everyone hugged Erin. We were in a group hug when Teresa came into the kitchen, holding an empty cup. Erin turned to her and said, "My birth mother wrote to my mother."

Teresa closed her eyes and nodded before reaching out to Erin. "I prayed you would find her."

I noticed it had only a partial return address: Dungory West, Kinvara, Co. Galway, Ireland.

Teresa asked Erin, "Do you think she's still alive?"

Erin handed the envelope and the letter to her.

Teresa sat down at the table and read the letter.

"I'm happy for you," Christine told her, as she began spreading chocolate on her eclairs.

Erin exhaled. "Thank you."

Teresa handed it back to her. "I think you're right." She looked at me, her face lighting up. "She... umm. You, know what? You should go to Ireland and see her."

My heart sank. As much as I wanted her to find her birth mother, I didn't want her to leave. *I'm not ready to let her fly away yet.*

Almost an hour later, I was standing in the lobby, saying goodbye to a guest. When she left, Teresa called me over to me. "The woman, Margaret, spoke as if she knew Erin's mother and father and their time in Ireland."

The front door opened, and a couple walked in. Teresa grinned at me before meeting them at the front desk. I went down to the cottage and said a prayer for both Erin and Kyle.

Wednesday morning, Michael, Dan, and Jesse went shopping for the holiday weekend. I asked them to pick up raspberry ginger ale, a jar of cherries, and a bag of pink cotton candy. When Lynnae heard about my cocktails, she promised she would make her famous popcorn.

Right after lunch, Lynnae started popping. She spread the popcorn on a cookie sheet, drizzled butter and dark chocolate, sprinkled sea salt and tossed in a large box of Junior Mints and a bag of M & M candies. Then she filled big red Solo cups with her decadent snack. We went downstairs to the media room for the first time since the furniture had arrived. I had no idea how they got the big flat screen through that door.

"Wow!" Lynnae said as she set down the tray of popcorn.

"I'm impressed," I said. There were twelve brown recliners with nail-head trim. Two loveseats and a matching sofa for six. I pulled the label off the sofa. "Overstock.com"

"I love the gigantic wooden compass clock. The spotlights are amazing." Lynnae bent down and pulled the tag from the rug. "Hmm, indoor-outdoor. Cool."

I put my stack of hearts next to her cups of popcorn. Then we set the drinks on the long table next to the wall. "I'm going to run upstairs before they get here and get some napkins."

"Okay, I'll wait here," Lynnae said, as she stretched out on one of the recliners.

When I got upstairs, I saw Amanda pushing the stroller with two sleeping babies. But I didn't see the boys. I opened the door for her to come inside.

From behind the counter I heard, "We were hiding on Amanda."

"Sam, do you think that's a good idea?" I asked, and then closed the door.

"I could see them the whole time," Amanda said.

"We won't do it again," Sam promised.

I kissed his cheek. "Thank you."

"Aunt Julie." I turned around to answer Max, but it was Kyle. I bent down and helped him off with his coat.

"Aunt Julie, we're going to the movies."

I laughed. "We're going to the media room but we're not seeing a movie. Maybe next time."

"Call me. I'll come back for them," Amanda said, as she turned to leave.

"You're not staying?"

"I have so much work to do for–" she pointed to Kyle. "School. I have to make sure we're meeting every standard. Next time, I promise."

I gathered the napkins and followed the boys downstairs. Within ten minutes, we were all together. I handed everyone a heart-shaped paper.

"Oh, my, God, this is so good!" Teresa popped another piece in her mouth.

"Yum," Erin said, as she took another sip.

"Okay, listen up. I want everyone to write five things you want to do in the near future. And then I want you to write your heart's desire."

When they finished writing, everyone set his or her paper on the table. I picked them up and my heart sank when I read the name on the top. I was holding Teresa's in my hand and after reading it to myself, 'To not be alone', I decided not to read them aloud. Instead, I asked Dan if we could watch a movie.

"Good idea," Jesse said, as he shook his head at me. "Unbelievable! Where do you come up with these ideas?"

"I love the idea," Sherry said, nudging Jesse in the side.

"Ooh, it's matinee time!" Kourtnee patted the seat next to her. Kevin sat down and handed her another cup of popcorn.

"How about *How to Train Your Dragon*?" Dan said.

"Yeah!" It was unanimous.

I sat next to Dan in the recliner and read every one of the hearts. Dan wanted to retire and enjoy life with his wife. Jesse wrote to live with Sherry for the rest of my life. Erin wanted a brother or a sister for Kyle. Kourtnee and Kevin both wrote to live at the inn forever! Lynnae's was similar to Barry's. They both wanted a family, home and happy life together. Sherry wrote to have Jesse's baby.

February thirteenth, I hugged Lynnae, Barry, Sam and Max goodbye.

Chapter 51

I woke up earlier than normal. Four-thirty, to be exact. As not to wake Dan, I slid out of our bed, and poured myself a cup of tea, so he wouldn't be awakened by the smell of fresh brewed coffee.

I was glad the embers in the fireplace were hot enough to reignite. I tossed in a few pieces of kindling and two more logs. As I sipped my tea, I read Michael's menu notes. I smiled when I read Swiss Kirsch cake, flavorful, yet sugar-free. Julie loves it! Chocolate hearts with orange cream and cape gooseberries. Christine even drew a picture of how she was presenting it. A sprig of fresh lavender and chocolate dots decorated in a half circle around the heart. And for the children, chocolate-covered strawberries adorned with eyes and spiked black licorice for hair.

First course, fruit plate thinly sliced strawberries, kiwi, and plum swirled on a plate so beautifully you wanted to take its picture prior to eating. Lynnae was correct. Christine was an artist. Every plate swirled, dabbed and artful. For dinner, Michael was serving kale with chestnuts. Glazed baby potatoes. Veal shanks with braised red cabbage with onions and apples in a wine sauce. Butter roasted lobster tails, and beef tenderloin with cracked pepper and red wine-thyme pan sauce. And a vegetable lasagna. "Hmm, the next page says 'salads' but..."

"But what?"

I turned around. Dan was holding a long box with a red bow on the top. "I want to say thanks for last night."

I inhaled. "It was my pleasure." I patted the floor.

"Let me grab some coffee," he said, and handed me the box. "Don't open it until I get back."

Dan came back, sat down next to me, and handed me my cup. "Happy Valentine's Day." He kissed me, and I could feel myself getting excited all over again. "Open it."

I lifted the top, and I saw Sabrina's architectural drawing of the house I had asked for.

Dan reached over and lifted the top drawing. Underneath, the entire layout of the property. Three cottages, one log cabin and one big farmhouse. Dan pointed to the end of the driveway. "Jesse said he's almost done with his design. Sabrina will draw it as soon as he gives her the details."

"You know how happy this makes me?"

"Family's important to you. And I can see why. They're good people, Julie. I'm happy for you." He smiled. "For us!"

"This is the best Valentine's gift…"

Dan drank his coffee, emptying the entire cup. "Good, now let's eat breakfast. I'm starving."

After breakfast, Dan told me to jump in the shower while he cleaned up the kitchen. When I finished, Dan showered and I made the bed. I heard Dan suck in a harsh breath. He leaned against the doorjamb. Our gazes locked. One second he was by the door, the next he was in front of me. He nipped at my ear. Rubbed his thumb across my lips. I could hardly keep track of my thoughts. My lips parted.

Dan whispered in my ear. "I enjoy being alone with you." His voice still sounded edgy and sexy.

A shiver ran down my body when I kissed him. His body responded quickly. I moaned at the sound he was making.

Dan carried love songs in his heart. "Happy Valentine's Day," he whispered in my ear.

Chapter 52

Erin had completed every assignment given to her. Her instructors were more than pleased with her work. If she continued at the pace she was going, she would receive her associate's degree in less than two years and be able to enroll in a local college to complete her bachelor's degree. For the time being, we were content with her studying from home. Kourtnee found her *several* local colleges willing to accept her associate's degree from Southern New Hampshire University.

I was in the kitchen eating a bowl of yogurt, blueberries and chopped walnuts, daydreaming about traveling to Italy, when I heard someone say, "Meow."

"I'm as frazzled as a cat," Erin said as she came into the kitchen. She glanced up at the clock, set her homework down on the table and added, "Sorry. Good morning."

I laughed. "Good morning, Christine made yogurt and there's oatmeal."

Turning away she said, "Thanks, but I better hurry."

Her skin was flawless. Eyes defined her beauty. Her long wet hair gathered into a thick ponytail at the back of her neck. I could smell her shampoo. Erin sipped her coffee, took two spoonful's of her oatmeal, carried her cup and bowl over to the sink, and washed them up. Said a quick goodbye to Michael and Christine, picked up her books, and away she went.

I sat there waiting for her to come back.

"Ummm," she said.

I laughed. "Yes, I'll drive you."

We stopped by the lobby to put our sweaters on even though the temperature was in the low sixties. Thankfully, the snow never stayed long in Rhode Island. I told Teresa I would be back in time to serve lunch. She gushed, "Sherry and I will be fine."

As soon as we got in the car, Erin told me about the letter she wrote to Margaret. "I'm not sure she'll answer me but it's worth a try."

"I'm proud of you." I glanced over at her. "Do you think she still lives at that address?" I stopped at the end of the driveway to wait for a fleet of cyclists to go by. "What address did you send the letter to?"

"I only have one. The one on the back of the envelope."

"You should—"

"Julie," she said, but then paused. "I... I found an old photograph of my mother when she was a teenager. She was standing next to a little girl. On the back." She stopped speaking and looked out the window before adding, "I think." Catching my gaze, she said, "I think Margaret is my mother's sister."

"Why do you think that?"

"Because I look just like her. And someone wrote their names on the back of the photo."

"Do you suppose they could have been best friends, or cousins?"

"Maybe?" She inhaled. "I hope she writes me back."

"I do, too." I turned down the road to Rose's office, parked the car, and we both got out in our own silence.

Rose opened the door. "Hello, come on in."

"Hi," Erin said, with a sigh.

"Good morning," I said, following Erin into her office.

"So Erin, I heard some good news. It looks like Josh will be in jail until his hearing on the twentieth."

"March twentieth?" Erin croaked.

Rose shook her head. "April. Judge Klingner has set a postponement for the last possible date." She pointed her finger at Erin. "She likes you."

Erin seemed deflated. Her mood had turned darker. She sat still, hands clasped in her lap. Suddenly she began tapping her foot.

"Erin, are you okay?" Rose asked and then added, "Tell me what you're thinking."

"Josh knows a lot of wealthy people." There was a long silence. "What if he asks one of them to bail him out?"

"Erin, I can't say for sure, but I don't think Josh will be a free man for a long time. They set his bail pretty high." Rose stood up. "I'll be right back." Leaving the room, she clicked the office door shut.

Erin rose from her seat, but sat back down when Rose came back in with a tray and handed her a glass. "Lemonade," she said, adding, "very little sugar."

I reached for a glass. I took a sip, and so did Erin. "Thank you," I said, holding the glass in my hand.

"Erin, I want you to take your time. I know this must be hard for you. At our last session, you said you fell for Josh for all the wrong reasons."

Erin nodded. "Because, I've been sleepwalking through life, pretending Josh loved me. But seeing him again will be like looking over a cliff's edge." She was trembling. "I never want to see him again."

I decided to tell Rose about Erin putting a chair up against her door at night. "I had no idea until Kyle said something."

"Erin, do you put the chair up against the door because you are afraid?"

Erin nodded and set her glass down on Rose's desk. I picked it up and set a folded tissue under it. Why, I have no idea. But I did.

"Erin?"

There was an even longer silence.

Rose was staring at Erin.

"She busied herself around the inn so much, I had no idea how scared she was... is. I'm sorry," I said.

"No, no." Erin cried. "You have done so much for me. I can never repay you."

I reached over and put my hand on her shoulder. "When I see the way you are with Kyle. Oh, sweetheart. That is the greatest gift you could ever give me. Seeing the two of you together warms my heart."

Rose's eyes moved from Erin to me.

"Erin, I would like to see you again tomorrow."

Erin shook her head. "I have online classes all day."

"You're taking classes?"

"Yes. Julie is paying for my degree." She smiled warmly when she added, "I'm going to be a teacher."

"That's wonderful! Best news I've heard all day," Rose said to her.

When Erin and I got in the car, I told her, "When they write your story, they're going to say that *you* were a very brave young lady. Erin, you did the right thing. You ran."

Chapter 53

Seconds after pulling out of Rose's driveway, I pulled over to the side of the road, got out and picked a branch from someone's front yard. When I got back in, I handed it to Erin and said, "With every new growth comes a fresh beginning."

"Forsythia?" she asked while fingering the delicate blossom.

"Yep!" I fastened my seatbelt and drove straight back to the inn. As soon as I turned down the driveway, I told her, "Jesse is building himself a log cabin." I pointed to the area where he would build it. "From now on, everyone will have to get by Jesse first. And I'm calling the Ring Security Company. I'll have them install security cameras anywhere and everywhere we need them."

Erin smiled confidently. "I'm glad I didn't leave. Thank you for telling me to stay."

"Let's go for a walk, I want to show you something."

"Okay," she said, sounding much better.

I parked the car. As soon as we got out, we could hear music coming from the lobby. I opened the door, and we saw Gina Marie playing the drums, another woman I had never seen before was playing the violin, Teresa was on guitar, and Lynnae was playing her saxophone. Teresa was singing "Proud Mary" and sounding more like Tina Turner than her quiet self. Guests were applauding.

Kyle, Max, Delilah, Kourtnee and Amanda were dancing in the center of the room when two knockout white-haired women joined them. Christine was sitting in a chair next to a young couple, smiling and swaying with Brin on her lap. I leaned over and asked Sherry where Dan and Jesse were.

"They're down at the pond with Kevin. I heard something about a fire pit and new Adirondack chairs." She too was swaying to the music. "This is so cool!"

More than any vacation in the world, I wanted a family. "I'll be right back."

"What?" Erin shouted. Smiling and waving to Kyle.

"I'll be right back," I said a little louder. I went into Kourtnee's office and called Ring.

Chapter 54

Outside, bluebirds were singing. Trees were blooming in shades of pink and white. Erin made an appointment for a psychologist to come to the inn and talk to Kyle. Dan was breaking ground for Kevin and Kourtnee's cottage. Kevin completed the memorial garden. Jesse was happier than I have ever seen him. Teresa was wearing Sal's engagement ring. Lynnae and Barry finally told everyone they were expecting a child. Gina Marie would be part of our team. Oh, wait; yesterday, I did almost catch Christine and Michael making love out on the back terrace at three in the afternoon.

I actually slept last night. I dreamt about Dan, me, and all that we used to do together. It would be easy for me to say I fell in love during one of our conversations while kayaking down the majestic Ten Mile River on a warm summer day. Hiking on our property every morning. Dan reaching for my hand, stealing a kiss along the way, but it was our solitude that I treasured the most. Quiet moments when he would reach for me or kiss me under an open sky. *Those are the memories I live for and dream about.*

At seven-thirty, I headed up to the inn to help Sherry and Erin serve breakfast. After learning how scared she really was, I began including her in on a lot more happenings at the inn. It broke my heart to think she was hiding in her room because she was afraid Josh would come through the door at any moment. Like an idiot, I thought she was trying to find her birth parents and doing homework.

I waved to Mr. and Mrs. Dickett as they walked to their car. "We'll be back by four," he said to me before getting in.

I gave him a thumbs-up. "Sounds wonderful!"

I felt good inside. A long time ago, I opened my bakery in a small town. It was so small no one thought I would succeed. But I did. If not for my old bakery, I wouldn't have met Lynnae. Because of her, I hired the sisters. And to think, today, Brooke and Stephanie are going to be on national television.

"Wow!" I said at the ground covered in ajuga. "Oh, my!" Kevin's bidens, violets, aquilegia and blue iris were popping up everywhere, reminding me that the gardens would once again awaken to the splendor of spring. I smiled at the lonely crusty snow patch. "You don't stand a chance."

I stepped up onto the porch, reached for the knob, but then let go. So much had happened. Dan found me. Jesse finding Erin and Kyle in the early hours of dawn. Lynnae marrying Barry, Teresa, engaged. Jesse finding true love. I became lost in the moment. Thinking, *I am blessed.*

I took a deep satisfying breath when I remembered tonight; everyone including my guests were planning to watch an episode of Cake Boss staring Brooke and Stephanie McGhee from Bella Napoli Bakery.

I opened the door and saw Teresa next to the front desk, on her knees. *Was she praying?* "Teresa?"

Teresa had tears in her eyes. I bent down next to her. "What's the matter?"

"Okay, Sherry, I'm ready," Erin said, as they passed through the lobby.

Over my shoulder, I watched as the two of them went into the large dining room. "Teresa?"

She put her hand to her mouth. I could hardly hear her, shocked by what I thought she was trying to tell me.

"Josh? She whispered.

"Josh? Did you just say?"

She nodded.

I reached out, taking her by her shoulders. We both stood. I handed her a tissue. "What? For God's sake, tell me!"

Teresa whispered in my ear. "Detective Kohl called and said Josh Rhimes is out of jail. Someone bailed him out."

I put my arm around her shoulder and led her to the library, but someone was sitting in the corner chair, reading. "Upstairs," Teresa said to me, so I followed her.

We went up to her room, where she took a piece of paper out of her pocket and handed it to me. I read it aloud. "Josh Rhimes is out of jail. One of his clients paid his bail. Detective Kohl is on his way." I collapsed onto her bed.

Teresa sat next to me. "I pray he doesn't come back."

"I have to call Dan." I thought for a second. "He'll never hear his cell phone. He's in the excavator. Damn it!"

"What are we going to do?"

"I don't know. My God, she just started to feel safe again. The poor kid finally comes out of her room, and someone fucking bails him out."

Teresa's eye were wide. "Julie.?"

"Don't Julie, me. I'll fucking kill him myself if I have to." I got up, and stood by the window for a second. "I don't understand! How am I supposed to tell her?" I spun around so fast I knocked against a side table, causing Teresa's Bible to land on the floor. "I'm sorry," I said as I picked up the Bible.

Teresa stood up. "It's okay."

"I have to find Erin," I murmured.

"I'll get Dan and Jesse," Teresa declared.

"Listen for the sound of equipment," I told her, hoping she'd know what she was listening for.

"I'll be fine. Goooo!" she shouted to me.

I ran past the large dining room and into the kitchen, where I informed Michael, Christine, and Kourtnee. Both Kourtnee and Christine told me to find Erin and get her out of the inn. "We'll cover the dining rooms," Kourtnee said adding, "Go!"

"Wait!" Michael shouted to me. "What about Kyle?"

"I'll get him, too," I shouted as I ran out of the kitchen.

I found Erin in the small dining room, and told her that it was time for our walk.

"But?" she started to say, stopping near the coat rack.

"Let's go!" I said, leading her out of the room. "It's nice out. You don't need it," I demanded, pushing her out the door. There was no time to put on a damn sweater. We walked into the daycare, and Kyle ran up to Erin. Delilah hugged my leg. I patted her on the head and told her to be a good girl. I scooped Kyle up, took hold of Erin by the hand and headed out the door. When I clicked the door shut, I saw Christine running toward us. I opened my eyes wide and shook my head, trying to get her attention. When she nodded back at me, I knew she understood.

I stopped for a brief second for her to whisper in my ear, "I'm going inside. I'll lock the door and stay with the children."

Without saying a word to each other, we ran toward the cottage as fast as we could.

Chapter 55

We met Dan, Jesse, Teresa, and Kevin near the pond. Dan and Jesse got out of the Kubota. Jesse reached out, taking Kyle from me. Dan told us to follow him. Kevin and Teresa continued up to the inn.

Dan opened the door to the cottage and pushed Erin and me inside. When Erin laced her fingers, held her hands to her mouth, and closed her eyes, I knew she was aware of the situation. She was trembling.

Jesse took Kyle to the kitchen and asked him if he was hungry.

"Julie, maybe you and Erin should make yourselves a cup of tea. I'll light a fire. Kyle, can you help me?" Dan looked directly at Jesse, motioning for him to come into the living area. "Kyle...?"

"Can Jesse help us?" Kyle asked, tilting his head to the left before adding, "Please?"

Dan cocked his head. "Yes, Jesse can help us."

Kyle smiled at Dan as he climbed down from the chair and said, "Come on, Jesse."

Dan handed Kyle three pieces of kindling.

Kyle tossed two of them in. "We're hungry," he said, waving the stick at Jesse.

Erin was standing in front of the refrigerator, twirling her hair. I asked her if she wanted a cup of hot or cold tea.

She was shaking. "Hot."

I had just filled the kettle when someone knocked hard on the front door. Erin screamed at the top of her lungs and I dropped the kettle on the stove. Kyle jumped and ran into Dan's arms.

Dan turned around and said, "It's my friend, Mr. Kohl."

Erin said, "Oh, my Lord!"

Jesse opened the door and let him in. Erin and I both moved into the living area and stood near the fireplace. Dan and Detective Kohl sat on the small sofa. Detective Kohl nodded his head acknowledging Jesse and called out to Kyle, "It's nice to meet you, young man."

"It's okay, Kyle." Erin said.

"Hello," Kyle said, extending his right hand to the detective.

Jesse nodded to the detective before taking Kyle back to the kitchen. He set Kyle down at the table with his back to the living area. We heard Jesse telling Kyle that Mr. Kohl was his friend, too."

"Friend," Kohl repeated, "Gotcha!" He nodded at Erin. "Is *this* where you'll be staying?"

I put my arm around her.

Dan spoke up. "Yes. No one knows about the cottage. This is my wife's private residence."

"Good," Kohl replied.

"How?" Erin wiped a tear from her cheek. Her brow furrowed, then she repeated, "How did he get out? He's out. Isn't he?"

"I don't know all the details yet," Kohl said slowly, shaking his head. "Erin, by any chance," he lowered his voice, "does Josh have more than one..." He held his hand out as if to imply a handgun?

"I've only seen the one he keeps in his desk drawer," she replied.

Kohl leaned in closer. "Can you describe it?"

Erin closed her eyes for a second, opened them and said, "It's all black."

Kohl sat back, pulled out his cell phone, and stood up. We heard him say, "Get me that search warrant." He looked at Erin. "I want you to stay right here until I come back."

Erin put her arm around me and rested her head on my shoulder. "I won't move," she cried.

When Detective Kohl reached for the doorknob, he told Dan he was leaving two officers on the property. He handed Dan a business card. "My direct number."

Dan rubbed his forehead. "You know something—"

The teakettle whistled, and Jesse screamed, "What the!"

After detective Kohl left, we sat in the kitchen. Jesse's idea of a snack consisted of chocolate chips mixed with almonds and coconut flakes. "Mmm, good. Try some, Mommy." Kyle held out his hand.

"No thank you, sweetheart," Erin replied, staring out the window.

Dan put his hand out. "Can I have some?"

"Uh-huh," Kyle said, handing him a handful.

"I know. Who wants to play Go Fish?" I opened a drawer. "Come on. We'll sit in front of a nice fire and play until it's time for dinner."

Erin appeared freaked out. Both lost and confused at my suggestion. "But...?" she said.

I shook my head and held out my hands. "I forgot," I said remembering our orders to stay at the cottage.

"No, let's make pizza!" Dan raised his eyebrows. "Tell her, Kyle, we want to stay home and eat pizzaaaa."

"With Jesse," Kyle announced.

"Sure." Dan picked Kyle up and brought him to the living area.

I handed the cards to Jesse. "Go fish."

Jesse took the cards from me and said, "These are regular playing cards." His phone buzzed. "Yeah. No! Stay where you are." Jesse walked into the bedroom. We could still hear him.

Everyone sat on the floor and waited for him to return with the cards. "Women! I'm telling you." He handed the deck to Dan and sat between Erin and me.

"Is everything all right?" I asked him and then took the cards from Dan.

"Sherry. Wanted to know *where* I am." He reached over and tickled Kyle. "Stay away from girls." Then he slapped my leg. "Maybe you should call Teresa and tell her to keep Sherry busy. No one needs to know that we're at the cottage."

"Got it." I called up to the inn. "Teresa, umm." Kyle was watching me. I handed the cards back to Dan and stood up. "Sherry is trying to find Jesse. Teresa, do not tell anyone about the cottage. He did? And...?" I let out a breath. "Thank You, Lord. See you in a bit." I set my phone down. "Erin, we're going back up to the inn. It's movie night, damn it!"

Kyle jumped to his feet and clapped his hands. "Yay!"

Dan and Jesse were looking at me as if I was crazy. "What?" I smiled. "Someone lied about how many toys he owned. He just got picked up for possession."

Erin's eyes filled with tears. I pointed to the bedroom, and I followed her in. We went into the bathroom where I closed the door and explained that Detective Kohl found a casing from a different bullet other than the gun he fired at the inn, and that led him to go back to the house. I handed her a cool washcloth. "You're safe."

By the time we got back to the living area, Dan had Kyle wrapped in a blanket. "Ready?" he asked.

"Yes, we are." I handed Erin one of my sweaters.

Jesse put his arm around Erin. "Ya all right, kid?"

Erin rested her head on his chest. Then she slapped his backside and through laughter and tears said, "Who you calling kid?"

We were almost to the inn when I remembered to tell Dan, "Your friend Mr. Kohl is on his way back to see you."

Dan opened the door, and Kyle ran inside. Sherry was standing next to the door. She blew out a long breath. "Everybody okay?"

Jesse gave Sherry a hug and told her to calm down. "I was gone for a few hours. What's the problem?"

"I missed you," she said, kissing him on the lips, his nose and cheek.

Kourtnee and Kevin came into the lobby. "Come on, let's go," she said as she pointed to the basement door. "Guests are waiting. Popcorn is popped, and it starts in fifteen minutes." She snapped her fingers. "Snap out of it!"

Teresa walked up to me, turned back around and said, "I love her."

"Go, we'll be right down." I put my hand on the small of Dan's back. "I want to hear what he has to say."

Dan nodded. "Kourtnee, I promise, we'll be down before it starts." Erin moved closer and stood between Dan and me.

Everyone went downstairs, except us three. When Detective Kohl arrived, he told us about finding an empty shell casing in Josh's car the day he was arrested. "The casing didn't match the gun used at the scene. When we arrived at the home, he wasn't there. We backed out of his driveway and passed a vehicle several houses down the road. I'm glad I glanced back. The vehicle turned into Josh's driveway. He had a nine-millimeter and an assault rifle in his possession. Judge sentenced him to jail *without* bail."

Erin rested her head on Dan's chest.

He patted her on the back. "You have an angel on your shoulder."

She let out a long slow breath. "Thank you," she said to the detective.

A second later, Kevin was standing at the top of the stairs, calling for us to join them. He cleared his throat. "Lynnae's on the phone. She said to tell you to get your asses downstairs."

"Mr. Kohl, we're watching an episode of Cake Boss. Would you like to join us?"

"No, thank you. Promised the wife I'd take her to dinner for our anniversary."

Dan shook his hand. "Happy Anniversary!"

I hugged him and said, "Happy Anniversary." This time, he hugged me back.

Together, we slowly made our way through the lobby.

We sat down just in time.

Chapter 56

At three in the morning, something inside me clicked. I knew the time had come for me to confront my fears. I was still awake when the sun started streaming in through the windows. I had decided to tell Dan about the nightmare, but first I wanted to talk to Rose.

"Good morning," Dan said. "How'd you sleep?"

"I saw that image again."

"Image? Oh, the clouds," he said as he threw back the covers. "Come on, coffee, shower, and I'll race you up to the inn. We have a lot to do today. Gina Marie's team is framing the first cottage and I'm excavating the foundation hole for Michael and Christine's home." Dan got out of bed and went into the bathroom.

I sat up, stretched my arms and asked him, "Do you think it is God?"

He peeked his head out the door. "Yeah, sure."

"I'm serious—"

"Julie, I'm sure you are." He sat down on the bed next to me. "I know your faith is strong. "I'm glad you have—"

"A relationship with God. Dan, you know what, I'm waking you up the next time I see it."

Dan knew I was upset. He didn't say a word the whole time we were drinking our coffee. I wasn't about to tell him that I only see the image when I have that damn nightmare with him making love to another woman. I'm sure he'd tell me not to be silly or those days are over, but I couldn't help the way my heart felt. Yes, I loved Dan and as much as I forgave him for the way he acted, I could not make the past go away. I couldn't help but feel this way. When Dan was in New York, I would dream about him, I longed for him to hold me, but seeing his face brought back the memories all over again.

The morning had fallen into an uncomfortable silence. Then we heard a knock on the door. Dan's voice was lower than usual. "Morning," he said, holding up his empty cup. "Coffee?"

"Please," Jesse replied, his breath warm and sweaty. "I ran down here. Don't ask me why."

I handed him his cup. "Who are you running from?" I jokingly asked.

"No one," he replied, smiling. "I thought I'd drop by and see if you're ready to check out my plans." He reached behind his back and held out a cardboard tube.

I snatched it from his grip, opened the top, and pulled out his plans. "Let me see," I said, setting them down on the table.

"Four bedrooms?" Dan said, "What? Why do you need…?"

Jesse sat back, took his hat off and said, "Just because I don't plan on getting married, doesn't mean I don't want kids someday."

"You would make a noble father."

"Yeah," Dan said, as he patted Jesse on the back. "Great grandfather!"

"Still not as old as you, old man."

"Stop, both of you," I said and then emptied my cup. "Jesse, I love your design and the thought of you having children."

"Yeah, well, one of your kids is up at the inn with news about the woman who gave her up."

"Erin?" Dan asked as he set our empty cups in the sink.

Jesse snapped his neck to the left. "Yeah, apparently she wrote a letter."

"I'll see you guys later," I said as I headed for the door.

"Come on, we have work," Dan said to Jesse and then added, "Let us know how Erin is."

I sat down on one of the rockers, watching the men head down to the construction area. They were talking and laughing the entire way. I was still on the porch lacing up my sneaker when I remembered my cell phone. When I went back inside, the message light was flashing. I read Frank's text message and smiled. "He misses me." I closed my eyes and whispered, "I miss you more!"

I was near the perennial garden and I could hear Dan's excavator crashing and banging on the ground. It sounded like he hit rock. *That's not good. Blasting is not in the budget!*

"Julie! Julie." Erin said, waving her arms in the air.

"Hello," I yelled back to her.

Standing only a few feet away from me, she grinned shyly. Our eyes met, and I could not believe how beautiful she looked. She appeared happier, and somewhere between fear and awe. She reached in her pocket and pulled out a small envelope, waving it in the air. "Margaret wrote back to me."

I took in a deep breath. "Oh, Erin. I'm so happy for you." And I meant it. I *was* happy for her.

We sat on the porch swing. "I want you to read it. I wanted you to be the first person to know," she said as a tear slipped from behind her sunglasses.

She handed the envelope to me. I looked at her face as she lifted her sunglasses, and rested them on her head. Her eyes were smiling. I pulled out a single piece of paper that smelled like gardenia and read:

Dear Erin,

I'm so glad you found me. I cried for days when I heard the news of your mother's passing.

I grew up knowing and loving your mother and your father. They were the sweetest individuals I have ever known.

As you know, they fell in love with each other in middle school. Every day, he would walk her home from school. It was during the eighth grade, when your father stole his first kiss. Or was it the other way around? I often teased the two of them.

A few years after graduation, a longshoreman named Jack asked your father to accompany him to America. He told him he would find him a job. A better paying job. I remember the day as if it were today. I was standing on the dock with your mother. We cried so hard that day. When your father saw us sobbing, he told Jack he was happy working as a dockhand. But Jack said he would pay for your mother's passage, and your father agreed. I was so happy for them. They were about to live a new life in America.

A few months had passed, and I received a letter telling me of the news. They were expecting their first child. Six months later, I received a telegram letting me know of the infant's death. A year had gone by without any word. After sending many letters to your mother, she finally told me she could never bear a child. I felt her pain. I loved her so.

By now, I am sure you know the truth. I am the woman who carried you for nine months. Erin, your mother and father loved you before you were born. They wanted you so much. They deserved the gift of a child. I love you, my darling. As I loved my sister.

Love,

Margaret

Tears were streaming down my face. I lifted my eyes. "This is wonderful news!"

With happy tears, she cried. "I was born out of so much love."

Chapter 57

Erin and I were sitting on the porch when we heard Kevin shout, "Julie, you got a minute?"

"For you, all day," I replied and then told Erin, "I'm so happy for you."

We both stood up. "Hi, Kevin!" Erin skipped her way back inside.

Kevin came up onto the porch and asked me, "Do you think it's too early to put the outdoor furniture out?"

"Whatever you think," I said.

"Good, because I have a lot more to do this year."

"More?"

Kevin cocked his head. "Let's see, I have to stack firewood, put all the brown resin furniture out on the terrace, the white wicker furniture, the porch rockers, the garden benches, and hang five new tree swings." He scratched his neck with the back of his hand. "And that's before the new stuff arrives."

"What new–?"

"Julie, you're the one who told my wife to order all the furniture *and* tents for the weddings."

"I'm sorry. I'll ask Kourtnee to hire someone to help you."

"Nah, I just want to be done with it so I can help Dan and Jesse."

Remembering it was his dream to operate heavy equipment, I said, "I'll ask Kourtnee to hire someone as soon as possible. In the meantime, you should go and help Dan."

Kevin smiled. "Are you sure?"

"Yes, now go!"

Kevin flew off the porch. I turned back around and saw an SUV pulling into the driveway. *Oh, a Mercedes SUV.* I waited for everyone to get out of the vehicle. "Hello, welcome."

"Hi, we're checking in for the week," he said, opening the hatch. "Can you tell?" he laughed and pointed to the luggage.

"Here, let me help you." I walked over to the vehicle and he handed me two small matching bags. In fact, *all* the luggage matched. "I'm Julie," I announced and then smiled back at the little girl with golden hair.

"We're the O'Briens. You know my wife, Tina," he said.

"Ahh, yes, you're a writer."

"Yes," she replied, and held out her hand. "I love your inn so much; I demanded we come to Point Judith for our vacation." Tina put her arm around the little girl. "This is our daughter, Molly, and our sons, Aidan and Connor."

"It's a pleasure to meet all of you," I said.

I opened the door and told Teresa, "This is the O'Brien family."

She smiled from ear to ear. "Welcome!" Teresa bent down, holding her hands on her knees. "Mommy's going to write a wonderful story and when she's ready, we're going to host a book signing event for her. Are you excited for your Mommy's new book to come out?"

"Yes, we are! Right, Aiden, Connor and Molly?" Mr. O'Brien agreed.

"Molly?" Teresa smiled. "I used to work with a young lady named Molly. Come on over, your rooms are all set."

"I'll see you all later," I said on my way to Kourtnee's office.

"What's up?" she said as I walked in.

"By any chance, do we have any male applicants?"

"Two, one I hired on the spot—"

"Seriously? For what position?" I asked.

"Everything and anything. He said he could do it all. Julie, he needs the work. He lost his job, his wife is pregnant, and they're evicting them from their apartment."

"Ooo..."

"I know, right! I asked him if he wanted to park cars or serve cocktails at our weddings. He said both. Then I asked him if he could help Kevin with the yard work."

"What did he say?"

"Yes, to everything. Thank you!" She raised her eyebrows. "You're going to love him. He's a younger version of Michael."

I smiled.

"Julie," she said, as she reached back and grabbed a piece of paper, "Guess what?"

"What?"

"I ran an ad for the corporate rooms for next year and got three replies."

"Seriously?"

"Yep, MetLife, Ford Motor Company and the Dime Savings Bank. They not only booked, they prepaid. I had an idea. Can I show you?"

"Of course," I said and sat down.

Kourtnee read her idea to me, "Baker's Confection 1765, White Horse Tavern 1673, Wiley 1807, Seaside Inn 1667, and Shirley Plantation 1613. What do you think a baker, restaurant, publisher, hotel and farm all have in common?"

I grinned from the inside out. "Tell me."

"They're some of the oldest businesses in American."

"I've heard of Wiley Publishing. They're in New Jersey. But..."

She waved her hands at me. "I know how you like to name your rooms." She grinned from ear to ear. "I thought these names were perfect for the corporate rooms—"

"I love it! Kourtnee, you're a genius. Seriously. Love, love, love the idea!"

"So, I should order the name plates for the doors right?"

"Umm, yeah!" I said, smiling.

"Sweet!"

"Okay, my sweetness, I have to go into town. Can I get you anything?"

She shook her head.

I got up to leave, stopped in the doorway and said, "Good job!"

When I got in my car, I realized, Kourtnee was the only person I told I was leaving. At the end of the driveway, I called Teresa to let her know I would be back in two hours. I drove to Rose's office, terrified. I was fifteen minutes early. I sat in the car, wondering why I even called her. It's not like she could change the past, erase the memories, or stop me from having the same damn nightmare.

As much as I did *not* wish to go, I got out of the car, opened her door, and went inside. The receptionist smiled at me and said, "Go right in."

"Thank you," I replied.

Rose was sitting on the other side of her desk, pouring water into two waiting cups.

"I made us a pot of tea." Then she sat down in the chair next to mine.

I sat down and she handed me a cup. "Mint. I hope you like it."

"Yes," I said, taking the cup from her. "Thank you."

"Julie, I want you to know you can say anything to me. As with Dan, everything stays in this room. Our—"

"I'm fine," I said and then shook my head. "Okay, *that* is one of my biggest faults. I have to learn to stop saying, 'I'm fine', when I am not."

"Most people come to see me when they need calmness, clarity, and structure. You, I'm thinking, are here for reassurance and hope. Am I right?"

Shock had a constricting effect, like a punch in the stomach. She knew what I was after. I blew out a breath and started with, "First, I want to say Dan is great. He's my world. So this has nothing, okay, maybe something to do with him. I don't know. All I know is, I can't shake the feeling. I keep having the same nightmare."

"How often?" she asked. And I was surprised she didn't get up and grab her notebook.

"Two to three times a week. Last night, I woke in a puddle of sweat."

"Tell me about the nightmare," she asked casually.

"I walk in to the same bedroom and, find Dan making love to another woman."

"Julie?"

"Rose, I almost didn't hire a young woman because I was jealous of her." I looked at her, wondering how many times she caught Dan's eye. "I don't want to lose my husband, not again."

She put her hand on my arm. "I assure you, Dan is going nowhere." She took back her hand. "You are all he—"

"He talks about. I know, and that is why I'm scared. I don't want to chase him away because of my jealousy."

"Julie, often we are quick to blame infidelity for the breakdown of our relationships when indeed it is communication. I understand you not wanting to tell Dan about these nightmares out of fear that he will see it as an act of jealousy. However, you need to open up to him. He can't help you if he doesn't know *what* is keeping you awake at night."

I closed my eyes for a second, wondering if I should tell her about the figure in the sky. "Sometimes, when I can't get back to sleep, I get up and look out the window. And when I do, I see Him and I know He is watching over me. Rose, why does God allow us to live in darkness?"

"By Him, you're referring to God?"

"Yes," I said.

"Julie, you have suffered a very traumatic experience. Perhaps God wants you to know that no matter what, He is with you."

I picked up my cup and took a sip. I blew out a long breath. "How do I stop the nightmare?"

Rose held her cup in her lap. "Julie, share with me the most traumatic event during your childhood."

I laughed.

"What?" Rose gave me a look.

"Now you sound like a therapist," I said, laughing.

"Huh, and you look… just answer my question," she scolded.

We both laughed and drank from our cups.

I sat back in my chair, trying to remember. "I was in the second grade. I had forgotten my lunch. My mother made the best lunches. She baked everything from scratch. Cooked all of our meals. I remember two things about that day. I was the only child who could spell Connecticut correctly. And I got caught stealing a cookie from someone's lunchbox."

I closed my eyes, remembering the green chalkboard. "The teacher, Mrs. Buck. Yes, that *was* her real name! I was putting the lunchbox back in the cubby when she caught me eating the cookie. She yelled at me, moved my desk to the front of the room, pushed it up to the chalkboard and made me sit with my back to the entire class for the rest of the school year."

Rose's hand went to her heart. "I'm so sorry. As a mother, I am deeply sorry. She was wrong on so many counts."

I shook my head. "Because of her, I opened a bakery. Every day, I set out a tray of free cookies." I glanced over at Rose, took a sip of my now cold tea. "With every mistake I learn something new about myself. That was the day I learned how to take a hit."

Rose stared at me for what seemed like forever. "By the way, I've seen Him many times."

I smiled at her. "Rose, Dan's not just kind, he's loving and giving. He has an infectious laugh that rumbles like thunder. To this day, I am still crazy about him. Dan is my soulmate. Why can't I stop the nightmares?"

"Julie, Dan loves you with all his heart. He knows what he did was wrong." She inhaled. "Promise me something. Don't let go of that little girl inside of you." Rose smiled warmly at me. "Seriously, sleeping is for dreaming. Tell that devil to go to hell!"

I stood up, as did Rose, and we hugged.

I pulled into the inn's parking lot as my cellphone rang. "Hello," I said without looking at the caller ID.

"Julie, your truck is ready any time you are," the man said.

"Oh, my. Thank you. How much do I owe you?" I asked. I wrote the amount down on a piece of paper and went directly into Kourtnee's office to get a check. Then I found my husband.

"Dan, can you drive me into town?"

"Now?" he asked.

"Yes," I said trying to contain my excitement.

"Give me thirty minutes," he said. "Wait for me up at the inn."

I wandered into the dining rooms and almost had a heart attack. The tables were bare. No one had filled the vases with flowers. I ran to the walk-in cooler and grabbed as many tulips as I could carry. It's not about the morning muffins or the flowers on the table, it's about the people. You have to care for your guests. I knew that, but I also knew how to make a room look pretty and welcoming. I liked flowers. They were my strength. Running the inn made my heart sing. I knew how important it was to assign the right duty early, and communicate with my staff about every task. Managing my staff was an inevitable part of the process, especially as the business grew. Keeping an orderly and efficient staff was one of the keys to making sure operations ran smoothly. I filled the last vase, knowing I failed to communicate this one task.

"Are you ready?" Dan asked standing in the doorway.

"I am now," I said.

When we got into Dan's truck, I gave him the address. I refused to tell him where we were going, until he read the sign on the side of the truck. As soon as Dan saw my logo, he knew why we were at the restoration garage. My heart lit up seeing the old truck. I had so many plans for the bed of that truck. I was so happy the way the decal turned out. A white anchor in the center. The words: THE INN IN RHODE ISLAND on the top and under the anchor: POINT JUDITH written on the bottom. She was beautiful. Candy apple red. I paid for the work and asked if I could leave Dan's truck there for a few hours. Then I handed Dan the keys. He drove down to Bay Bluff. He parked near the wild beach roses. I kicked off my flip-flops as Dan turned the radio on. To our right, grasses danced as the wind billowed from north to south. We were holding hands and singing, *Sweet Home Alabama*. Then he kissed me, jarring me, reminding me why I fell in love with him. I wanted to throttle him, right there out in the open, under blue skies and with a wind that smelled like roses and ocean air. When "Can't Help Falling In Love" came on the radio, I sang every word to Dan. When I stopped singing, Dan smiled warmly at me and I thought he was going to cry when I said, "You're the only man I ever loved."

We drove back to Classic Restorations and picked up Dan's truck. I offered to drive his truck, but he insisted I drive my new restored classic. Before I got out of his truck, Dan reached for my arm. "That's the most beautiful Ford, I've ever laid my eyes on. I'm so proud of you." He kissed me and I melted once again. "I love you so much." Then he smiled and said, "That's a great truck!"

I leaned over and kissed him. "As soon as I saw the old F100, I knew I had to have it." I winked at him. "I'm planning on transporting a lot of flowers in that truck bed. Right after I take a picture of it in front of the inn."

Chapter 58

Dan left the cottage immediately after sunrise. Last night, I could hear the excitement in his voice as he spoke about excavating the last cellar hole. I laughed when he said Gina Marie's men were not normal. They were working machines. Jesse was super excited to see his log cabin erected. Frank called me again to say hello and to check on the progress of the cottages. I was heartbroken when he told me, "I had a setback. I won't be home until next week."

"Frank, I love you. I'll be right here waiting for you."

It was seven-thirty-five and that meant I had ten minutes to get up to the inn. We had more than our normal amount of children running around. Teresa said they were here for the Springtime Family Fun week at the Confreda Greenhouse and Farms.

I ran up to the inn. Despite Sherry and Kourtnee telling me they could handle serving breakfast, I needed something to do. I was worried sick about Frank. When I entered the lobby, Teresa told me we were having a family picnic down in the orchard at lunchtime.

"Who came up with that idea?" I pointed to the dining room full of people laughing and children asking for more.

"No one will be here for lunch. We checked. Besides, you know Michael. He has his team on standby."

"It is gorgeous outside."

In the small dining room, I met the new young man, Robert. I could see why Kourtnee thought he reminded her of Michael. He smiled when he spoke. "Thank you for helping Kevin with the outdoor furniture," I said.

"You're welcome, ma'am, thank you for the job. I appreciate it."

The morning went off without a snag.

Under delicate blossoms of pink and white flowers, we all gathered in the orchard. Delilah was sitting on a blue blanket, laughing as Kyle tapped her on the head, saying, "Goose, goose, duck." Instead of duck, duck, goose.

Kourtnee, Erin, Cathy and Amanda sat in Adirondack chairs sipping Moscato. I smiled at them when I saw the size of the wine bottle.

Teresa sat on a larger red blanket, playing her guitar. To her right sat Sal, Jesse, Sherry, Christine, Brin, and Lady. No more bandages and her hair was coming back nicely.

Kevin and Robert arrived carrying picnic baskets. I was wondering where Dan could be. A moment later, Michael put his hands on my shoulders and said, "April Fools."

Dan was driving the Kubota, Gina Marie was sitting in the middle and Frank was on the passenger side.

Everyone hugged him before I could get to him. I laughed when he said, "I'm the building inspector. I'm here to see what kind of job you're all doing."

He was thinner. His face drawn. His gray hair gone. But his smile was still the same. I hugged him. "I've missed you so much."

He whispered in my ear, "Not as much as I missed you."

After lunch, Dan and Frank sat in the Kubota while Gina Marie and I rode in the back. First, we drove over to Kevin and Kourtnee's, then to Michael and Christine's, and then to an empty lot.

Frank pointed to the lot next door. "Is that?"

"Mine?" Gina Marie said. "Yes. Dan's starts excavation next week."

Frank pulled back his chin. "Where's?"

I smiled. "We've decided to stay in the cottage for a little while longer."

Dan tapped Frank's leg. "She wanted to wait for you."

Chapter 59

At four o'clock, Gina Marie drove an exhausted but happy Frank back to his home. Dan and I promised him we would stop by the next day, and show him the plans for our new farmhouse. A few minutes later, everyone headed back up to the inn. The inn was so busy; I needed all the help I could get. Besides, when the inn was full to capacity, the outgoing laundry stacks were heavy. So when Dan, Jesse and Kevin volunteered to strip the beds and do the laundry, I obliged.

I gave Dan a kiss and thanked them all for assisting me with the chores. Dan groaned, "The things I do for you."

Kevin's forehead furrowed. "Yeah, me, too." Then he laughed and added, "Actually, I'm better at doing laundry than Kourtnee. Ask Delilah."

"I'm ready," Erin said to me.

"So am I," I said, adding, "time to make the beds." The king-sized beds were so much easier to make with two people.

We were making our last bed when Erin said to me, "I'm glad that woman couldn't take the job. I like working here. Gives me something else to think about besides homework."

I glanced up from the bottom of the bed and it dawned on me. She deserved a raise. I made a mental note to stop by and see Kourtnee. After we completed the dusting, vacuuming, cleaning and making all the beds, I asked her "How are your school assignments coming?"

"Great! As far as I can tell."

"I'm glad to hear that," I said and then asked her if she was planning on going to Josh's court date.

"Do you think I should?"

"No. I was just wondering."

She sat down. "Julie, I don't want to be married to him anymore. Frank told me he would help me file for divorce. He said I could hire a friend of his. She works for the South County Public Assistance Office."

I sat down on the corner of the bed. "I don't want you to ever worry about that man again."

"I can't tell you how terrified I was that night. Julie, I think Josh is capable of murder. He beat me so hard. I think he intended to kill me."

It was the first time she spoke about that night without shedding one tear.

"Julie, I have no idea how or where I found the strength to crawl up two flights of stairs. If not for Kyle, I don't think I could have made it through the night."

I swallowed hard.

Erin took a deep breath. "Maybe I should go. Show him just how strong I am. Will you and Dan go with me? I'll go if you go with me. Julie…" she laced her fingers together, brought them up to her chin and said, "Yes! Damn it! I've decided I want to be there when the judge sentences him." She glanced up at the ceiling and then back at me. "I want to see Josh's face when the judge locks him up."

April 24, 2011. Erin, Dan, Jesse and I sat in the Narragansett Municipal Court room.

While Erin sat quietly between Dan and me, I prayed for the judge to serve justice. A moment later, two officers walked in. Josh standing in the middle, hands and ankles held together by transport restraints. Better known as cuffs. Josh glared at Erin. Dan tapped her on her leg. She was staring right back at him. She appeared stronger than ever. And when Josh said, "Who the fuck are they?" A grin appeared on Erin's face.

I answered him. "We're her fairy godparents!"

An officer put his hands on Josh's shoulder and forcefully sat him down in his chair. A moment later, a bailiff called out "All rise," and Superior Court Justice Andrew Rice entered the room.

"Josh Rhimes, you have committed an act of felony for which life imprisonment may be imposed." He went on to say, "Committed in a manner creating a great risk to more than one person by means of a weapon." Then he pointed to the district attorney.

The district attorney stood up. "The young lady did the right thing by seeking safety for herself and her young son. She found a secure home with her family and friends, only for Mr. Rhimes to track her down and unleash unspeakable violence and fear." He went on to say, "We are very fortunate that both victims were not more seriously injured, and ask for this defendant to rightfully spend a significant time incarcerated for his violent crimes."

The entire room sat in silence. Judge Rice lifted up his eyes and said, "Josh Rhimes, I see a plea bargain has been entered in this case."

When his lawyer stood, so did Josh. I could only assume he took the deal because of his past record.

The room fell silent.

"This court finds you guilty of two counts of assault with a deadly weapon in a dwelling with the intent to commit murder. I hereby sentence you to twenty-five years for the attempted murder of Erin and Kyle Rhimes. Twenty of which are not eligible for parole. Take him away."

"Yes!" I heard someone say from the back of the courtroom.

Dan and Jesse stood, followed by Erin and me. We turned around and saw Teresa, Rose, Gina Marie and Frank sitting in the back of the room. Gina Marie and Frank got up and hugged Rose. Teresa opened her eyes and said, "Amen!"

The world suddenly felt safer.

Chapter 60

At a quarter past seven in the morning, I wandered over to the new garden. Sat down on the bench and told them how much I missed them. "Dad, oh, Mom. So much has happened. I miss you with all my heart."

I saw Lady coming my way. No one else, just my baby girl. When she sat down in front of me, I told her, "I know why you leaped in front of him. I'm proud of you, baby girl. I love you."

Behind me, I could hear water trickling past rocks. I closed my eyes. Crickets. Frogs and the wonderful sound of birds. I opened my eyes. Lady's head was resting on my lap.

Life can be full of heartache, headaches, and numerous setbacks. But if you create a plan. Write it down. Every detail. Believe in yourself enough to show it to your family and friends. Together, you can make it happen.

I lifted my face to the warm sun. I was thankful for the life the Lord had given me. Accepted every heartfelt joy and pain. Acknowledged the headaches along the way. Somehow, through it all... I survived because of Him.

Lady and I made it as far as the pond when we saw Frank stepping up onto the front porch of the cottage. "Frank!" I shouted.

At the sound of my voice, he turned around. "I thought I'd find you down here."

I hugged him and asked if he would like something to drink.

"A glass of Dan's lemonade would be nice."

Frank sat down in one of the rocking chairs on the porch while I went inside the cottage to pour our drinks. I handed him his glass. "I'm so glad you stopped by. Thank you for everything you did for Erin. She's so happy."

"She told me she's been accepted to the University of Rhode Island."

"That was Kourtnee's idea. She needed to get back to society so next fall she'll be attending URI. She works her tail off around here. Ooh, did I tell you, Kourtnee put her on payroll."

"Business is good," he said, then drank his lemonade. "Not me, no more work. I spend my afternoons chasing a little white ball. Judge Abrams insisted it was time I started playing golf. I think I might get used to it."

"I'm so happy to hear this."

"Yes, well, I told Abrams I can only play golf after I've checked up on you."

I laughed. "Did I tell you why Gina Marie decided to build her new home here?"

Frank chuckled. "So she can live at the best little retirement community in Point Judith?"

"Ha ha ha! She's going to enjoy her retirement by offering classes. She's going to teach my guests how to paint landscapes."

"And ride her Harley," Frank said to me. "Don't forget about her love for riding."

"Oh, she'll have plenty of time to ride and fish. Apparently, she and Dan have a fishing contest going on."

Frank emptied his glass. "He sure does make a good lemonade."

I refilled his glass. "That's not all he's good at." I laughed.

Frank reached over and took my hand in his. "I told those southern doctors I had a woman to get back to up north. Had to build her a house before I go and meet my Maker."

I tapped the top of our hands. "I'm so glad you came home. I was afraid you would fall in love with that warm weather."

"Nah, not me. Already got me a nice tan," he laughed. "Tell me about this new she shop you want me to design."

"Ahh, yes. Did you ever go to Debi's Devine Love?"

"A sex shop?" Frank blurted out. "No!"

I laughed. "No, not a sex shop! She's a spiritual medium. She believes in angels, peace and love."

"You scared me for a minute there," Frank said, shaking his head.

"Well, Sherry told me because of high rent, Debi is closing her storefront."

"Sherry?"

"Jesse's new girlfriend. Yep, and she's moving in with him. The old man is settling down."

"How long was I gone?

We both laughed.

"The building is for Debi. It was actually Jesse's idea she open her new shop here at the inn." I sat up. "Are you hungry?"

"Starving," he replied and I thought, *All men think about is food.*

Arm in arm, we strolled up to the inn. "It is gorgeous out today," I proclaimed, feeling extremely happy.

We were almost to the inn when Frank and I stopped walking. We both stared at the inn. While Frank admired his handy work, I couldn't help notice Robert's work. He had everything in its place. The cast iron rocking horse on a vintage walnut wooden stand, side tables, white wicker rockers, both cast iron urns filled with cascading flowers, and enormous matching hanging baskets. Then I saw it. A new personalized stoneware-pickling crock. I read it aloud, "Welcome to The Inn in Rhode Island."

"Do you like it? I asked Kourtnee to email me a photo of your anchor."

"It's perfect. Just like you!" I kissed him. "Thank you!"

Chapter 61

Frank and I went out to the side porch and sat down next to Dan, Gina Marie, and Cathy. A moment later, Teresa came outside. I smiled when she rested her head on Frank's arm and said, "Gosh, it's good to see you."

Next to us, the window in the small dining room was open and we could hear the children laughing. "So, Julie," Cathy said, "Did Amanda tell you, she wants to hire Jessica to assist her in the daycare?" and then took a bite of her Caesar salad.

"My Jessica?" Frank asked.

"Yes. Apparently, she has a teaching degree."

I raised my eyebrows at Frank and said, "One surprise after another."

He smiled. "It appears my entire staff wants to work for you."

Dan laughed at Frank's gesture and then waved to Jesse and Sherry to join us.

We moved our chairs over so there would be enough room for them to sit down.

Frank finished the mustard greens that Michael had prepared especially for him, and his baked marinated ham steak. He admitted he had a round of golf to play, but he sat back down when Christine said, "Frank, don't you move. I made you a coffee-poached pear with chocolate whipped cream."

After dessert, no one wanted to move. Gina Marie stood up. "Come on Frank. This chauffer's got a schedule to keep."

I didn't want Frank to leave. I hugged him goodbye and thanked him again for my gift.

Dan stood and shook Frank's hand. "You take care of yourself. When we get back from Italy, we'll bring the plans over for you to take a better look at them."

Frank touched my cheek. "Young lady, you're getting that pool and your farmhouse, or my name isn't Frank the Builder!"

Everyone laughed.

Jesse gave Sherry a kiss and informed her he'd see her at five.

I told Dan and Jesse that I would walk with them as far as the cottage. "I still need to pack."

"Oh, yeah, that's right. You're finally going on your honeymoon. It's about time," Jesse teased.

"Yeah, and I can't wait to get away from you," Dan replied. Then he put his arm around me. "Just think, your wish is about to come true."

"Wait, when do you leave?" Jesse asked.

"Two weeks from today," Dan replied.

"Why she packing now?"

Laughing, I said, "We're sending our luggage to the hotel ahead of time." I kissed Dan goodbye, and waved Jesse off.

It was so warm outside, I decided to open all the windows. Before I knew it, it was four-thirty. I put the book I was reading down on the window seat. Sat up and heard footsteps outside; they were moving toward the front door – *no, now they're moving away.*

"Where's my sunshine?" Dan hollered in the bedroom window.

As soon as I heard his voice, my heart smiled. My husband was home. I met him at the front door and my heart lit up. Dan was wearing only his underwear.

"My boots and my clothes are full of mud," he said. "I left everything by the garden hose on the side of the house."

Dan stepped inside, kissed me twice on the lips before heading for the shower.

I went to the kitchen and poured him a glass of lemonade. When he returned to the living area, I patted the cushion next to where I was sitting. His scent made my heart race and I wanted to make love to him right there on the sofa.

Dan took a sip of his drink and asked, "What's for dinner?"

Food? My insides are tingling and you want to eat. I rolled my eyes, knowing I would have to wait. "Tonight, we are serving cucumber and mint salad, baked monkfish, carrots and cauliflower purée, pasta with crawfish and for dessert, Christine made a blackberry roll and homemade vanilla bean ice cream."

Dan nodded. "I'm starving!"

Outside, Dan reached for my hand.

We were in the lobby when Erin approached us. "I filed for divorce today."

Dan let go of my hand and hugged her. "Good for you. We're proud of you." He leaned back. "You know that, right?"

She kissed him on the cheek. "Thank you. That means the world to me." Then she reached for his hand and told him. "Dan, my mother didn't give me away." She blushed before adding, "I was born out of love."

"Thant's great. Julie told me about the letter your mom wrote to you."

"I was thinking if I save every penny, maybe Kyle and I could go see her next summer."

"That is a wonderful idea!" Dan told her, but looked directly at me.

"Okay, I better get Kyle ready for dinner," she said, and off she went.

Dan cupped my face in his hands, bringing his mouth to mine in a slow, lingering kiss that sent a shiver through me. He deepened the kiss, dragging me into the billiards room, making my heart thump. "Mmm," he murmured against my lips and then added, "I know what you're thinking."

"We could always go next year, after we build the farmhouse," I said.

"I'll call the airline and see what I can do." He shook his head. "You'll never change. Always thinking about the other person."

I smiled, and kissed him. "I believe with all my heart, everything happens for a reason." I squeezed his hand. "I needed each and every one of them."

"Maybe God put them in your path because they needed you more than –"

"Mwah!" I said pressing my lips to his.

Acknowledgements

I'd like to thank the many successful self-published female writers before me for paving the way on the road to success. Such a joy discovering fellow writers who are willing to answer my concerns and guide me along my writing journey. From publishing to advertising and marketing campaigns, I'm grateful to the women of Women's Fiction Writing Association and to 20BooksTo50K for creating professional sites open to all writers.

To my beta readers, critique partner, copy editor and book doctor, thank you for your reading time, comments and suggestions. A big "thank you" goes out to Jan Kardys and Barbara Ellis, my agents for their unrelenting support of my novels, and for their never-ending friendship. Much appreciation to my team, Susan McGurl, Natalie Butka, Natasja Hellenthal, Donna McFarland, and Karen Sheff for their help, guidance, and reading time!

In my personal life, I have been blessed with a circle of close family and friends. It is their support that fuels my soul and pushes me to be the best writer I can be. I thank you all for believing in me and in my stories. To the many fans of my first novel *Still Crazy*, thank you for reading, writing your reviews and recommending my work to all of your book friends. Because of you, I am a bestselling writer on Amazon. I'm proud to say my writing has won two awards. The Readers' Favorite award and an American Book Fest award for women's fiction. Thank you for your continued support. I love you all more than you realize! Thank you for being my book friend! My heart lights up every time I open one of your cards, or letters. They mean the world to me. Shout out to my sponsors: Lilly's Family Foods, Sunflour Bakery, Harney Tea, and the RISE Brewing Company!

If you follow me, you know I love a good giveaway. I invite you to share the joy of receiving with your book friends. Everyone is welcome to sign up for my monthly newsletter, follow me on social media and join my book club. I would love to be a guest at your next meeting. Via Zoom or in person. I promise, we'll have fun.

Book club kits are available for the asking. To join my street team email me at judyprescottmarshall@aol.com

To learn more about me please visit my website.

www.Judyprescottmarshall.com

COMING MARCH 2023
THE COTTAGE

Book Three
Be Strong Enough Series

Chapter 1

Our evening stroll was beautiful. Dan and I toured the property holding hands, laughing about how many times we said one day we would own a bed and breakfast. Our plan was to host hiking, fishing and kayaking adventures. We never talked about a twenty-five room inn, cooking for fifty to seventy-five people on any given night, or hosting weddings for three-hundred people. Honestly, we wouldn't change a thing. As long as Dan and I are together, we can handle whatever exploration comes our way.

After we strolled past Michael and Christine's cottage, Dan asked me if having all the children living at the inn made me happy. "I know you wanted to have children," he said looking into my eyes. "I'm just wondering if seeing them brings you joy or makes you feel sad that we never had any of our own."

"Dan, God has blessed me with so many wonderful people, and they have given me more children than any woman could ask for. There isn't a day that goes by where I'm not thanking Him, especially for you. You are all I ever wanted. Needed in my life." I took two steps, stood in front of him and said, "You are an answered prayer. I'm so grateful to share this life with you.

You make me happy. I plan on spending every day discovering something new with you by my side."

He nodded before kissing me. "I love you so much." Then he reached for my hand and said, "You make every day feel like

Christmas. We're going to enjoy our retirement one day at a time." "Yes, we are," I replied, squeezing his hand.

Under the nautical twilight, a warm spring breeze blew by as we approached Kevin and Kourtnee's home. I smiled when I saw the post and rail fence, chicken wire, gardens filled with flowers, herbs and fresh, tender spring greens, including baby lettuces. "She's such a good mother," I said.

Dan laughed, rolled his eyes and added, "She makes all of Delilah's food."

"Really? I didn't know she made her own baby food. How do you know that?"

Dan laughed again. This time a little louder. "Kevin. He told me he has to pre-wash the babies clothes for an hour or the food stains won't come out. Beets are the worst." Dan began swinging our hands in the air as he sang, "A Kiss To Build A Dream On".

When Teresa decided to live with Sal, but continue to work for me, I was happy for her. Marrying Sal meant she wouldn't be alone at night. Sal assured her he could handle his four-room bed and breakfast all by himself.

On the days when Dan and Jesse go fishing or when they join Gina Marie on their motorcycles through Newport, Teresa and I got to share a soothing cup of tea. I was glad when Gina Marie bought the property next door. She's been a godsend lately. Keeping Dan under budget, teaching our guest how to paint landscapes and filling in wherever needed at the inn.

I looked over at Dan, inhaled the night air and said, "We have the best family in the world!"

Chapter 2

Thursday morning, Dan and I both woke up excited. First, a breakfast meeting with my entire staff, then lunch with Frank, followed by a going away party in the large dining room. At midnight, Jesse's taking us to the airport in Providence. Our flight should land in Italy sometime around ten Friday morning.

"Would you like another cup of coffee?" Dan asked holding up an almost full pot.

"No." I shook my head. "I'm so excited I don't need any more caffeine. I picked up my notepad and the list of things for Kevin to plant while I was gone. I wanted him to wait for me to return, but he insisted he could do it on his own. I only agreed because of the warm June weather approaching.

"I'm going in the shower and then we better get a move on," Dan said as he emptied the coffee pot into the kitchen sink.

"Okay, and then I'll take mine, but first I want to check my email to see if Erin replied."

While Dan showered, I read Erin's email. I took a deep breath knowing she meant every word. I was happy for her. Glad she located her birth mother. Thrilled she had decided to stay in Ireland and make a new life for herself and her son.

"Good morning," Jesse said as he entered the cottage holding a case of nitro cold brewed coffee for the RISE Brewing Company.

His and Dan's new favorite morning beverage.

"Dan's in the shower. Take a seat. I have a few more things to do."

Jesse sat on the sofa with his feet kicked up on the footstool, telling me all about his dinner at Mulligan's Irish Pub. "Sherry loved it. She made me promise to take her there every Wednesday night."

"Better than George's?" I protested.

"You're early," Dan said to Jesse as he tapped me on my derrière, adding, "You better get in that shower now or wait until after the meeting."

"I'm going," I replied and headed for the bathroom.

I took a quick shower, made the bed, dressed and sat on the bed to tie my sneakers. I was near the bedroom door when I overheard Jesse telling Dan that Rose had sex appeal. "Not bad for –"

"Knock your shit off!" Dan said. "Don't ever talk to me about another woman in that manner again. Rose is my therapist! And that is all she is. Got it?"

"I got it," Jesse said. "I'm sorry. I didn't mean anything by it."

"What's wrong with you? You of all people know how hard it was for me when Julie left. Why would you even bring another woman up?"

"Dan," I hollered for the bedroom, "is my pocketbook out there?" I knew exactly where it was. Hanging on the back of the kitchen chair. When I entered the kitchen, both Dan and Jesse stared at me. "I found it," I said and grabbed it. "I'm ready if you are."

We were still on the front porch when Jesse patted Dan on his shoulder. I heard him say, "It won't happen again."

Dan closed the door and reached for my hand. "Jesse and I have a few things to go over before the pool guys get here. I'll catch up with you after your meeting and we'll go see Frank."

I kissed him goodbye and told Jesse I would see him later, too.

I inhaled, taking in the scent of hyacinths and primrose planted in the garden bed along the path leading up to the inn. I knew Jesse felt bad for saying what he did about Rose. Truth be told, Rose was a sexy woman.

My staff meeting went well. Everyone assured me they were in total control of the next three weeks.

"Oh, one more thing," I said before ending the meeting. "Erin and Kyle have decided to live in Ireland. She's going to school full time and help her mother on the weekends in her dress shop, Erin's

Threads."

"That's wonderful news!" Kourtnee said.

"Oh, my goodness! Her mother named her dress shop after Erin," Christine said, smiling.

At eleven-thirty, Dan and I went to Frank's for lunch. He was much thinner, but still happy-as-ever Frank. We ate our lunch, laughing about Dan hanging up on Frank the first time he called him. I said thank God for caller ID, then I told him. "I'm excited about going to Italy, but knowing you, Dan and I will be working on a project together, which is better than any trip in the world."

"I'll be ready," Frank said to me and then shook Dan's hand. "Have the time of your life. You both deserve it."

On our way back to the inn, Dan told me what Jesse said to him. "I shouldn't have yelled at him, but–"

"It's okay. Jesse knows you love him. I'm glad you put him in his place. Seriously, Rose is a married woman."

Before we knew it, we were celebrating and toasting to our long-awaited vacation. I noticed Jesse and Sherry sitting at the corner table. I went over and asked them if they needed a drink.

"You and Dan are a perfect couple," Sherry said.

I smiled. "There's no such thing as perfect, but as long as you have love in your heart, faith in your home and forgiveness in your soul you'll have all you ever need in your relationship." I felt Dan's hands on my shoulder. "Are you guys ready?" "Yep." Jesse and Sherry both stood up.

"I'm coming to the airport with you," she said.

I hugged everyone goodbye one more time. Kissed Lady on the head and told her to be a good dog for Jesse.

After Jesse and Sherry waved us off, we grabbed a few snacks and something to drink. I forgot about the no water rule at the airport and had to toss two brand new bottles in the garbage. As soon as we boarded, we both took a deep breath, put our heads back and thanked God for traveling with us.

About two hours into our flight, Dan was watching the news on his tablet when he read aloud, "Prominent Narragansett divorce lawyer Donato Russo was found dead in his car outside his law office earlier this evening. Russo leaves behind a wife and three children. Rose Russo had no comment."

Made in the USA
Middletown, DE
26 March 2022